THE OUTFIT:
TO HELL AND BACK

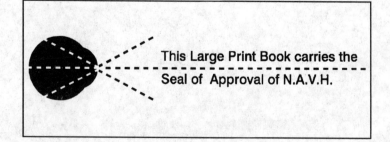

This Large Print Book carries the
Seal of Approval of N.A.V.H.

THE OUTFIT SERIES, BOOK 1

THE OUTFIT: TO HELL AND BACK

MATTHEW P. MAYO

THORNDIKE PRESS
A part of Gale, Cengage Learning

GALE
CENGAGE Learning·

Farmington Hills, Mich • San Francisco • New York • Waterville, Maine
Meriden, Conn • Mason, Ohio • Chicago

GALE
CENGAGE Learning®

LIBRARY OF CONGRESS CATALOGING-IN-PUBLICATION DATA

Names: Mayo, Matthew P., author.
Title: The Outfit : to hell and back / by Matthew P. Mayo.
Description: Waterville, Maine : Thorndike Press, 2016. | Series: The outfit series ;
  #1 | Series: Thorndike Press large print western
Identifiers: LCCN 2016039996| ISBN 9781410481641 (hardcover) | ISBN 1410481646
  (hardcover)
Subjects: LCSH: Outlaws—Fiction. | Large type books. | GSAFD: Western stories. |
  Adventure fiction.
Classification: LCC PS3613.A963 O88 2016b | DDC 813/.6—dc23
LC record available at https://lccn.loc.gov/2016039996

Published in 2016 by arrangement with Cherry Weiner Literary Agency

Printed in the United States of America
1 2 3 4 5 6 7 20 19 18 17 16

To Rose and Larry Sweazy, true pards.

"It is one of the blessings of old friends that you can afford to be stupid with them."

— Ralph Waldo Emerson

"If a man does not make new acquaintance as he advances through life, he will soon find himself left alone."

— Samuel Johnson

OUT·FIT (noun): A group of people engaged in the same occupation or belonging to the same organization, occasionally with the implication of being unconventional or slightly disreputable; a collective of cowboys employed by a cattle ranch.

PROLOGUE:
THE END

A man stands in a fresh-dug grave, cold autumn rain pools around his mud-sunk boots, pelts the mounds of earth above. He is tall, broad of shoulder, and the muscles of a toiling man glisten through the soaked shirt that clings to his lean form. His broad-brimmed hat sags with the weight of rain.

To one side the dirt pile slowly slumps, dissolves with the ceaseless cold drizzle. To the other side, two bodies lay wrapped in sodden blankets. One form is smaller than the other. Both are smaller than the man. He gently pulls the larger of the two to the edge of the grave, lifts it down, holds it close for a moment, the blanket parts to reveal the face of a dark-haired woman now cold and still, her skin the hue of snow in moonlight, lips and eyelids gone bluish like river ice.

The man's shoulders convulse at the sight of her. Too soon he lays her at his feet in the bottom of the grave, repeats this with the

11

smaller form, a little boy. He crouches low over them, kisses them each in the cold rain. Where he has caressed them, his big muddy fingers smear their foreheads, cheeks with mud. He wipes them clean, places the little boy on the woman, as if cradled in her arms, then with a moan drags himself up out of the grave.

It takes him a long while to fill it in. After that he mounds it with rocks, jams a charred arm-length of timber into one end of the grave, straps another to it with his leather belt, forming a crude cross. Nothing is carved into it.

Behind him, the charred remains of a log ranch house, barn, and other buildings sizzle and smoke in the rain. A last leaning log falls in, heavy black ash flurries up. Only a stone chimney and fireplace remain and the walls of an adobe bunkhouse, with a caved-in roof, still stand.

Two federal marshals sit their horses, watching the man. He looks up at them, waits for them. One marshal climbs down, manacles the man, then escorts him to a third horse. They lead him away, toward the southwest.

CHAPTER 1:
SWING WIDE THE GATES

Five years later.

"Barr."

Clang clang clang!

Rafe Barr's eyes snapped open.

"Hey, Barr!" It was Mossback, the old man, whispering from the adjoining cell. "Wake your ass up. You're keeping Feeney waiting. I'd say Timmons wants to see you."

The prisoner lay unmoving in the dark. He sensed it was past midnight, had been for some time. He shifted his eyes and saw the thick plug of a guard, Feeney, waiting outside the bars. Mossback was right, Warden Timmons only ever summoned prisoners in the middle of the night. But why would the warden want to see him? He'd had no such request in his five years at Yuma Territorial Prison.

As with so much in his life, the more he thought about it, the less sense it made. Rafe swung his feet to the cold stone floor, tugged on his striped cloth prisoner's cap, and stood. At least whatever it was they wanted would be a distraction from the endless hours of night in his cell.

Feeney clamped the manacles on Rafe's wrists and feet, locked them, and prodded him in the back with the barrels of the shotgun. Rafe shuffled forward. Again Feeney jammed him. Five years of guards' shotguns poking him in the back. Rafe wanted to drive a fist into the man's face, choke him with the chains connecting his wrists, but he'd learned early on that such thoughts only led to frustration, and that made the time pass slower. But if he ever got out . . .

Barr's clothes hung off him, and what flesh he carried was hard, seared onto the bones of his tall, wide-shouldered frame from five years of busting rock and chipping tunnels and carving chambers in the rock face of the cliff that made up walls of the place. He was built of lean, hard muscle, corded arms with sinews like steel, and hands that gripped a fifteen-pound sledge as easily as soft men might grab a pencil or a whiskey glass.

Soon they were at the door to the warden's office. It swung inward, and there stood Warden Timmons . . . smiling. The same

14

man who had made the first five years of Rafe's life sentence a hell on earth.

"Come in, come in."

Feeney poked at him again, and for the first time since they left the cell, Rafe swung away from the kidney-aimed gun barrels. The bull-necked guard growled a thick sound deep in the back of his throat. He rarely sullied his hands through direct contact with the prisoners. He usually followed the warden around the compound, cherished sawed-off double Greener cradled in his arms, and a scowl wrinkling his pug face like an angry sunken apple.

"Now, now, Feeney. The man is my invited guest. I must ask you to refrain from rough-handling him."

Again, the thick man's chest rumbled, but he backed down, kept a short distance from the prisoner.

"Coffee, Mr. Barr?"

Rafe stared at the warden, brows pulled tight, no readable expression on his chiseled face. The prisoner's short, gray-peppered hair, trimmed close, high around his ears to help keep lice at bay, gave his lean face a grim cast, as if he were rough-hewn from stone, all shadows and planes.

The warden's smile dissolved and he moved behind his desk, selected a cigar from a carved wooden box atop the desk. He sniffed its length, snipped off the end, then dragged a match along the underside of his desk and lit the cigar. All the while Barr stared at him, no expression on his stony face.

The warden removed the cigar from his mouth. "I don't know or care if you are guilty of the crime you are in here for. Hell, most everybody in this place claims innocence." He sank back into his padded leather chair with a sigh. "Once they get here, it's a moot point." He looked up at Barr. "That means —"

"I know what it means." Barr's deep voice held an edge like honed steel.

"Of course you do. How silly of me to assume that all men stuck inside these walls are dolts — there are exceptions to every rule. That is in part why I summoned you here." He sighed. "I'll cut to the chase, Barr. I have need of the skills you gained during the War Between the States as a northern spy."

"I wasn't a spy."

The warden waved a hand as if to shoo away an irksome fly. "You were, but quibbling about it is of little use now. You were also a field-titled fighting general who refused to leave his men in battle, even

16

when you were wounded, what . . . seven times, I seem to recall? Which, incidentally means you are either reckless or clumsy. It could also be that you are a masochist. At any rate, I leave that up to history to decide."

He puffed the cigar in silent scrutiny a few moments more before continuing. "In addition to your skills as a covert operative and a combat fighter, you also have estimable skills as a tracker. I have been told that during the war, you gained a reputation on both sides for your ability to infiltrate opposition forces, then seek out and extract information others were unable to get."

The warden leaned back, blew smoke at the dark-paneled ceiling, not once taking his eyes from Barr's face. "You haven't denied much. I'll take that as an admittance. Pity you ended up turning your back on all that promise before . . . ah, how to put it gently . . . killing your wife and son."

From his standing position a man-length before the polished slab of a desk, Barr launched himself straight at the warden. His big hands were shackled at the wrists, but not attached to a waist chain, and they sought the warden's throat even as he sprawled atop the desk, sending an unlit oil lamp crashing to the floor. Stacks of papers scattered, two inkwells and several writing implements shot outward.

Rafe's thick hands encircled the warden's throat — one quick squeeze and he could crush the man's windpipe, collapse the muscles against the top of the spine. The warden's eyes popped wide, his cigar slipped from his mouth, fell to the floor.

Two cold steel holes pressed tight to the back of Rafe's head, the singular sound of both hammers cocked all the way back echoed in his skull. Rafe's face, inches from the pasty warden's, showed emotion for the first time since he was brought into the man's office. He smiled a death's-head grin, his steel-gray eyes staring straight into the warden's.

"He pulls those triggers, Timmons," growled Rafe. "And we both go."

"Back off, Feeney!" whimpered the warden as Rafe's fingers tightened.

The burly bodyguard stayed put.

"Damn you, Feeney," gagged the warden. "Back off!"

A few more moments, then Barr released the man's throat, slid himself backward off the desk, and stood as he had, as if nothing had happened.

"That was unwise." Red-faced, Warden Timmons tugged at his shirt collar and retrieved his smoldering cigar from the carpet where it had singed a tidy little ring by his boot.

"I could say the same to you."

"Agreed," said the warden, and though Rafe heard the conciliatory word, he saw nothing but contempt on the man's face.

"Despite this" — the warden waved his hand at the mess of the desk, the papers spilled on the floor — "I still have a deal to offer you." He paused, watching Barr.

"You have my interest." What man in his position could afford otherwise?

The warden steepled his fingers, puffed on the now-bent cigar. "The daughter of the governor of California has been kidnapped, brainwashed, forced into, shall we say, a lifestyle undesirable in the extreme. She must be rescued."

"You mean a lifestyle unbecoming the daughter of a politician with his gaze fixed on the national stage."

"Then you understand."

"Is this coming from the governor himself?"

"In a manner of speaking. You see, he is . . . distraught, as one might expect. And —"

"And if you were to be instrumental in the retrieval of his daughter, he might well

19

look favorably on you and your career."

"Again, you understand."

"What do I get out of this?"

"I should think that would be obvious." The warden began straightening the mess on his desktop.

"By all means," said Rafe, plunking down in the stuffed leather chair before the desk. "Enlighten me and state the obvious." Behind, he heard a throaty growl from Feeney. "Easy boy," Rafe said in a low voice.

The warden smiled at the comment. "I will grant you early release in exchange for the successful return — alive, whole, and to my custody — of the governor's daughter."

"Tall order, considering I don't know what sort of hell she's been through, what shape she'll be in, or if she's even alive. What if, despite my best efforts, I am unsuccessful?" asked Barr.

The warden smiled slyly. "Then, Mr. Barr, you will be tracked down — for you will surely try to maintain your grasp on your newfound freedom, but trust me it won't work — and you will be dragged back here. Then you will spend ample time in the Dark Cell. You know the one, don't you? The dank snake- and scorpion-filled pit at the center of this complex."

You know full well I'm familiar with your

little pets, thought Barr. He regarded the smug warden for a long minute, then stood. "No deal. Back to my cell, Feeney." He turned. "I need my beauty sleep."

Behind him, he heard a sound, part gasp, part growl, from the man in charge. As Rafe shuffled down the stone hallway, Feeney in tow, the warden's strangled oaths boomed at him: "You will regret this, Barr! No one turns their back on me — no one!"

The chains of his ankle manacles clinked on the stone floor as he shuffled down the hallway, and Rafe Barr smiled, really smiled, for the first time in five years.

An hour later, he was back in the warden's office. The mess he'd made of the man's desk had been tidied, and it seemed the warden had indulged in a drink or three of whiskey in the interim.

But the warden slurred nothing when he said, "You will be freed regardless of the outcome of your quest. Success, of course, will be looked on favorably. But I caution you — anything less than that will be . . . well, we'll cross that bridge when we come to it, eh?"

Rafe held out his chained arms, shook them, did the same with his leg irons, the links offering a dull clanking sound. The warden nodded once to the burly bald guard. Feeney's tree stump of a head bent low by Rafe's feet as he unlocked the manacles. Once freed, Rafe slowly strolled the room, working his shoulders, rubbing his wrists.

"Far as I'm concerned, Warden, we've already crossed that bridge. You require certain services and skills and apparently I'm the man for the job, otherwise you wouldn't stick your neck out so far. You don't trust me and I sure as hell don't trust you. So we're even. I will do my utmost to bring the girl back, but no guarantees. Then we're done with each other, take it or leave it." Barr stood in the center of the room, the warden glaring at him from behind his desk, Feeney growling by the door.

"You're not in any position to negotiate, Barr."

"And neither are you, Warden." Barr's jaw muscles tightened as he recalled unbidden one of his wife's favorite saws: In for a penny, in for a pound. "I'll need a few supplies."

Rafe stepped to the desk, flipped open the carved-wood humidor, and plucked up a long, thick cigar. He took his time, mimicking the warden's earlier ritual of sniffing, snipping, and lighting. Puffing, he nodded in appreciation. "I don't care what the inmates say about you, you have a fine taste in cigars."

"Are you about done?"

"On the contrary, I am just getting started, Warden." Rafe poured himself two fingers of bourbon from the cut-crystal decanter, sipped, swirled it in his mouth, and inhaled the heady vapors. "Nearly there." He winked, then sat back in the plush leather divan, spread his arms along the back cushions, taking care not to spill his whiskey.

"I'll need a solid riding horse, a gelding, and a packhorse. Plus full trail supplies for two weeks, a hefty wad of cash, a Winchester repeating rifle, a Greener double-barrel, and a counter-signed, notarized, and dated document stating I have been lawfully released from this fine establishment. Oh, and my own set of Colts back. You know the ones Feeney here has been wearing for the past couple of years? I'm guessing they were a gift from someone."

They both looked over at the plug of a man glaring by the door. He stood spread-legged as if ready to drive himself at them like a human battering ram.

"Yes, I'd recognize that double rig any-where. I believe you'll find my initials, R. B., carved into the steel beneath each gun's grips, and inside the belt, too. Shall we

23

check, Feeney?"

"That won't be necessary," said Warden Timmons. "Feeney, take off the guns."

The guard's eyes narrowed.

"Lay them here." The warden gestured at his desk.

"No, Feeney. Bring them here."

The warden closed his eyes. "I think not, Mr. Barr. Have you forgotten you are an inmate of Yuma Territorial Prison?"

"Not anymore, Warden."

The warden nodded at Feeney. The squat man complied by dumping the guns on the floor at Rafe's feet, growling at Rafe the entire time.

"Now, Mr. Barr, aren't you going to ask what I know of the abduction? Where the girl might be?"

Rafe blew out a plume of smoke and sipped his whiskey. "I figured you'd circle around to it before too long. And besides, I have a pretty good idea of where not to look. That's usually enough to open the ball."

"Yes, well . . ."

The warden looked to Rafe to be less confident of himself than he had a few minutes before. "As near as we can tell, she was lured to Deadwood by Al Swearengen, owner of the Gem Variety Theater in that

24

rat hole of a mine camp."

"Pimp, bully, beater of women, and worse. Yeah, I've heard of him."

"How might that be, Mr. Barr? You've been incarcerated for five years, during which time he attained his somewhat dubious level of power in Deadwood."

"Let's say I'm acquainted with the man and his escapades. Now if you'll excuse me, gentlemen," he downed the last swallow of bourbon, set the glass on the floor, stretched out full length on the leather couch, and tugged his cloth cap down over his face. "I'm going to get a couple hours of sleep. I have a full day tomorrow."

The warden shook his head, exchanged unbelieving glances with Feeney.

Rafe tipped the cap back up. "Oh, one more item. I'd like hot coffee and a full breakfast in the morning. About five, I'd like to make an early start."

Little more than two hours later, Barr smiled at the scowling guards as he rode a decent buckskin through the front gate of Yuma Territorial Prison. His belly was full, he wore fresh duds, and trailed a pack animal laden with his requested goods. He didn't need to turn around to know the warden was watching.

Only one of them was smiling.

Chapter 2:
Look Behind You

Behind him, the warden heard a number of men file into his office. Still he did not turn from the high window that offered a long view of the entry gate and the surrounding landscape.

I tortured that man for five damn years in this hell hole, thought the warden. And he's the one who rides out of here a free man. And I'll bet he's wearing a grin on his face. Warden Timmons sighed silently, pasted on a smile of his own, and turned to face the newcomers.

"Gentlemen," he said, taking in the bizarre assemblage. "Considering what I perceive as your relative intolerance for mental challenge, I have made your task a simple one."

The assembled group, ten plus Feeney by the door, stood before him, bristling with knives, handguns, tomahawks, rifles, and shotguns. They were known as El Jefe and his Hell Hounds — a harder-looking batch of men the warden had not seen outside of the cells.

They were a motley collection of hired thugs, former prisoners, bounty men, and guards, all of whom had committed crimes far worse than what many of his inmates had been incarcerated for — the difference being they hadn't been foolish enough to get caught. And that is why he hired them.

"I want you to trail Rafe Barr, but keep your distance."

The thugs' leader, El Jefe, gestured toward the warden with his chin. He was a thick-featured brute with shoulders as wide as a door frame, and with a pockmarked face sporting a drooping moustache, all framed by lank black hair. Bandoliers of brass shells crisscrossed his wide chest, two knives and a tomahawk hung from a broad leather belt, as well as two heavy Colt Dragoon revolvers, their worn walnut handles nicked and gouged, but polished.

The thick fingers of his left hand, poking from fingerless black leather gloves he rarely took off, gripped the forestock of a repeating rifle, the barrel cut down by a foot. The savage-snouted weapon drew questioning glances wherever El Jefe went. Jigged-bone knife handles protruded from the tops of his worn, mid-calf black boots.

27

"Why not hire us to find the girl? Why bring that gringo into it?"

The warden sighed, turned back to the window. "Because you are all idiots who can't find your asses with both hands."

As he expected, his hired thugs growled oaths and sounded for all the world as if they might jump him then and there. But the sound of Feeney's double hammers clicking back stopped their seething.

"Understand me, men. Finding the girl is the easy part." Timmons watched the black dot grow smaller on the horizon. "Barr is a master tracker, a master marksman, a master soldier . . . a master killer." The dot disappeared from view.

One of the Hell Hounds laughed. "I don't care how good he is. I'd like to see him stop a bullet in the back!"

The warden spun on them, glared at the laughing man. "You idiot, that is precisely why most of you won't make it back alive. You get too confident with Rafe Barr anywhere around and you'll end up dead."

"Nobody's that good."

"Barr is. That's why he'll find the girl for you. In a way, it's a shame you'll have to kill him."

"You almost sound as if you like him, Warden."

It was El Jefe again. Smarter, more perceptive than the rest, thought the warden. Though that wasn't saying much. "Like? No. Admire? Perhaps. He is one of a kind, and his war record is beyond belief. But it would indeed be unfortunate should he return alive to Yuma Territorial Prison. Are we clear on that, gentlemen?"

"As a bell," said El Jefe, and laughter, subdued in tone from a minute before, rippled through the group.

The warden smiled and handed El Jefe a sack of coins, then to each man, a cigar.

Minutes later, from his office window he watched them ride out. Fools, he thought. Or am I the fool for trusting in fools? So much rests on their success. If they don't triumph, all my plans will be for naught. And Barr will hunt me down . . . for setting him up to fail.

CHAPTER 3:
FANCY MEETING YOU HERE

Northeast of Yuma by a week, Rafe breathed deeply of fresh morning air. A sudden hammer blow of thunder pulsed outward from a spot miles to the west, in the rangy foothills of southern Utah. It was followed a second later by a massive ragged ribbon of smoke that plumed upward then spidered out, marring the clear blue skyline. Rafe reined up on the buckskin gelding he was riding. The packhorse, a sturdy Morgan, fidgeted.

The sound pulsed outward and though it began miles from him, Rafe waited one, two seconds, and then he felt it in his ears, fluttering his shirt sleeves, stirring the grit of the alkali flat and trembling the sage. "Damn, that was one hot charge, horse." The buckskin flicked an ear.

Miners, maybe? Or a railroad? Rafe recalled someone from his past, someone who liked to set hot charges, then shook his head, dispelling the notion. He rode on, easing away from the explosion. A series of three smaller blasts issued from the same spot, followed by a succession of measured gunshots — rifle fire. He reined up again.

Rafe looked northeastward, as if he could see Deadwood in the distance, and within the vision, a dingy room with a sad little girl, barely a teenager, perhaps chained to a ringbolt in the floor, surrounded by squalor. His cheek muscles worked. The blasts weren't all that far out of his way.

As if to convince him, another small explosion sounded. He sighed, not sure if he was about to make a mistake. "In for a penny," he said and booted the horse into a lope.

He also knew that it might confuse the ten clumsy riders backtrailing him. That alone would be worth the time spent.

It took him a half hour to draw near the spot, but it wasn't difficult to find — random small blasts and rifle fire guided him. Then he heard shouts, as if there were men up ahead celebrating something.

Rafe tied the buckskin to a gnarled mesquite. The Morgan seemed content to not challenge the endurance of the lead line. From its boot, Rafe shucked the Winchester, then stood still a moment, listening. The laughs were those of men who sounded as if

31

they'd been drinking and were now shooting. But at what? Or who? And how did the explosions figure in?

Rafe low crawled up the last gravel bank that separated him from the rowdies. At the top, he took in with a glance a scene that answered most of his questions. Three men, two wearing the raggy working garb of miners, and a third decked out in slightly finer, though no less dusty duds, stood below him, a rifle and pistols drawn. They stood around a wooden crate, suckling on a shared half-full bottle of tea-like liquid. Had to be whiskey.

The man in the fancier garb raised his rifle and aimed toward the west. Rafe followed the sight line and saw a massive tumble-down of freshly scarred boulders, still smoking — the result, guessed Rafe, of the first massive explosion he'd heard. And seated at the base of the pile of smoking rock, a bald, naked old man looked to be trussed up. His legs were spread, but bound again at the ankle, his arms tied behind him. There was something on the ground at his crotch, but it was too far for Rafe to make out. Even from that distance, Rafe could see the man's skin had taken on a boiled hue from the sun. He was also squawking like a flustered chicken.

Rafe edged closer to the top, tipped his hat forward to shield his eyes, and squinted. "Can't be."

One of the drunk men strode forward, a slight wobble to his gait, holstering his pistol as he walked. He also held the bottle.

"Hey!" one of the other men shouted. "You took my drink!"

"It's to make sure you don't shoot me, huh?"

They laughed. The staggering man made it to the tied-up man, and though it was too far for Rafe to make out specific words, the tone from the trussed old man was unmistakable — he was irate. Then Rafe saw the man with the bottle pull something from his waistband — sticks of dynamite? He wedged them in the shouting man's mouth, three, four, five of them. The bound man made feeble bugling sounds and thrashed his head in an effort to shake loose the sticks.

"Uh, uh, uh!" The man with the bottle shook his head and wagged a finger as if scolding the bound man. Then he walked back to his drinking buddies. "I'm getting bored. First one to hit the bottle of nitro by his pecker wins."

Rafe stood over them, jacked a shell into the chamber. "Wins what?"

The three men spun, looking in different directions.

"Up here, boys."

"Who are you?" one of them said, squinting up at Rafe.

One of the men smiled. "Who cares? Hell, it's only one of him and three of us."

Rafe held the rifle to his shoulder, trained down on them. "Let's see if I understand your logic: I have the high ground, I have a repeating rifle pointed at you, a couple of you'd have to clear leather . . . oh, and I'm not drunk."

They exchanged glances, then the one in fancier garb said, "I tell you what, mister! You should come down here. We'll take you on — *mano a mano mano mano!*" They laughed again, and the speaker half turned, palmed his pistol and dropped to one knee. Rafe was quicker and a single shot rang out. The man's revolver pinwheeled away. He screamed and clutched his gun hand with his other, a ragged hole welling red in the center of the clawed appendage. He collapsed to the sand, writhing and weeping.

"You shot Carlton!"

Rafe levered in a fresh round and cocked the hammer. "Looks like it. Now, what say you tell me why that old naked man deserves to have his parts and the rest of him pasted all over this desolate knob of rock."

"He make much work for us, señor!" The man waved his arms.

"That's good — I like that. Keep the arms up high. You, too. Good, now please, continue with your story."

"Look at that rock, señor! How we going to move all that now? And without the use of Carlton's hand! This morning, it makes many times that the old man blasts too much, we must work extra hard to clear it away. This leaves us no time to get ready for the track layers."

"Oh, I see. You all are the advance blasting team for a new railroad line, am I right?"

"Sí, sí, señor, that is it."

Rafe made his way down the slope, came up close to the two standing men. "I'll tell you what. I'm a believer in doing unto others." He looked at the faces of each man, and they seemed confused. Carlton, still mewling in the dirt, was a gringo, the other two were Mexican. They all sweated something fierce, and from the stink of them, Rafe guessed they'd been long on the bottle and short on baths.

"I'll make this plain. You all shuck your duds, toss them in a pile over here." He waited through their protests and eventual compliance. At last the two Mexicans stood before him, looking smaller and misshapen and defeated. "Good. Now help poor Carlton."

They did, and one of them said, "If it's money you want . . ."

"Naw, I'm full up on that. What I need is good old, honest-to-god retribution. Then I'll be moseying along."

Rafe toed open the top of the wooden crate they'd been using as a boot rest and tabletop. Inside was a stack of sticks of dynamite, coils of fuse, a coil of rough hemp rope, and three bottles of a clearish liquid that quivered with each slight movement.

"Hmm," said Rafe quietly, easing off on his rough handling of the rest of the crate's contents. Nitro — not a tincture you want to get too rambunctious around.

He tied the three naked men seated on the ground, their backs to each other, their ankles bound, and set the bottles of nitroglycerin between their legs.

They set up another round of hueing and crying, with Carlton howling the loudest, but Rafe only smiled as if they'd told him a long-forgotten joke. He finished off by stuffing as many sticks of dynamite in each howling man's mouth as he could fit: four in each, and five in Carlton's.

Next, he made his way down toward the

initial object of their ire. "You lay around in the sun like that, old man, you're bound to blister." He eased the dynamite sticks gingerly from the old timer's mouth.

"Rafe?" The man's eyes opened a crack. He squinted up. "That you, boy?"

"Yep, reckon it is, Cookie. I won't insult you by asking how you've been keeping yourself."

"I'd be obliged if you'd cut me loose, Rafe. Getting a mite crampy."

"Yeah, and that scorpion on your shoulder might not take it too kindly should you start twitching."

"Oh, lord."

Rafe unsheathed an Arkansas toothpick, shifted his cigar to the other side of his mouth, and flicked the venomous arched creature off the man's crimson shoulder. He sliced through the ankle ropes, then they both looked at the bottle of liquid between the naked man's thighs. It looked angry in the sun. Rafe tweezered the squat neck of the bottle and in one quick motion flung it far northward. It spun high, glinting in the sunlight, then disappeared over the hill before erupting in an orange-black cloud of roiling flame and smoke. They were pelted with blasted rock bits.

He helped the old man to his feet and cut

his wrists free, then walked back to the other men.

He lifted a shirt from the pile of clothes, puffed on the nub of his cigar, and got the shirt good and lit. The rest of the clothes — boots, and hats, too — soon caught fire.

"Oh, no, señor! You have no heart. You are *el diablo!*"

"That's true, I might indeed be ol' Scratch himself. You never can tell with strangers."

He scooped up their gun belts and the rifle, and by then the old naked man had ambled up beside him. "You got the rope around the wrong parts of 'em."

"Where's your camp, Cookie?"

"Back yonder, over that hill I made." Cookie smiled, his wrinkled face stretching wide at the memory. "You shoulda seen it, Rafe. Quite a blast."

"I did see it — from about five miles away."

"Good! You want something done right, don't do it by half measures!"

"Packed it hot, huh?"

"Could be I got a little carried away. Gets the job done, and it's so purty to see rocks start off in one piece, come down in a million little ones."

"Made your friends mad, though."

"They ain't my friends, neither. I hope

38

never to see 'em again, in fact. Might be, though, that they'll follow."

"Might be."

They made it to the small camp, Cookie drained a canteen, his Adam's apple working convulsively. Then he put his gear together, donned his clothes from the pile his three compadres made when they had him strip down, and led his two horses out of the little, semi-shaded corral. There were three other horses and a wagon left. Rafe turned the remaining horses loose, carried the guns with him.

"Hot horse?" said Rafe, indicating the beast Cookie had saddled for himself.

"Huh?"

"Mustang's are generally hot. They like to run."

"Oh, Stinky here? Nah, someone done rode the starch out of her before I come along. She pokes at a good pace, though. Same with that squirly brown thumper I got haulin' pack."

They rode northeast for a while in silence, then Cookie asked, "Where we aimed for?"

"To find a girl."

"Well, that makes sense. You have been in the calaboose for five years."

Rafe smiled and fired up a fresh cigar. "Good to see you, Cookie McGee."

"Good to see you, Rafe. Mighty glad you happened by when you did."

CHAPTER 4:
WHERE WE HEADED, AGAIN?

Late afternoon of the day Rafe found Cookie in his rather odd situation, the two men still rode northward at a brisk trot, pausing now and again to cool the horses. They'd quickly settled into their routine of years before of riding long distances, sometimes all day, without speaking. One of them, anyway.

Cookie knew most men grew uncomfortable in such a situation, wanted to fill the air with all manner of words, palaver and cackling. Yes, sir, he knew there were a good many men who felt that way, because he was one of them. But it was an urge he tried to keep lidded, lest it annoy Rafe more than he knew it did.

The younger man didn't seem to mind if Cookie flapped his gums or not. If he did mind he never said, so Cookie took that as a sign the whippersnapper liked his chattiness, though Rafe himself was a pitiful conversation-maker. But even Cookie had been quiet lo these last twenty miles or so.

"Out with it."

Rafe's sudden command caught Cookie by more than a little surprise. "What are you on about?"

Rafe barely cut his eyes toward the little man jostling in the saddle on the mustang beside him. But he knew he'd gotten to him when, soon enough, he saw Cookie's shoulders slump — a sure sign the man was about to get chatty.

"You know I don't like to pry none," said Cookie. "And I'm only too happy you helped me yarn my way outta that fix back there in the rocks with them railroad boys. Course I was about to kick up a fuss and really let them have it." Cookie's bushy eyebrows rose and he glanced at Rafe. Their eyes met for a moment, then Rafe almost smiled. He puffed on the cigar and shook his head.

"You don't think I was? Why, you hadn't happened along those boys would still be picking up pieces of themselves from here to San Jacinto and back. I was that mad, I was."

Rafe said nothing. Let the old man cool down, which he did presently.

"Way I see it we're riding due west."

Cookie rubbed his bristled chin. He suspected he could use a shave, a bath, and a bottle, not necessarily in that order. Still, there were no offered words from Rafe, so he tried again. "Yessir, I'd say we're . . ." He licked a fingertip and stuck it in the air. "Stompin' west, all right."

Cookie nodded at his deductions. All around them gold-topped scrub grass waved lightly in an unfelt breeze. They'd topped a rise and as Cookie glanced behind them he saw a ragged, strung-out line of black dots, maybe a dozen, tops. Puffs of dust like small clouds bloomed with them. Riders.

"Rafe, I hate to bring you raw news, you being so recent to the land of the free man again and all, might be you've lost some of your ability to see distances. But I seen —"

"Mounted men, ten. Been trailing me since Yuma."

"What?"

"And Cookie?" Rafe reined up and squinted over at Cookie. "It's not so easy to tell our direction by licking a finger and looking around. That's for figuring out where a breeze is coming from."

"Worked though, didn't it?" Cookie grinned. "Got you to open your trap!" He cackled and slapped his thigh. "Now, you gonna tell me how we come to be followed?"

"What's this 'we' stuff, Cookie? You have a mouse in your pocket? It's me they're following. You can cut out anytime, I won't think ill of you."

Cookie recoiled as if Rafe had backhanded him. He blinked, narrowed his eyes. "Now that's a fine howdy-do! You save my hide and now you don't allow me no way to repay you in kind?" He nudged his horse forward. "No, sir, you ain't gonna lose ol' Cookie that easy." He pointed a bony finger at Rafe. "You hear me?"

But Rafe was smiling, shaking his head, blue smoke rising slowly from his cigar. He plucked it from his mouth, held it atop his saddle horn, a thick finger curled around it. "Cookie, I swear. You haven't changed at all in five years."

Before the little man could respond with what Rafe knew would be a flurry of righteous oaths, he urged his own mount forward. "I'll fill you in as we ride . . . northeastward."

"Nor— wha?"

Rafe licked a fingertip, held it up, nodded. "Yep, northeastward."

Cookie's face settled into a deeper scowl, but he said nothing.

"And you're right, you know," said Rafe. "We're both in this, for good or ill. Those three men I helped, ah, liberate you from are bound to be along anytime, too. So that makes at least thirteen men to contend with. About right for our luck."

"Why don't we start with your ten. We already know what mine want."

"Yep, I reckon they didn't get a clear shot at it back there. Lucky that bottle of nitro was hiding it."

"Oh, you are testing my patience, whip-persnapper."

Over the next hour as they rode, and peppered with frequent head swivelings by Cookie to keep an eye on the men back-trailing them, Rafe told Cookie everything Warden Timmons told him. When he finished, he relit his cigar.

Cookie was uncharacteristically quiet for a spell. Then he said, "Ain't you worried? Those men are likely lawmen, or a posse of some such, fixing to nab you and hang you high."

"Sounds like maybe you weren't listening to me, Cookie."

"Not listening? Could be you didn't read that Timmons weasel the right way, Rafe. This whole mess stinks of a put-up job. He's setting you up for a fall, a short one down the hangman's drop."

Rafe puffed thoughtfully, blew out a cloud. "No, I don't think so. Timmons wanted me dead he'd have killed me a hundred times over in Yuma."

As he said that last word his voice thinned, tightened down on itself, sounded to Cookie like sand grinding between sheet steel.

"No, he's frying bigger fish and using me as the flame."

"You gonna singe his hide, eh?"

Rafe turned a grim face on Cookie. "That's the plan, my friend. Now let's make camp." He jerked his square chin forward. "That arroyo looks promising."

"You think camping down a gully is wise, Rafe, considering those rascals are back there?"

"Yep, because I want to know who they are. And besides" — Rafe urged his horse, with a cluck, in a zigzag trail down the scree-strewn slope — "we won't be down there when they come."

Cookie touched his nose. "But they'll think we are."

Rafe nodded and rode down to the bottom.

As they stripped their saddles and rubbed down their horses with scraps of burlap sacking, Cookie said, "You ever wonder what was behind you finding me like that?"

Rafe's eyebrows rose. "Why, Cookie, did you get religion while I was away? I take it you mean did some divine hand guide me to your aid?" One corner of his mouth rose.

"Confound it, Rafe, you are about the worse fella I ever did try, I say try 'cause I ain't actually ever succeeded, mind you, to have a conversation with! A genuine, one-hundred-percent conversation! Not that you'd even know what that word means."

They were quiet a while longer, then in a low voice Rafe said, "Oh, I reckon I've talked plenty in my time. Me and . . . me and Maria, we spoke all the time. Some-times without saying a word."

Cookie leaned against his horse, closed his eyes and nodded. He remembered Rafe's wife, the boy. "Never was there a sweeter woman, Rafe. I'm sorry I wasn't there —"

"Forget it." Rafe turned from his horse, snatched something from his saddlebag and made his way up the far side of the arroyo, sending narrow runnels of gravel down the slope as he climbed.

Cookie sighed and toed rocks and gravel into a tight ring, enough to hold a small fire for coffee. Should have known better. He cursed himself for talking so much. His mother, bless her ancient heart, had long ago told him his jawboning would be the death of him. He reckoned it had cost him a few friends over the years, too.

Cookie heard a clicking sound and looked up toward the top of the slope, thirty, forty feet away.

Rafe stood skylined against late-day blue, the last wispy remnants of far-off clouds stretched away forever, it seemed. The big man aimed a brass spyglass, twisted it, puffed once, twice on his cigar. A few moments passed, then he lowered the glass, but kept squinting toward the south.

"They still back there?"

Rafe didn't answer, but Cookie knew he would. The big man collapsed the glass, strode back down the slope. "Yep," he said, stuffing the brass tube back into his bag. "Ten of them. Hard-looking lot, from what I could see. And toting more weapons than a platoon could use." He swigged water from his canteen, swished it around in his mouth, swallowed.

Cookie nodded as he unstrapped the grub sacks. "Figures. Why can't we attract a passel of pretty doves making their way to a mine camp somewheres?"

"What are you doing?"

"Fixing to make supper," said Cookie.

"Don't know about you but I am peckish."

"What I mean is . . . have your cooking skills improved any?" Rafe knew what sort of response that would draw from the man, but he couldn't help himself. "You got that name of yours because you liked to cook up a hot charge under bridges in the war, remember. Not because you're a trail chef."

"Course I remember, you back-talkin' whelp! Now quit your jawin' and fetch some burnables."

Rafe did as he was bade, shaking his head and chuckling. Ol' Cookie never changed — and he hoped he never would. He'd missed the old codger while he was stuck busting rock in Yuma. There were few folks he'd missed, though the only other ones that really mattered were gone, long gone. And unlike Cookie, he'd not meet up with them again.

Some time later, Cookie hunkered over a small fire that crackled and snapped its greedy flames around dry sticks of mesquite and sage Rafe had gathered. He dished up a tin plate of runny frijoles and charred, leftover biscuits.

Rafe spooned up a sloppy dollop and shoveled it in. Truth be told, it was awful, but he was so hungry he suspected he could eat the southbound end of a northbound mule. Turns out even that determination wasn't enough to help him plow through Cookie's offering.

"How you like it, Rafe?"

Rafe chewed, swallowed — trying to not make a show of it. "The good news is you're consistent. The bad news is nothing's changed."

Cookie narrowed his eyes. "What's that supposed to mean?"

"Means you could burn water, old man."

"Who you calling old?"

"I notice you didn't deny my claim."

"Course not." Cookie grinned. "That's why I'm so lean."

"Because you're old or because you're a lousy cook?"

Cookie shrugged. "Take your pick."

Rafe ladled up another spoonful of beans. "Cookie," he said, around a mouthful of piping hot, scorched beans. "Don't ever change."

"Not a prayer. I'm consistent, remember?"

By the time they'd finished cleaning their dishes and had settled back for a smoke and a cup of hot coffee, the sky to the west began tugging on its evening colors, purpling like a fresh bruise. The thought turned Rafe's mind to the girl, daughter of the governor of California. How had she fallen into the clutches of someone so raw and rank as Al Swearengen?

From what little Rafe knew of the man, he was the human equivalent of boot scrapings. Even that had some value as fertilizer in a flower garden. Swearengen and his ilk were weeds taking over the lives of good people.

"How long you reckon we have before they make their move?"

Cookie's voice startled Rafe and he snapped out of his reverie. "Oh, I'd give them a couple of hours after dark. Maybe longer."

Cookie nodded, drew on his pipe. "Know their type. They're likely to be jackals, night fighters who'll count on us being wrapped tight in our bedrolls, snoring to high heaven, and dreaming of hot times with buxom lady folk." He cackled and slapped a hand on his leg, dust rising from his gray wool trousers.

"But we won't be."

"Right. So what's the plan?"

Rafe stretched his long legs out, crossed them and puffed on his cigar. "Couple of hours of rest. We'll be safe here in camp, unless I misjudge them. Then I'll low crawl up thataway." He nodded toward the rise to their northeast. "I have the Greener scatter-gun, plenty of shells, two Colts, and my skinning knife. I'll leave the Greener over there, hidden at the base of that boulder."

He looked to Cookie who merely nodded, so Rafe continued. "I was thinking you could position yourself behind the rise at the top of that hummock there." He gestured toward the west. "I don't for a second think they'll come in single file, chatting and whistling 'Dixie,' but these spots should give us plenty of room to catfoot around this little campsite. Surround them as best we can."

"How about the horses?" Cookie looked over at the four beasts, two his, two Rafe's.

The big man nodded. "Tricky. Don't want to move them too soon, lest they think we're rabbity, but I don't want them hit by any stray shots, or run off."

"Or stolen!" said Cookie. "I've been afoot in places worse than this, but that don't mean this stretch of . . . where are we at, anyway?"

Rafe half smiled. "Still in Utah, I expect. We'll be riding northeast soon, through Wyoming, then eastward."

Cookie nodded. "What was I talking about?"

"About how you were going to curl up yonder. I'll wake you when they come."

"No siree. I reckon I'll take first watch,

Rafe. You don't mind me saying so, you ain't built up your wind yet. That place took more out of you than you care to admit. And since I'm going to need your brawn should it come to a scrap, I'll ask you to kindly get a good rest in. And make it quick. They won't wait all night."

Rafe was set to argue. It was in his nature not to take anything that even faintly smacked of a favor, but he had to admit Cookie was right. He was still working to build himself up to his old self again, and wondered if he ever would. As if to prove Cookie's point, a yawn, unbidden, rose up and out of Rafe's mouth.

"There, you see?" Cookie stood and whacked the spent bowl of his pipe against his palm, smacked the soot against his leg. "Now get your shut-eye. I'll wake you when the time comes, and tend to the horses, too."

Rafe nodded, laid back, head on his saddle, and tilted his chaw-brown flatbrim hat over his eyes. "Cookie?"

"Yeah, Rafe?"

"I don't care what they say, you're a good egg. Can't cook worth a damn, but you're okay."

"Rafe?"

"Yeah."

"Shut that yapper or I'll button it up for you."

Both men grinned. Within a minute, Rafe was snoring softly. Cookie gave him one last look, concern creasing his plenty-lined face. The boy ain't all home yet, he thought. Wonder if he ever will be? He sighed, checked his own stock of weapons — a much-nicked carbine with a rawhide-wrapped stock, more repair than wood at this point, two blades on his person — a Green River skinner and a short-handled tomahawk, good for close-in swinging and kindling work.

And in a worn leather holster where most men carried a six-gun, Cookie McGee had loaded a bundle of dynamite short sticks. In the left breast pocket of his chambray work shirt, he carried extra lucifers. Had them in most pockets on his person, in fact. He was of a mind that a man couldn't have too many sources of flame, nor items to light and make loud sounds with.

Satisfied, Cookie climbed to a hidden vantage point provided by a sharp jut of sandstone ledge. From there he could detect even the slightest movement for miles in three directions. The fourth, he'd have to guess at. He settled in to wait.

This was a position he was accustomed to

where it concerned Rafe Barr. The big man was a straight shooter, and because of it would rarely bend his thinking to suit those who wronged him or who he knew had wronged others. A time or twelve in the past this trait had resulted in such a situation — them being dogged by malcontents, as Rafe called them. It had never ended well for the malcontents.

Cookie recalled, sucking a breath in through his teeth, that there had been a couple of times when they had also nearly nibbled off more than they could chew. Still, what was the dish of life without a liberal dose of chili powder now and again?

He readjusted his legs so they wouldn't cramp, but wouldn't feel too comfortable, either — didn't want to doze off — and settled in for a long wait. Night was all but upon them. Various critters of the dark commenced their stirrings. Cookie knew diamondbacks and sidewinders were testing the cooling air with flittering tongues, wide-eyed kangaroo mice knew it too, and were doing their best to avoid the darkest crevices where misfortune happened in the desert at night.

The quick yips of a coyote brought a musical string of others, like gemstones you can hear, thought Cookie. He'd long been partial to the sounds of coyotes. They worked that middle ground between being homesick and being in love, and made a man think deeper thoughts than he had a right to.

And so it was that Cookie and Rafe passed the early, small hours waiting for what, they didn't quite know. But someone did.

CHAPTER 5:
UNLEASH THE HOUNDS!

"You . . . you . . . stupido!" El Jefe's tin bowl of spicy frijoles sprayed its contents across the face of the man next to the one he'd been aiming for. No matter, they were all idiots who deserved much abuse. He had decided only that day, hours before, that he was far too easy on them.

The man who'd received the ill-thrown food stood and swatted at the dripping brown mess dribbling down his sweat-stained smock. "Why did you do that, El Jefe?"

The Chief saw the man's teeth, saw the bunched muscles in the whiskered cheeks, knew he wanted nothing more than to lunge at El Jefe. And El Jefe wanted that, too. He knew now why he had been so angry these past days on the trail. He wanted a fight. He had been far too long away from their hometown of Yuma. Or at least their adopted hometown. No matter, it was a town he could bloody his knuckles in anytime he wanted.

Ever since they became the servants of Warden Timmons he had chafed nearly raw under the never-ending demands of that pious head jailer. And now here was their biggest undertaking yet. One he knew he had to make the best of, had to do something that would separate them from Timmons for good.

If he didn't this time, there would be more of the same. Timmons took everything and gave them nothing in return. Well not this time. And if it meant El Jefe had to ride his men harder, even lay low a few them to get the job done, then so be it.

"Why is he stupido, El Jefe?"

El Jefe sighed. Would they never learn? "Because you all are. You most of all, though, Tepito." El Jefe stood, squared his bulk, and crouched enough to drive forward like a small lumber train. God, but he wanted to fight. Might take his mind off the man they were following.

He'd caught sight of him a handful of times, knew, too, that the man had seen them, but didn't believe for a minute the stories the warden told them about how impressive this Barr was. No man was that bold nor as skilled as Timmons told them.

Still, the bastard was big. And he had picked up a scrawny *viejo*. The old one would be easy to pinch out. But Barr, he would require more thinking.

It had taken El Jefe much of the day, but he concluded that, in case Timmons was even half right, he had to beware. Mostly, though, he thought about why Timmons hired Barr to find the girl. And the answer he kept circling back to was that Timmons did not think El Jefe and the Hell Hounds were up to the task. After all they'd done for him!

Still, El Jefe was torn between waiting for Barr to snatch the girl from the man in Deadwood, or lay into Barr now, kill him, and steal the girl from the mine camp himself, then hold her for money. Lots of money. Put the real squeeze on the warden.

Why would Timmons want her bad enough to release a murderer from prison? There had to be something in that. He would think about it later. But for certain, he would charge the warden no small amount for return of the girl. How much to charge though, he had no idea. It would come to him. But not before he had some fun, though, eh?

First, he would have a dustup with one or two of his men, remind them who he was and who was in charge. Then maybe they would pay a call to this Rafe Barr and the skinny old man. It would be good to figure out the cut of their cloth, as an old cowboy had said to him some time back. That gringo trail bum shared his whiskey bottle with El Jefe. Then, when the cowboy was good and red-eyed, El Jefe also made him share his purse.

Of course, even drunk the man had put up a fuss, so the Chief had slid his long knife, the one he called Needle, *Aguja,* for the fine, slender blade that slips, fast as you please, deep into a man's most hidden places, the heart, lungs, the guts, depending on how quickly El Jefe wanted a soul to die.

As it happened, the purse was hardly worth the effort, but the old cowboy had brought on his own death. He should not have fought over such a pathetic sum.

El Jefe grinned and smacked his thick hands together as if squashing a moth in midflight. "Tonight, you worthless bastards, we will see how their cloth is cut, eh?"

The men stared at him, their swarthy brows wrinkling. He knew they wanted to ask what he meant but were too afraid of him to say so. Good, at least they knew he was still the head of this gang. But he was also a little concerned that he had said something stupid.

He should not use these gringo ways of speaking, especially from the foolish cowboys, who never came right out and spoke their mind but talked around it. El Jefe sighed. "We will visit their camp tonight, sí?"

"Ah, yes, yes," murmured the men, smiles creasing their curly, food-flecked beards as they finished their meals, lit brown-paper cigarettes.

Coyote spoke first. "So you have finally decided we should kill them now, eh?" He nodded to himself and tilted his tin plate up before his face, licking up the last of the greasy mess like an animal.

El Jefe's teeth ground together so hard he felt something in his jaw pop. He brought up his boot fast, drove the sloped heel straight into the middle of the plate. A grim smile played on his face as he felt Coyote's nose snap behind the plate, heard the strangling "Gaaak!" cry of surprise churned with pain.

"Anybody else? Huh?" El Jefe's stance suggested any response at all would be ill-advised. His broad legs were bowed, wide shoulders rising and falling with his hard breathing, not from the brief burst of exertion but from the tingle of excitement he felt twitching deep in his gut.

Anytime he could lay a man low, reduce him to a squealing, sobbing, broken beast, El Jefe was pleased. It put him on top once more, and was something he enjoyed whenever doubt of his leadership crept in around the campfire.

"You worry too much," Rosa the *puta* had told him. She had been right, of course, but he still had treated her to a dose of his tattooed knuckles. He had given her an up-close look at the scarred joints that read D-I-O-S. But, next time, if she kept her mouth shut, he might give her the left hand, the black ink on the knuckles spelling out D-E-I-S.

A priest at the friary in Chihuahua had told him that word meant "God" in some language or other. El Jefe liked it because it played nicely on the hand opposite the other God word. And that's what he wanted his men to think of him — not their boss, but their god.

"El Jefe?"

The seething man focused, shook his head as if to dispel an irksome bee.

"El Jefe?" the voice was small, timid. It was the Kid, a half-Apache, half-something-else whelp he had all but raised after finding him tortured and tied to a wagon wheel, left by his own kind to bake to death in the sun far south in the Sonoran Desert.

"What?" El Jefe eyed the youth, now grown to a chinless, stringy, wolfish-looking boy, one gray eye, dead to the world of sight, one green, round and glittering like that of a turtle. But sometimes at night it seemed the boy's eyes were both the same, both black as forgotten pools of water at midnight.

The Kid was timid, as El Jefe had intended. But he was also devoted to El Jefe to the point that he emulated El Jefe's mannerisms and style of dress. This El Jefe did not mind — it made him feel some pride in the Kid. He was certain he had left a number of mewling creatures behind over the years that various women would tell him were his own offspring, but they were less than nothing to him.

But the Kid was different somehow, and useful in various ways. He was willing to put up with the womanly duties of cooking and clothing repair when they were on the trail. He was also the only one of the men El Jefe would tolerate as a go-between when his blood was up. As now.

"El Jefe, the men are confused." The boy's voice came out in his high-pitch, raspy whisper, the only way he ever sounded since being found, something to do with the arrow he'd taken in the throat, El Jefe was certain of that. "We will visit these men, but we will not kill them, sí?"

The leader let his eyelids droop, his breathing evened. "Sí." His great fists relaxed and he looked at the cowering men. "Sí, nothing more than to put a fear in them. Once it is full dark. I am not convinced the warden told us the truth. And besides, are we not the Hell Hounds?" He grinned wide and nodded.

Eager to once more be on the good side of their harsh leader, the men smiled and nodded with vigor. "Sí, sí, sí!" Their chorus tailed off as El Jefe rummaged in his saddlebag, and lifted out a nearly full bottle of mezcal. He tossed it to Tepito, who cradled it expertly, not daring to risk the loss of such a fine gift.

"You all take a pull, pass it around, but no more. Else you will not be in good shape to dance with the two gringos later tonight, no?" El Jefe chuckled as he wandered off to make water on a stunty sage bush. He gave fleeting thought that he might step on a hunting snake, but figured he would hear its buzzing in enough time to piss on it and drive it off.

It was his practice following one of his

frequent black moods to walk the camp, circle it from afar, though keeping the fire in sight. Long ago he had adopted the practice and it had saved his life a number of times over the years. Twice he was able to hear various members of the Hell Hounds plotting dark deeds against him.

He had suspected they were up to no good, but wanted to find out for certain before he began killing his own men. They had been between jobs, roving from one outpost to another, taking at will, both women and money and food and goods. But the men were bored, that much he knew.

El Jefe did not let on to them that he suspected their betrayals, but should his suspicions prove right, he was armed with enough power to kill a few. And that's what happened that dark night.

He'd played up the character they most wanted to see — an ineffective man losing his clawhold on his gang. "That spicy mess has done me false. I must go find a tree to lean against." That was one of their ways of saying they had to empty their guts of previous meals.

He went to his saddlebags to retrieve whatever he might need at the latrine, but it was a ruse. He'd palmed a stick of dynamite, then catfooted around the camp, sidling low and finding a comfortable spot behind a boulder. Soon enough he heard their voices telling each other that El Jefe was long in the tooth, past any usefulness, and should have his throat opened wide in his sleep.

That was all El Jefe needed to hear. He waited a few seconds more, and when the men were giggling like children at their plan, he flicked to brilliant life the head of a wooden match. He touched it to the short fuse of the thumb-thick stick of tight-packed hell.

The vicious paper-wrapped cylinder sparked and hissed in his hand, and as one of the men said, "What's that sound — hey . . ." El Jefe tossed the stick of dynamite, and watched it as if time had slowed, arcing end over end against the blue-black of the night sky, trailing spits of light until it descended in the midst of the campfire around which the men were seated.

It seemed to El Jefe as if all the hunting creatures, all the bugs in the sky, the stars themselves, all the night around them, held a soft breath for less than a moment. Then . . . *KA-BAM!* And the desert night erupted like what he imagined a volcano would look like.

Flame and jags of hot rock and clods of sandy earth and burning wood blasted in all directions, driving into and through wide-eyed men caught on the cusp of screams.

Though the stick only needed a moment, sounds of the explosion seemed to last for many minutes, though he knew that was impossible. He grinned — the men who planned to slit open his neck in his sleep were gurgling screams through blood-filled lips, writhing in bloodied clots on the ground.

He'd heard the horses thunder off into the night, but didn't care. He would catch them in the morning. For now, El Jefe strolled among the dead and dying of his gang, gazing down at them from the light of a half dozen tiny fires, one of them a dead man's hair. The stink was rising, but two of the men appeared to still be alive, one for sure. It was Monte, the bastard El Jefe had heard voicing the plot.

The men caught sight of each other, El Jefe from on high, grinning down at Monte. The man on his back on the ground convulsed as wet coughs wracked him, blood gouting from his mouth. But his eyes were not infirm. The narrowed slits spat venom at the man who had caused this.

"Oh, you are angry with me, compadre? Sí, sí." El Jefe nodded in sympathy. "I, too, would be angry had you done something

67

like this to me." He bent low, close enough that his rank breath clouded the dying man's face. "We are somewhat alike, you and me. But there is one difference, Monte. You see" — he stood again, sighing — "from now on, you will be dead. And I will be El Jefe." He walked to the edge of the wrecked campsite and bent to retrieve his tumbled saddlebags.

The last sound Monte heard was a low, throaty chuckle that rose to a full-belly laugh, moving slowly away into the otherwise quiet night.

All this El Jefe recalled as he puffed a black dog-turd of a cigarillo. He strolled the perimeter of this camp as the sun made its way down the sky. This latest group of Hell Hounds was a mess, some of the worst he'd ever had, a few not so bad. Not counting him and the Kid, there were eight of them.

All could be counted on in a scrape to at least fight for their own lives if cornered, maybe throw in with their fellow Hell Hounds at least in defense of whatever loot they had made off with. What more could he ask of a gang of simpleminded fools? None of them, save maybe for the Kid, seemed to have the gumption to survive alone in the world, much less kill him and take over the gang.

That was good, for if he played this hand right, this Warden Timmons deal he had working in his mind, he might be able to get rid of this batch of Hell Hounds, though maybe not the boy, and go it alone.

Making sure his men were obeying his orders was becoming a pain in his ass. Had been for a long time, but he wanted more of the nice things he'd only tasted now and again. He wanted good clean whores, and fat cigars that did not smell like animal leavings. Plus, he had a yearning for tasty gringo whiskey and crisp, tailored clothes, not these layers of smelly black leather. It was tiresome to wear all the time.

And maybe one day a nice hacienda not far from a good little town, some place he could visit each day and spend time playing at cards in a cantina. Maybe a cantina he owned! With his own stable full of whores! Hey now, that was not a bad dream.

El Jefe puffed the cheroot, his nose wrinkling out of habit at the stink of it. But to pull off the plan, and to snatch the amount of money he truly needed, would take more of his brain's ability than ever. With someone like the warden, he had to be smart. He did not trust the jailer any more than he trusted the sincerity of a woman's whimpers, or the dedication of any of his men, the Kid included.

El Jefe wanted it all, and the way he figured it, he could have it all. He had to choose the best moment to strike. He plucked the cigarillo from his mouth and blew on the tip to revive it. Then a new thought occurred to El Jefe, and his eyes widened.

What if the warden would pay not only for the girl but for Barr, too? From the way the warden spoke, he would dearly like to have Barr back, alive, no doubt so he could stomp him into a pulpy mess himself.

A spreading smile halted as yet another new thought chewed the heels of the previous one. What if he went directly to whoever the girl belonged to? For it had occurred to El Jefe that the girl was merely a card in Timmons's hand, not the entire game of play. So how to find out who that might be? He pooched out his bottom lip and made his way back to camp slowly. This matter would require more thought.

But in the meantime he would send the boys in to roust the gringos in their sleep. El Jefe would watch from a place of hiding and take stock of the skills of this fellow Rafe Barr. Then he would better be able to tell what he was facing. If he was as good as Timmons said, maybe Barr would cull a few of the weaker Hounds from the pack, eh?

All this thinking was driving him crazy, chasing his tail like a starving fleabag dog in the street. El Jefe strolled back to the campfire light and within paces of the flames he knew something was wrong. He squinted, looking at each of the men in turn. "Where is the bottle?"

No one answered, then Tepito held up the nearly empty glass vessel. "It was a long day, El Jefe, and the men have been so thirsty and hot."

"Stop making excuses. You are men, are you not? Men who should know better than to disobey me. Now you will have to fight with the mezcal muddying your minds? Make ready and saddle your horses. We have business to tend to."

Each of the men groaned and glowered at him, at least until they caught his eye. Then they lowered their gazes and went about their tasks as El Jefe sighed and saddled his own horse.

Once they were ready, they stood together, in a ragged ring, facing inward, all eyes on El Jefe. "I will not say much about the mezcal. That is not going to be helpful. It would have been better if you had not sipped more than you did. But for that I blame myself. You are weak and stupid men and I should not have handed you the bottle. Now, here is what we are going to do. We are going to ride to Barr's camp, not to kill him, but to prod him as if he were a sleeping rattler. That old man who is with him does not matter to me, but don't kill him yet. For if we do, then this Barr might not follow through with finding the girl. So I have decided we will only see what he can do, no more than that. Understood?"

"Sí, sí, that is good, El Jefe," said Coyote. "Then if he is not any good, we can kill him and consider it a headache we will no longer have. Then we'll go to Deadwood ourselves and rescue the gringo girl and make money off her."

El Jefe listened to all Coyote had to say. Despite the mashed-in nose, which made him sound as if he were speaking through a wad of cotton mattress ticking, Coyote was in sound shape. That bothered El Jefe. He was the one Hell Hound he trusted the least, and that was saying something.

"And how did you come up with all this information, eh, Coyote? You have been listening in on my thoughts, maybe?" El Jefe pasted on a wide, insincere smile and circled the puffy-faced man. "Yes, yes, that must be it. And since that is the case, I will need to think about you more. Much more. But for now, you will do as I say, no killing. Now we ride."

Chapter 6:
Somethin's Hinky

Rafe felt the not-so-gentle nudge of a boot on his shoulder. For the sliver of a moment it took to awaken from his slumber — deeper than he would have allowed but a few years before — his uneasy mind was convinced that he was still in Yuma Territorial Prison, and something was bent on rousting him. Rage, nested deep in the angry knots of his sleep-addled, angry brain told him to strike hard, fast, and with finality.

His muscled arm lashed out and snatched tight the source of the offense — a man's boot. Even as he came around fully to wakefulness, Rafe's steel-band grip tightened as if fired by great pistons, and clamped ever tighter.

His eyes snapped open, seeing little in the full dark save for a vague outline of something thrashing close by. He pushed himself up to a sitting position with his free arm, still maintaining his grip on the thrashing form's leg.

"Lay off me, Rafe!" The voice came out as a growled hiss.

"Cookie?"

"Who in blazes you think it'd be?"

Rafe's clamp-like hand released and the old man sank back on his butt, massaging his ankle through the boot.

"Sorry, Cookie."

"Keep your apologies for the morning," the old man whispered. "And keep that voice down." He moved closer. "I got me a hinky feeling, Rafe. You were right. Something's on the move this way. I figure we got a few minutes yet."

But Rafe was already on his feet, crouching low. He leaned his hat on his saddle, stuffed his saddlebags under a thin wool blanket, and Cookie did the same. Then he slowly poked three slender sticks of dry sage into the coals, knowing they'd tinder up after a few minutes, give them as much light as they could hope for.

He turned to tell Cookie to get to his position, but the old man was already angling that way. He gave Rafe a quick salute. Rafe heard Cookie's low chuckle as he settled into his spot.

The big man felt little nervousness at the

coming fracas. Whatever the reason behind it might be, he'd find out soon enough. Instead his gut twinged with excitement and anticipation of action. It had been far too long since he'd allowed himself to cut loose, really cut loose, and deliver on another man.

From what he'd seen earlier through the spyglass, these scurvy-ridden desert rats were out for a dose of something and he was only too happy to oblige. And he knew Cookie felt the same way. Still, he did worry a smidgen about Cookie. He was his oldest friend, hell, the cantankerous billy goat was his only friend. But he was no kid.

Rafe would, by instinct, do his best to draw the fight to himself. He had little worry that others would turn the tide away from him. He was not a boastful man, merely confident of his abilities. He perked his ears. When Cookie says he has a hinky feeling, something's in the offing, and soon.

Rafe didn't have long to wait. After a near-silent ten minutes, almost part of the shadows, yet peeling from them, a tall, thin form, taking little effort to bend low, moved with snaky silence toward the campfire, skirted it. As it did so, from his vantage point above the scene, Rafe caught sight of the barest of details — dark trousers, perhaps tucked into tall boots, equally dark. The shirt was of a lighter-color cloth.

The person's head was too far above the low glow of the dim campfire to see facial details. But he did catch sight of one long arm swinging, something gripped at the end, weighting the hand like a pendulum.

That would be a knife, for close-in work and silent gutting. The only reason to carry one into a strange camp at night was for evil purpose. Other footsteps, less careful than the first person's, came to his ears. The boots ground and smeared sand beneath the soles. This may have been near-quiet for most folks, but Rafe's hearing had always been impressive.

He was able to pick out the flutter of a bird's wings in a thorny mesquite from afar, and his long experience in the field clued him in as to the cause of the bird's alarm. So the sound of careless, heavy-footed prowlers was no challenge for the big man.

Rafe waited for three more shadows to join the first, knew that was less than half of the gang he'd seen earlier. If he waited any longer they'd discover the ruse, so he cat-footed his way closer to the campfire, and the middle of the coming action. He would not hesitate to kill should the need arise. These looked to be dark men bent on dark deeds and he would match their intent with his own.

He also was not worried about Cookie opening fire and accidentally hitting him. They'd agreed that quiet was the key, only opening up with a firearm should they have no choice, and then only if they knew for certain where each other was located.

Rafe stepped once, twice, not getting as quiet a step as he'd like in his boots — he wished he had his old soft-sole camp moccasins. Still, he made little noise until he stepped on a small flat rock that grated against a larger one. He paused, knew the tall, skinny invader had done the same. Rafe was bent low and risked a slight movement. With two fingertips, he tweezered up a nugget of rock, flicked it off his thumbnail. He heard it land six or so feet away. It worked.

The tall stranger bent lower and circled wide of the spot where the stone landed. Rafe wasted no time, but dropped nearly to his belly and swooped low, the momentum from his forward lunge propelling him straight at the tall figure.

Even as his shoulder drove into the man's midsection, his left hand reached up and clawed at the face. He felt scraggly whiskers, a bony face, no chin, and he clamped his big mitt across the mouth.

Rafe let his momentum carry him forward.

He slammed the man's head to the ground where it bounced off the hard-packed earth. Dazed, his lanky victim's head lolled with weak efforts. For a moment he caught the dull glint of moonlight off dark eyes. The sight chilled him.

Rafe shook off the feeling — he knew the man was a second from a shout or scream. He drove his big right fist into the bony face, felt something collapse, the flesh smear as the man's muffled mouth whimpered. One snapping punch ushered the man into long, painful dreams.

A sound like a quick breeze through a length of lead pipe bloomed behind him in the inky dark. Trouble suspected, Rafe dropped low and rolled onto his back. Another man, shorter and thicker than the first, stood above him, outlined against the purple sky.

"Gringo!" spat the man, before he shifted his weight to his left leg. The movement was telltale enough that Rafe knew he was going to deliver a kick. Rafe sat upright, pivoting on his backside, and snagged the right leg as it began its backward motion.

The kicker barely had time to utter a grunt of surprise when he found himself rising backward through the air. Rafe drove the burly man's girth upward, then with his own legs beneath him, used his considerable power as leverage.

He guided the brute up, shoving, and was rewarded with the sound of the man's hard landing. A shout of strangled surprise cut off in mid-bark as the attacker's shoulders hit the packed ground, his neck and head bent at an unnatural angle.

"That you, Rafe?"

Cookie had revealed his cover, but it didn't matter to Rafe, he was in his element. Once again he dropped low, one knee to the ground, scanning the night for sounds, movement, shifting shadows.

He smelled sweat, possibly of the brute he'd upended. Heard stuttering breaths of someone trying in desperation to quiet loud breathing. It wasn't working.

Hurried footsteps, off to Rafe's right, closed in fast. No time to think — only react. The big man watched an arm rise, arc back over his head, then whip downward. Close by, Rafe heard Cookie shout, "What in the hell's he . . ."

Cookie's question was cut short as Rafe's big arm raked him down hard to the ground. The old stringy warhorse bubbled with rage — until their world exploded in a stormburst of gravel glinting in the campfire's glow.

Someone out of the dark spun a high kick, drove it down at Cookie's bald, moonlit pate. The crotchety man caught a glimpse and dropped, feeling something popping in one knee. Worry about that later.

The driven boot whipped inches above him — he felt its breeze. "Hey! You bastards!"

"I . . . ," said Rafe beside him as he drove a ham-fist into another leering face. ". . . don't think they . . ." Rafe ducked to avoid a fist, then clawed free a Colt, tempted to trigger it smoothly, longing to hear the throaty clicks, knowing they'd be a tonic to his ears. ". . . give a shit about your insults, old man!"

Instead he flipped the gun, the barrel landing smoothly in his palm. He raised it up, brought it down like a hammer on a nail, and heard the dull *whump* as the butt of the revolver crushed bone.

"Who are you callin' . . ." Cookie bit off the tail end of the words as he rolled over on his back twice, feeling the spines of a clot of prickly pear cactus pierce his shirt and sink into his bony back. He missed the gleaming Bowie blade that whipped out of the dark and sunk with a dull thunk into the gravel beside him. ". . . old, you whiny sprout?"

Cookie drove a harness boot straight at the fingerless-gloved hand clutching the brass-and-wood handle. Quick as a striking copperhead, the dynamite expert snatched the Bowie. Keeping his momentum hurtling forward, through gritted teeth Cookie hissed as he felt the intruder's blade pop its owner's sweaty, hairy hide.

"Gaaaah!" The man's scream dissolved into a gurgle, tailed out with a weak cough. By then Cookie had dragged the knife back out of the hot, gushing wound and whipped around low. The move was fruitful, offering up another scream as yet another man's hamstring snapped like a sliced lynch rope.

The moment left Cookie grinding his teeth, nostrils flared. He heard a low, mannish chuckle beside him, and a grim grin crossed his face. Rafe was back, all right. And so was Cookie — old man, like hell.

The two men hunkered low behind the southerly boulder, listening sharp and scanning the dark. So far neither had heard any commotion anywhere near their horses.

"Why you think they're not shooting?" whispered Cookie. "Ain't like we don't know they're here by now."

"This is a lull. I'd guess those three were the advance guard. Still seven more out there somewhere."

"We kill 'em?"

"Likely that last one, not sure of the other two."

As if in response to their question, they heard a commotion down by the campfire. They peeked around the boulder and saw two, maybe three dark shapes bend, muckle onto the unmoving forms, hoist, and haul them off. Cookie growled and began to rise, but Rafe gripped the old man's forearm. "Hold steady."

"What? Why? They're going to get away!" He continued to whisper, but barely.

"Something tells me this was a test."

"What? Are you crazy?"

"Think, Cookie. They could have tried, really tried, to kill us, but they didn't. Instead they sent in a few men who don't know any more about fighting than you do about cooking. Let them go. I expect we'll learn more from them later."

Next to him in the dark the little man clucked like a perturbed hen.

"Besides," said Rafe. "It gave us a chance to work our muscles."

"Speak for yourself. I'd as soon have my beauty rest."

Rafe shook his head and continued to listen to the dark. They stayed that way, two veterans of many scuffles and skirmishes through the years, together and separately. As dawn lit the landscape once more, it found the men red-eyed but alert, and with a full view of their surrounds. Their horses stood hobbled where they'd left them hours before, and their gear appeared unmolested, other than what had been trodden on or kicked out of the way in the melee.

As they stood and stretched their backs, Rafe said, "I plan on scouting the area, see what I can learn about our guests."

Cookie nodded. "I'll tend the horses, tidy up, get a coffee fire going."

Rafe set flame to a cigar stub he plucked from his shirt pocket and set off down the hill, following the footsteps and drag marks the retreating attackers took no care to hide. They led to the southwest, back toward where he'd seen their camp in the distance the afternoon before.

Rifle cradled across his chest, the big man strode willfully alongside the tracks, scanning ahead for sign of a belated ambush. Along the trail, bloody splotches, dark and drying in the coming light, further accentuated the route. The blood would be from the man Cookie had all but eviscerated. Of his body there was as yet no sign, let alone the other two they'd laid low. Rafe continued on, puffing on his cigar only when he

84

had a clear sightline ahead and to each side.

He topped one last rise, suspecting he would soon be at their campsite. And there below sat stomped, churned dirt and a still-smoking campfire. Most curious of all was the flopped body of a man. It lay stretched out, face up, alongside the fire's huffing remains.

Rafe glanced around, all his cautions on high, though he knew with certainty born of long experience in such matters that the varmints had long since skedaddled. He walked to the corpse, looked down at it. There were the knife wounds, gut and hamstring, where he suspected they'd be. But it was the man's head that interested him.

A distinct boot print marked the side of the man's face, turned away from Rafe as if ashamed. The severity of the turned head was telltale. A snapped neck. The boot print told it all. Someone had not wanted to be saddled with a dying man and so had done either the most vicious or the kindest act that could be done in such a situation, depending, of course, which end of the boot you were on.

Rafe puffed vigorously on his cigar, glanced up at the new day's sky, and saw the first far-off wheelings of buzzards. He looked back to the dead man. "Everybody's gotta make a living, fella. You had your chance, now it's theirs."

He walked back to camp. Over a breakfast of warmed biscuits, dried apple slices, and good, hot coffee, Rafe told Cookie what he'd found. None of it particularly surprised the older man. "Sleep with dogs, I reckon you'll get fleas."

Rafe nodded and sipped his coffee.

"I declare!" Cookie smacked his thigh. "I ain't had that much fun in years. Not since Selma the Bear — you remember Selma, down Houston way? I recall that time she chased me around that breakfast table in the boardinghouse, each of us wearing nothing but a smile."

"As I recollect, you wore the smile, she wore a growl, and carried a cast-iron skillet. She caught up to you, too, you seem to forget."

Cookie ribbed the back of his bald head. "I don't remember all of that morning, truth be told. Might be it wasn't as fun as I remember."

"Speaking as someone who was trying to eat breakfast, I can safely say no, it wasn't all that much fun. Especially when you flopped facedown in my flapjacks, your bony old ass wagging in the air."

"Hee hee!" Cookie downed the last of his coffee.

"Don't ever change, Cookie."

"What makes you think I would, even if I wanted to?"

CHAPTER 7:
THERE'S GOLD IN THEM HILLS

For five days they traveled at a hard pace. Cookie kicked up a fuss over it, but he knew enough to stop short of riling Rafe's feathers. They had to make time, had to get to the girl. Cookie knew Rafe had given his word to that Timmons character, no matter the backhanded sort of man the warden was. He also knew that the girl, likely not so innocent any longer, was held against her will. They would no doubt find her in a drugged, sloppy stupor. The situation was an unacceptable burr that worked away at Rafe without cease.

Still, Rafe's silence was annoying, and Cookie could take it no longer. "You got a plan in mind once we get to Deadwood, or are you going to waltz on in there and make it up as you go?"

They rode a half minute more, the only sounds the soft creaking of saddle leather, the thumping of hoofbeats, the random soft *ching* of a shoe on stone.

The land in which they now found themselves, somewhere in the middle-eastern edge of Wyoming, had altered from the raw jags and crags of the Rockies days before to a vast scape that stretched in slow rises for as far as they could see. It was a pretty place, with its low green valleys, the grasses of summer topped with seed heads the color of Rafe's sweat-stained, dust-rimed hat.

The landscape was familiar to them, and they knew soon the land would begin to fall away, subtly at first, then with more intensity as ravines opened in the earth, revealing shadowed slopes. Above would be those unforgettable rising hills clotted with dark pines, the sight from a distance giving the Black Hills their name.

"The plan," said Rafe so long after Cookie had asked that even Cookie had forgotten what he'd asked. He had given up on an answer and allowed himself to sink into the beauty of the terrain they loped through. "Is to find this Swearengen fellow and persuade him to let the girl ride on out with us."

Cookie smacked his dusty trouser leg. "Now don't that beat all. I know you're a man of few words, Rafe Barr, but if you'll allow me to comment, that ain't much of a plan."

"Got any better ideas?" Rafe thumbed alight a lucifer and set flame to the end of a fresh stogie.

"Might be I have, you never know. And you know why you don't know?"

Rafe rolled his eyes. "No, why?"

"Because you never ask, that's why."

"I'm asking now."

"Okay then. What if Swearengen — who I hear is one nasty piece of work — what if he won't go along with your plan, hmm? You ever think of that? What then?"

"Oh," said Rafe, letting a plume of cigar smoke trail out the side of his mouth, spit a fleck of tobacco from the tip of his tongue. "You mean like a Plan B."

"Yep, that's exactly what I mean." Cookie nodded with vigor.

"Didn't I mention? That's where you come in."

"Me? What?"

"Yep. You provide a distraction and I'll get the girl."

"Like old times, huh? I do all the hard work and you get the glory jobs."

"Yep." But Rafe glanced at Cookie and could tell the old man was already warming to the idea.

"Might be I could cook up a little something to take his mind off his brood mares for a spell." He rubbed his whiskery chin.

"Make sure whatever it is you cook up doesn't leave Deadwood more dead than alive. Be nice to depart without leaving behind a smoking downtown and the law on our tail."

"Speaking of that, you reckon Seth Bullock is still cock of the walk there?"

"Last I heard he was."

"That's good," mused Cookie. "I think. Not sure I recall exactly how we left off with him."

Later that day they came upon a couple dozen mounds of gravel and rock, each the size of a buggy. It looked as if a mammoth rock chuck had been hard at work. And in the midst of it, baking in the sun, leaned a shanty dwarfed by the nearest gravel piles. Out front, propped back on an old nail keg, snoozed a skinny, bowlegged old man. Only the top of his head was still shaded.

"Reminds me of someone," said Rafe.

Cookie narrowed his eyes but said nothing.

Rafe rode up close, eased one boot out of its stirrup, and nudged the old man's keg. It slid sideways and he slid with it, catching himself with a squawk before he ended up on the ground.

"What you go and do that for?" The old man struggled to stand up, and shocked his visitors when they realized he was fully upright, so bent by rheumatism was he. "Can't hardly crab along no more, and you come along and torment me."

Rafe gestured at the various piles and at the shanty, against which leaned all manner of picks, shovels, lengths of chain, a ragged sluice box, its boards sprung and snapped, and other assorted tools and worn-out, used-up implements of the small miner's trade. "Interested in selling any of these tools? A couple of picks, shovels?"

The man's sullen, crotchety demeanor changed immediately. "You got cold cash, the sort I can spend in a saloon, might be I could part with some of these high-quality items."

"High quality, my foot," said Cookie. "These tools are either nubbed from too much use or else their handles are plum snapped in half. Rafe what do we want with this old rock hound's junk, anyway?"

But Rafe had already swung down from the saddle and was in negotiation with the crippled codger. He dropped several coins into a wrinkled, callused hand, and tossed a pick, a shovel, and a much-battered sieve to Cookie. "Tie 'em on. These, too." He tossed him three well-used small canvas sacks.

He did the same with a few implements onto his packhorse, then climbed back into the saddle.

The bent old man looked up, squinting. "Say, you fellas wouldn't be interested in a prime claim, now, would you?" He gestured expansively at the desolate mess he'd created over years of grubbing for gold. "Molly's Folly might not look like much, but she's been a steady producer of high-grade ore!"

Cookie spat to one side. "Gettin' a mite windy around here for my taste."

Rafe and the old man ignored him. "Thanks, old-timer," said Rafe. "But we have commitments elsewhere."

"Oh, I get you. Already got a fortune waiting, eh? Just needed a few tools to dig it out?"

"Something like that." Rafe saluted the old man, who licked his lips like a parched man in a desert. He had trouble taking his eyes off the more-than-adequate compensation he held in his hand, but managed a head wag and a wave.

They made their way up and out of the old man's claim and back to the trail, which for a few hours had begun to look like a well-traveled lane.

"Getting closer," said Rafe.

"Confound it, Rafe! You feel bad for that old rock hound or what? Buy all this junk, anyone would think we was going to pass ourselves off as . . ." Cookie stopped talking, his jaw opened. "Oh, I get you now. Going to play-act. Like the old days."

Rafe puffed on his stogie. "Something like that."

They rode into Deadwood mid morning of the next day. Like all mine camps that survived their first formative, balls-out lawless years, the plank- and log-sided structures had begun to outnumber the canvas tents. Despite that march of progress, the street down which they rode, once removed from the town's main route, was a churned affair of shit-stomped muck, shards of smashed pottery, tree bark, and jags of rock. Here and there at random intervals rough planks and halved logs had been laid end to end across the street in an effort by the citizenry to keep their feet from squelching into the boil of filth bisecting that wedge of town.

Rafe and Cookie guided their horses over the boards and came to stop in front of a log-fronted affair with a sagged canvas sign above the door that read: "Dinky's Bar."

"Nice place." Cookie, not yet dismounted, eyed the leaning boardwalk out front. "Any chance we're going to have a drink or two before we begin this rescue mission?"

"Yep. One drink," said Rafe. "Long enough to get information."

"Like what?"

But the big man was already off his horse, so Cookie swung down, too, stomping square in a fresh pile of steaming green road apples.

"Nicely done," said Rafe, with a nod toward the old man's boots.

Rafe slipped his reins over the hitching rail, patted the buckskin's neck. "We'll get you and the others to a stable in a few minutes, fella."

He shucked his rifle from its scabbard and laid it across his shoulder. Taking plenty of time, he lifted two small bulging canvas sacks joined by a length of hemp rope that he'd dallied around the saddle horn.

He scanned up and down the street from under his hat brim for sign of loafers who might swoop vulture-like on their gear and animals. He saw they'd attracted the attention of at least a half-dozen threadbare gawkers, and as many more hard-bitten men with enough gall to stare right at him, their greed for the content of those sacks barely contained.

Satisfied he'd been seen, and that their goods were safe, if only for the time being, Rafe said, "You coming?" Without a second glance at Cookie, he mounted the steps and pushed through the door of the establishment.

Grumbling, Cookie paused on the bottom step, shifted to his other shoulder the gravel-stuffed sack he carried, and scraped horse muck from his boot. "Why these shenanigans we get up to have to be in dirty towns is beyond me. You think these people ever heard of a shovel? No, course not . . ." His mumble trailed off as he stamped his way up the steps and into the dim interior of Dinky's place of business.

It was a dark affair. Dry-sprung planking on the floor squeaked and cracked as they walked toward a table along the far right wall. The stink of dried man sweat and old, spilled beer warred with the rank, nostril-twitching tang of vomit.

The small round table sat propped on a stack of flat rocks and firewood. Three chairs clustered beneath it like sickly calves. Puffing his cigar, Rafe nudged one outward with the toe of his boot. It was a dainty-looking affair with a curved back and turned legs.

What this chair, obviously a prized possession hauled out here by someone from back East, was doing in the confines of the dumpy bar was anyone's guess. The once-fine rush seat had been kicked, punched, cut, burst, and frayed beyond use. Rafe nudged the chair further until it rested against the wall.

He toed another next to it, a crudely built concoction of pegged boards and bark-on branches. But it looked stout and serviceable. He tested it and found it would hold him. Cookie inspected its twin across the table and it, too, was up to its designated task as a chair.

As Rafe dropped his two filled sacks with a thud by his feet, a short greasy-aproned man, as round as he was tall, shuffled over, his feet clad only in wool socks that were more hole than stocking. Chaw juice dribbled down each corner of his puppetlike mouth, staining furrows pocked with a splotchy beard of twisty red hairs. Atop his pate sat a brown, moth-eaten derby two sizes too tiny for his fat head.

Cookie half wondered if he were to knock the hat off, would flaps of fat slip down over the man's dark, deep-set piggy eyes.

The fleshy mountain stood before them, staring down at the table, not at either of them.

Rafe cleared his throat. The man didn't move, save for his slow, bovinic chewing.

"Why thank you for welcoming us to your fine town," said Cookie, slapping his canvas sack down atop the table, which wobbled accordingly. "I believe me and the boy here will have two cool glasses of beer. Prospecting is thirsty work."

The round man grunted and tottered back to the bar.

"I can only assume that must be Dinky his own self. Nice sort," said Cookie. "Not sure you're going to get much more out of him than a fart and a belch."

Rafe said nothing, but leaned back and puffed on his cigar. "Might be someone else here who can help us."

Cookie looked around, spied a lone man hunched over a drink at the bar. Despite the month, he wore a buffalo coat with numerous bare patches where hair should be. The fat barkeep leaned toward the man, grunted something, and the shaggy-coated gent rose, his stool squawking backward against the wood floor. He clomped over to the door and took his leave.

Rafe and Cookie exchanged glances.

In two minutes, another man came into the bar. His gaze swept the room, and he strode to a dark corner to his right, along the streetside wall. He sat on a tall stool, half hidden in the shadows. Cookie saw thin-striped trousers tucked into black stovepipe boots. Light from a begrimed window slashed across a matching vest over a white shirt. Both looked impeccable. A silver watch chain hung in a curve across the dapper man's trim middle.

"What's his story?" said Cookie lowly through unmoving lips.

"Don't know yet. But we're about to find out." Rafe stretched his legs and removed the cigar from his mouth as the fat man set down two headless beers, slopping them on the teetering tabletop.

"Where can a couple of newcomers to your town," said Rafe in a none-too-quiet voice, "get a decent game of faro and a couple of girls, the younger the better? This once, I'd say expense be damned." He toed the sacks by his boots, then winked and in a low voice said, "Had some luck at the claim."

The fat man's eyes shifted beneath the drooped lids, looked at Rafe, then rolled to the right toward the well-dressed gent in the shadows.

Rafe nodded, tossed a couple of coins on the table. "Thanks."

Cookie lifted one of the beers and looked at Rafe over the rim. "You mind filling me in?"

"Nothing to tell yet." Rafe sipped.

Both men grimaced at the taste of the bung-sprung beer, but quaffed it nonetheless. They'd had many long, hot days of riding and this one had barely reached midday.

"Here we go," said Rafe through a soft belch, setting down his glass.

Cookie heard bootsteps behind him. He tensed slightly, his right hand inched along his leg to his Green River knife.

"Excusez moi," said the stranger, standing before them where the fat man had been. "I could not help overhearing your, ah, request."

Rafe puffed the cigar, squinted through the smoke in one eye. "And?"

The stranger smiled, held his hands up before him, palms facing them, but his eyes skittered to the sack by Cookie's elbow on the table. "I am merely trying to help, you see? I have no, how do they put it? No horse in this race, eh?"

"Yeah," said Cookie, "and you still ain't got to the point neither."

"Ah ha, yes, yes. But of course, you are impatient. That is understandable. If you will follow me, after you finish your beers, I can show you to a lovely place here in Deadwood, the loveliest in all the town, in fact. It is a place of infinite variety, offering all manner of gentlemanly sport."

"Such as?" Rafe eyed the man narrowly.

Cookie played along, but was growing impatient with all this palaver.

"Ah, but you are blunt, no? That is good. So, the place I mention is the Gem Variety Theater, and it is the finest such establishment in all of Deadwood."

"That ain't saying much, Frenchy."

Rafe flashed Cookie a quick look of annoyance.

"While it is true this town has its, shall we say, rough edges . . ." The dandy looked about him and shrugged. "The Gem offers refinement in the form of fine whiskies, virtuous ladies, and sporting games of chance, unparalleled in all the West."

Rafe nodded. "That's a tall order, but if it's as you say, then it sounds like the place for us." He hoisted his glass and looked at Cookie. "Am I right, partner?"

"I reckon," said Cookie, matching Rafe's glass-emptying with his own.

Soon they were hefting their sacks and following the chattering dandy out the door. Outside, a quick raking glance showed Rafe that their horses were still in place, nothing seemed amiss. There was a handful more folks now than before, all men, loafing about the fronts of businesses, their casual ways betraying their true intent.

Cookie sensed it, too, but nudged Rafe and nodded to the boardwalk before them. The French dandy clicked his tongue and a dappled horse walked up alongside the wooden sidewalk, enabling the man to climb aboard the fine saddle without getting his polished black stovepipes soiled in the funk of the street.

"So that's how he stays so dapper." Cookie chuckled.

"Might want to take note of his technique," said Rafe, nodding toward Cookie's still begrimed boots.

"Bah, ain't no dandy can show me anything I don't already know."

They mounted and followed the man up the busy street, receiving a few glances, then second glances as people caught sight of their bulging sacks.

Cookie leaned toward Rafe. "You'd think none of them had ever seen bags full of gravel before." He winked and settled in for what was shaping up to be a promising afternoon.

Presently they reined up before a large, three-story building with the words "Gem Variety Theater" painted across the front. Broad steps led up to double etched-glass doors through which a number of men passed in and out while they watched.

"Busy place," said Rafe.

"Ah, oui, and for good reason. The Gem is the crown jewel of Deadwood, no?"

"You're spreading that jam mighty thick, pard," said Cookie. "We ain't yet seen hide nor hair of them gentlemanly pursuits."

The man closed his eyes and pinched the bridge of his nose as if he'd eaten a handful of snow too quickly. "All in good time, my . . . impatient friend. Please direct your gaze to the corner. There, you see ahead?"

The two men looked to where he'd gestured and spied a bustling livery.

"Your mounts and pack animals will be well cared for there, I assure you. I have business to attend to, but I would be happy to meet you here, on the steps of the Gem, in, shall we say, one quarter of an hour?"

"Sounds fair," said Rafe.

Cookie cocked his head like a bird eyeing a suspicious insect. "Thought you said you ain't got a penny in the place. Why are you so fired up to show us the Gem and its treats?"

The Frenchman sighed. "Oui, it is as you say odd, no? But trust me, I am merely trying to help strangers to our fair town. I am something, how would you say, of a politician, you see. I have hopes of becoming mayor one day. So every bit of good will to others counts."

"Sounds fair. We'll meet you back here in fifteen minutes, then." Rafe nudged his horse up the lane.

Cookie rode up alongside. "You believe that palaver about wanting to be mayor? Ha."

"Not hardly. More likely he's in Swearengen's employ. And that will get us in deeper than we could on our own."

"Especially if we make like we're fixing to spend our . . . gravel."

Rafe nodded. "Maybe even consider selling off our nonexistent claim, should the price be right."

"All well and good, Rafe, but this ruse won't last long once they get a sniff of what's really in these here bags."

"Hopefully by then we'll be long gone with the girl." Rafe looked over his shoulder, but the Frenchman was gone, presumably inside the Gem.

Cookie angled toward the livery the dandy had indicated.

"Hold up, Cookie. We're not going there." Rafe rode right, up a side street, then right again. This landed them at the head of a street roughly a couple of lots behind the Gem. The lane was much less traveled, and a small feed depot sat close by.

"You know that was here?"

"Nope."

"Must be you're living right, then."

"Could be," said Rafe.

They made a deal with the old, burly black man who ran the place. For a generous sum he gladly agreed to strip off the saddles, bridles, and blankets, give the horses a good rubdown, and feed and water them. "Not too much," said Cookie. "Stinky don't like to be ridden if she's been treated too well."

"Mister," said the liveryman. "I been at this for a whole lotta years. Ain't nobody never complained about my job yet."

"See that I don't become the first."

The man chuckled and shook his head as Cookie looped the rope of his bag over his shoulder.

"If you could have them saddled and ready to go in . . ." Rafe lifted out a slender pocket watch from a front pocket of his trousers. "Three, no, make it two hours, I'd be obliged."

"Not a worry, young man." The black man ran a horned old hand over the rump of Rafe's buckskin. "Fine beast you got here."

Rafe nodded, then said, "These picks, shovels, you have any use for them?"

The old man nibbled his bottom lip. "Might be I could get my grandboy to clean 'em up, sell 'em."

"Then they're yours."

"Obliged, mister."

As Cookie and Rafe walked down the street to scout the Gem from the back side, Cookie said, "That watch the same one that —"

"Yep."

"Huh. Figured they'd have took that from you in Yuma."

"They did." Rafe looked at Cookie. "Found it way back in a drawer in Warden Timmons's desk."

"Hmm. Kinda hinky, ain't it?"

"Kinda."

A few minutes later they climbed the steps of the Gem, toting their sacks of gravel around their necks, and smiling for all the world like two lucky rubes who could not wait to spend their loot.

CHAPTER 8:
UNEASY LIES THE HEAD
THAT WEARS A CROWN

"You disgust me, Kid, you know that, don't you? You went into that fight with a knife pulled. Do not deny it, I saw you. I can see in the dark like an owl, and I saw your knife."

"Sí, El Jefe." The tall, skinny Kid's head still throbbed with each step his horse took. He hadn't said much since that early morning at the campsite when El Jefe had stomped Raoul's head. The sound of the man's neck, like jicama snapping, echoed in his head. It was not a pleasant sound.

Raoul had deserved the wrath of the boss. He had been warned, they all had, and now he was dead. Perhaps the boss had done the man a favor? After all, Raoul had been bleeding from stabs, and his leg was in bad shape. There was no way he would have ridden for long, let alone live through the journey of pain his wounds were taking him on.

El Jefe was still talking, ranting once again since the attack, about what a poor mess of fighters they were. It was true, Pepe's arm was in a sling he'd fashioned from two bandannas, and Tepito was limping when he wasn't riding — and his face still looked bad, the colors of sun-spoiled meat. And the Kid had a head that felt like it was filled with boiling water. All he wanted to do was find some shadows and lie down there. He didn't even care if he had to share the spot with a snake.

"Are you listening to me, boy? How are you ever going to learn to be a jefe one day, hmm?"

The Kid lifted his head, looked through bleary eyes at the wide-faced sweating man who had saved him years before from being eaten alive by vultures while tied to that wagon wheel.

"Yes, yes, now you show some spirit, eh? Now that I have mentioned the goodness a man can get in life if he works hard." El Jefe waved a hand. "Bah, I do not think you have it in you. At one time, yes, maybe you did, but now? Now you no longer impress me."

"But I did, El Jefe?"

"Did what?"

"Impress you? Once?"

"You twist my words, boy. Nothing more.

Now, stop by that stream there. We will rest the horses and eat." He half turned in the saddle, raised his voice. "We are making poor time, riding slow because you are all sickly women who need nurses to attend you! I am ashamed of you all. Never have I ridden with such pathetic Hell Hounds."

El Jefe dismounted and handed his reins to the Kid. "Not too much water, remember. These dumb beasts will bloat and die."

The boy nodded.

The boss shook his head as the others groaned and flopped to the ground, wincing and crying out as if they were being kicked to death by mules.

"I am going to see what is making that dust behind us." El Jefe squinted at their back trail. Yes, there were riders there. Cutting the same trail the Hell Hounds made. "We will see what it is they want of us." He smacked his hands together and strode back to the camp.

"We have guests arriving soon. Three riders. You make them welcome until we find out what it is they want, eh?"

The tired men nodded, a ragged chorus of "Sí, El Jefe" greeted him. That was more like it.

They did not have long to wait. Within twenty minutes the three riders were in sight, and slowed as they approached the camp.

"Ho, the camp!" one man shouted.

"Hello, hello," shouted El Jefe, rising to his feet, smiling and gesturing. "Come on in and have some grub with us, eh?"

The three men looked to be conversing, then walked their horses forward.

"Perhaps they have whiskey, El Jefe," whispered Tepito.

"Yes, and perhaps they will do me a favor and kill you for being an idiot. Now shut your mouths and let me do the talking."

The three strangers, two Mexicans and a gringo, by the looks of them, rode to a stop yards from the seated men.

"Howdy," said the gringo.

El Jefe smiled, nodded. "Yes, welcome, have a seat here by the fire. We don't have much, but we can offer you biscuits with bacon, and a cup of hot chicory."

"Obliged," said the man and stepped down from his saddle with a grunt. His horse whickered, eliciting response from two of the Hell Hounds' beasts.

"You see, the horses are already fast friends." El Jefe's laugh sounded forced, but only to the men who rode with him.

The two Mexicans were slower to climb down, but did so after a few exchanged glances. Still holding their reins, unsure whether to lead the horses behind them to the fire or hobble them where they stood. El Jefe made the decision for them, with a quick-drawn Colt Dragoon.

The men often smirked at his fondness for the old revolver, but it had served him well and had taken its share of souls. El Jefe kept his smile in place as he wagged them over to one side. The Kid snatched up their reins.

"Your bellies have made you stupid and bold. I can safely tell you that our food is not worth risking your necks over. The Kid made the biscuits, and his efforts are passable, but you don't see any of us gobbling down the rest, do you?"

"Now look here, mister, we don't want no trouble." The blond cowboy stood with his hands up by his shoulders. One hand was wrapped in a grimy bandage. "We're riding through, that's all."

"No, you're not. You are riding to this spot, and you have done that. So now . . ." El Jefe looked to his men. "You have put up with my bad moods for days. Why don't you have some fun, eh?" He motioned with his head toward the three newcomers, as if he were offering a great indulgence.

The three riders began shouting, protesting, eyes wide, as they backed up. One pivoted on his heels and bolted for the horses. El Jefe's Dragoon roared and the man's right leg whipped forward, upending him. He howled, but was cut off by El Jefe. "You have not been shot. But the heel of your boot is not so good now, eh?" His tobacco-raspy belly laughs were soon joined by a volley of the same from his men.

As soon as it began, when El Jefe spoke again, the laughter ceased.

"Why were you following us, you three men?"

The newcomers looked at each other, then the gringo spoke. "We wasn't. Only riding, figure we'd make for the goldfields over in Dakota Territory."

"Ah, to make a fortune, eh?"

The three men nodded eagerly. "We can let you in on it, if you want." The white man's voice shook.

El Jefe furrowed his brow. "Hmm, let me see, a percentage of nothing, or . . ." He snapped his finger and his face brightened. "Or my boys can have a little fun with you. Hmm." He ran a thumb back and forth across his chin.

"Okay, I tell you what. You three get on your horses." He watched their faces in turn as they filled slowly with relief. "No, no, no!

I am kidding!" Again, his braying laughter filled the air above the little creekside camp. "Do what you will with them, Hell Hounds!"

Within minutes the three prisoners' clothes, boots, hats, as well as their saddles, bags, and bedrolls, were stripped from them and their horses. The goods were divvied up among the Hell Hounds in a whooping frenzy. Then the newcomers were forcibly remounted on their bareback horses. All the while El Jefe puffed a stinking black cheroot and chuckled.

It wasn't until the three men had been gagged that their shrieking abated to sobs and pleas that escaped through their stretched mouths, distorted by their own bandannas twisted and tied tight across their faces. The Hell Hounds looked quite pleased with themselves once they had their three prisoners loaded.

"Now what?" said El Jefe.

"Now we will hang these skulking dogs!" Tepito smiled broadly.

El Jefe nodded, puffed thoughtfully on his cigar. "I see." He regarded the cigar a moment. "And how will you hang them?"

"From a tree, boss!"

El Jefe nodded again. Then looked around him, squinting. "Ah, good. As long as you are thinking, that's all that matters."

Tepito and the rest followed El Jefe's gaze around the rocky, rolling landscape, nothing rising but rocky knobs from the sea of sage along the paltry stream.

"Well," said a red-faced Tepito, "we will string them up when we get to a tree."

El Jefe had grown tired of this foolishness and was about to kick the man in the face when the white prisoner offered a hard, vicious glare that had not been there before. He stared straight at El Jefe and shouted something muted but forceful through his gag. The man's neck veins throbbed like worms under his skin.

Something about him made El Jefe pause, perhaps he should reconsider robbing and killing these three. He could use new recruits to the Hell Hounds, after all. And if they did not prove up to the task, he could kill them later. Besides, what would it hurt to listen to whatever the gringo felt was so important to tell him?

The gringo looked uncomfortable in his ripped long underwear and one sock hanging loosely off a foot, the other bare. Rings of sweat and salt from dried sweat bloomed around his grimy underwear's underarms, neck, and crotch. El Jefe walked closer, not close enough that the man could reach him

114

with a kick with an untied leg.

"Kid, untie this one's bandanna. He would like to tell us something."

"Sí."

The Kid grabbed the man's shirtfront and dragged him off his horse. He hit the ground with a hard, dusty thud. Even El Jefe winced. The Kid slid a wide-blade skinning knife, honed to a glittering keen edge, between the man's sweaty, stubbled cheek and the blue bandanna and, with a flick, sliced the cloth free. The gringo worked his jaw open and shut.

"I am a busy man, mister," said El Jefe, a drop of sweat closing one eye in a squint. "What is so important?"

"We can be of use to you."

Tepito snorted a laugh, began to speak, but El Jefe held up a hand. "How?"

"We are after two bad men, banditos, who . . ." The man swallowed, realizing he was talking about the very sort of men he was now faced with, but he regained his voice. "Who got the drop on us. Tied us up, robbed us."

"It seems to me you are not so good at staying untied and safe, no? Tell me, who are these bad men and what do you think you are going to do with them once you find them?"

"Well, there are two of them, a big fella, tall, wide shoulders, a mean look on his face, didn't talk much. The other one, well . . . he was smaller." The man looked away from El Jefe, then looked back. "We aim to kill them."

He looked at his two Mexican cohorts, still sitting their horses, sweat stippling their faces. They nodded with much vigor. The gringo continued. "They tied us up, robbed us blind! Our boss found us and fired us on the spot! Wasn't our fault, those two men cost us our jobs with the railroad!"

El Jefe nodded, as much to tell the man to shut up as to acknowledge what he'd said. "I think there is some nugget of truth in what you tell me. Some of it is bullshit." He shrugged. "How will keeping you alive help me?"

"I don't doubt there's a bounty on them two. That's why we're riding out after them. Cost us our work, ain't got nothing else cooking."

"Oh, so it's work you need, eh? Well, as it happens I have need of two, maybe three more Hell Hounds." El Jefe gestured at the ragged group of men with confused looks on their faces. "That is us, by the way. We are a gang of, how did you put it earlier? 'Bad men, banditos.' Yes, that is us, eh?"

116

The gringo nodded, swallowed. His two compatriots did the same, nodding eagerly from atop their horses. Their hands tied behind their backs.

El Jefe pooched his lips, regarding the trio for long moments. No one spoke. A breeze eddied dust by his feet, then spun off. "Untie them, give them back their clothes."

The Hell Hounds protested loudly, Tepito gestured at his feet. "But boss, I have already put on these fine new boots. They are better than the ones I had!"

"Then keep the boots, the man you took them from can wear your old ones. But do not let them have their weapons." El Jefe faced the three prisoners. "I will decide if you are useful to us or if you are likely to kill us in our sleep, eh? Until then, you are warned. El Jefe will be watching you." His voice was a low, purring growl.

He turned away and smiled. It would not have troubled him to kill the men, but perhaps they could be useful to him. He wanted new blood in the Hell Hounds, at least for a little while longer. Men who would be grateful for the work instead of whining all the time.

And besides, he could not let them go — they were angry and might well kill Rafe Barr and the old man who traveled with him. That would not do. And there was more to the gringo's story than he was telling. Perhaps he knew something that would be of use to El Jefe. If not, he would kill them before he got to Deadwood.

CHAPTER 9:
WHAT ROUGH GEM

As soon as Cookie stepped through the doors to the Gem Variety Theater, he knew there was something odd about the place. What that was, he wasn't sure yet. At first glance, it was like a number of other such gambling dens he'd been in throughout the West over the years.

It was filled even at midday with folks from all walks, wizened old miners like the man they'd bought their shovels and picks from, and portly men in fine suits puffing cigars and rubbing their brocade-covered bellies. The room's light was dim, not uncommon, and made thicker with layers of slowly drifting smoke from countless cigars, cigarettes, and pipes.

In a back corner, a grinning man in arm garters and a bowler pounded a piano with great thumping arm motions. He looked to Cookie as if he were a clockwork mechanism in a carnival show.

Here and there through the crowd drifted women in low-cut dresses that on first glance looked fancy. When one strolled by without a glance, Cookie saw frayed seams and mended tears in the still-gay fabrics — purple and gold and crimson, trimmed in black lace.

Brass chandeliers, smudged with soot, hung low and guttered with ill-trimmed wicks. What the place could use, at least to begin with, decided Cookie, were a few windows. Still, he decided there was something off about the place. Something he couldn't quite lay a finger on.

"I can smell it," he whispered to Rafe as he scanned the room.

"Smell what?"

"The stink of something off, like a carcass hid under your cabin. You know . . ."

"Hinky?" said Rafe.

"Yeah, that's the word."

The Frenchman, a couple of steps ahead of them, paused. "Well, what do you gentlemen think of the Gem?"

Rafe nodded, eyebrows raised as if he were impressed. "Now, this is what I had in mind."

"Grand, *mes amis.* This is, as I mentioned earlier, a far superior place to that dump where I happened to find you, don't you agree?"

"Happened, my foot," mumbled Cookie through a smile. "Yeah, looks good to me, too."

"Bon, c'est bon," said the Frenchman. "Now, before I turn you loose to indulge in all the Gem has to offer men of your" — his eyes raked Cookie up and down, a slight sneer quivering the dandy's top lip before resuming its earlier stiff smile — "caliber, ahem, I would like to introduce you to a good friend of mine. The man who happens to be the proprietor of this fine establishment, a man who has — how do you say? — a vision beyond measure for the town of Deadwood and beyond."

"Sounds to me like he's the one ought to be runnin' for mayor." Cookie gave the Frenchman a wink.

"Yes, well, um, please follow me to the bar. I will find Monsieur Swearengen."

He led the way to the bar, hard to miss as it was the largest feature in the room. Already it was half filled with elbow leaners in animated conversation, hugging glasses of beer.

"Mes amis, please, order yourselves a drink. My treat. I shall return forthwith." He smiled at them a last time, then ducked

behind the bar and disappeared through a dim doorway.

Rafe set the laden sacks on the bar top, making sure they thudded well. Cookie did the same with the one he carried. A bartender made his way down to them.

"What'll it be, gents?"

"Whiskey for each," said Rafe, with a nod.

"These folks are being mighty accommodatin' to a pair of grubbers like us, huh, Rafe?"

"Yep. This is going smoothly. Maybe too much so."

"How do you mean?"

The door behind the bar swung inward and a swarthy man with widow's peaks accentuating his slicked-back salt-and-pepper hair stepped through. He wore a white shirt with the black arm garters of a businessman interrupted at a task.

He was not overly tall, but looked to be in moderate condition. Rafe noted he carried himself with assurance, stepping boldly toward them, a confident smile already pasted on his face, below an oiled moustache, blacker than the hair on his head.

"Gentlemen, gentlemen." He stood before them, extended a hand and gave each of them, Rafe first, a quick, tight handshake. "Al Swearengen, owner of the Gem Variety

Theater, for good or ill." He offered a quick snag of laughter, then his eyes took in the sacks on the counter. "It would seem you have been . . . how shall I say this without sounding envious? . . . busy."

The smile broadened, noted Rafe, but the man's brown-black eyes weren't up to the effort. They watched him like those of a serpent. And Rafe knew he could have picked Swearengen out of a crowd without an introduction.

"Might I interest you gents in locking up your obvious valuables in the Gem's state-of-the-art vault? It's a recent arrival all the way from Saint Louis. There isn't another like it for thousands of miles, I dare say. Safer than a bank."

Rafe sipped his whiskey, set down the glass. "Who has the combination?"

Swearengen smiled, thumbed his vest's lapels. "That would be me."

Rafe nodded. "And what happens if you end up dead?"

The proprietor's smile drooped. "I don't think I like your tone much. That wouldn't be a threat, would it?"

"What?" Cookie cut in. "Naw, why Rafe here is looking to protect our investment is all. Wouldn't you ask the same question if you was in our boots?"

Swearengen rolled the cigar in his lips. "I reckon I would at that." His cat smile spread on his face again. He smacked his hands on the bar top. "Offer still stands, you think on it. In the meantime" — he nudged a stack of chips across the bar — "enjoy yourselves — girls, booze, games of chance, pick your poison — on the house. If you'll excuse me, I have matters to attend to. A saloonkeeper's work is never done!"

Rafe nodded, eyebrows raised. "Much obliged, sir. Be seeing you." He raised his glass. Swearengen left through a door behind the bar. Rafe's fake smile vanished. "Cookie, you blew it. We have to move fast."

"What? What do you mean? All I said was . . . oh lord, no, I said your name."

"Yep, and I saw something in his eyes. I bet two-to-one he knows who I am, maybe heard of me from the war, or in passing from Bullock. Who knows? Hell, who cares. Right now we have to get that girl. I'll sneak upstairs and find her. I'm thinking all I have to do is follow Swearengen." He leaned closer to Cookie. "And that distraction we talked about?"

"Yeah, Rafe," said Cookie, cheeks still glowing red from spilling the beans.

"Now's the time."

"You got it, Rafe."

The big man stood, hefting the sacks.

"And Rafe?" said Cookie. "For what it's worth, I'm sorry."

Rafe smiled. "Are you kidding? We're about to have ourselves one unforgettable afternoon. Remember, stick to the plan."

"What plan?" Cookie's hairy eyebrows rose together like two caterpillars squaring off for a round of fisticuffs.

"Exactly." Rafe grinned and waited for Cookie's surprise — whatever it might be.

Chapter 10:
Where There's
(No) Smoke . . .

Cookie knew Rafe was biding time to allow him to cook up the distraction. Whatever it might be. In truth, he was fretting as he had given little thought to what he might do. He had hoped it would involve something exploding, maybe a bit of flame, a fireball, if he was lucky.

He thought he'd have more time to dither and think on it, maybe chat with Rafe over a cold beer or three. But he'd gone and spilled the beans about Rafe being Rafe. And Rafe being Rafe, well, Cookie didn't doubt that Swearengen had heard tell of him some time ago. Most folks had.

The war, it all kicked off with that damnable war. Never was a man more quiet about his life than Rafe Barr, then that all-too-public kerfuffle painting him as a spy, then a double spy. Then the US Government got its pantaloons so twisted up in knots. By the end, no one, least of all Cookie, knew what it was they were trying to accuse the man of.

But Cookie and Rafe knew the real truth, and the fact that the US Government, even after all those missions and escapades they'd had during the war — all on behalf of the government, thank you kindly — none of it seemed to matter to those fools in fancy suits in Washington, DC.

Railroaded Rafe is what they did, but it hadn't seemed to slow him down none. He went on being Rafe, traveled back to his version of heaven on earth in that little valley in Colorado. Built up a herd, married an angel, had the boy, life was fine and dandy.

Cookie, he'd drift in and out of their lives, didn't want to be a fifth wheel on a three-wheel cart, let the young family have its privacy. Lord knows Rafe deserved happiness, after the hell of the war.

It was while Cookie was gone on one of his solo jaunts across the Great Basin in Nevada to explore its wonders when the word reached him. Seemed that a famous spy from the War Betwixt the States had been arrested, found guilty of murdering his family.

Cookie's gut had clenched like a shaking fist when he'd heard that. He'd cautiously asked that man, a grimy little drunk of a cowpoke looking for a handout in a hole-in-the-wall bar in a nameless dust-heap of a town what the spy's name was. That worthless whelp had smiled out of the side of his face, said, "How much is it worth to you, old man?"

Cookie saw red like he hadn't seen the color in years. He flew at the bastard with both spurs flailing. Took four men to pull him off the weasel.

But Cookie knew, knew it had to be Rafe — weren't no other spies from the war so famous as Rafe Barr. But only because the damnable US Government told the world about him. Dragged his good name through the muck before slapping him on the wrist.

By the time Cookie made it, riding hell-bent, to Rafe's hidden ranch, there was nothing there but a blackened ruin where the fine home used to be. The barn was cinders, too. About the only thing left standing was a half-scorched bunkhouse. The cattle had scattered to the four winds.

He had found a grave with a ragged cross, the crosspiece barely held on by Rafe's old leather belt. The place had an eerie, churned-mud look with nothing living in sight nor hearing but a cold, howling wind.

Cookie recalled all this with a renewed grimace as he cast his gaze about the Gem's great room filled to brimming with laughing, half-drunk gamblers. Couldn't blow up the place, not yet, anyway, as Rafe would need time to find the girl. They didn't even know what she looked like. But if ever there was a man capable of finding her, it was Rafe Barr, bet good money on it.

Cookie knew he needed to . . . then he snapped his fingers. That was it, the best way — and not one he'd ever have thought of had he not been mulling over the past at rifle-shot speed. The past, the present, Deadwood — who did they know? Why, none other than Seth Bullock himself.

"Time to call in the law," mumbled Cookie to himself with a grin — and maybe a touch of regret that he wouldn't be blowing up the place. Not yet, anyways.

Rafe watched his older partner amble off toward the middle of the place. He'd bet a week's wages Cookie didn't have a clue as to what distraction he was going to lob at them. And oddly enough, Rafe didn't care what the crazy old coot cooked up. He reckoned it would involve sparks, smoke, maybe flame, and damn sure a dose of gunpowder.

Was a time not long ago — five years, to be precise, though at times it felt like a lifetime — that Rafe cared more about what the results of Cookie's actions might be. Oh, he damn sure didn't want to hurt anyone, and he didn't want to inconvenience innocent folks when he could avoid it, but he trusted Cookie enough that he knew the explosives expert felt the same.

Beyond that, Rafe's outlook over the past few years had changed. It was now bent and warped. Pounding rocks into smaller rocks, bending his back to any foul task Warden Timmons forced on him, from distasteful to humiliating, had done it to him.

Blow off a corner of the room, send the long front porch of the place skyward, he didn't much care. Anything that might distract the gamblers and barkeeps long enough that Rafe could slip behind the bar and trail after Swearengen. That'd do the trick. Didn't have to be a grand production. Come on, Cookie. Get on it.

Back across the room, Cookie mulled over the fastest way to get Bullock over here on the double. Something grand and danger-ous and life-threatening. A man next to him dragged a match across the thigh of his befouled trousers and a flame sprung alight. He touched it to his pipe, shook it out, and tossed the match to the sawdust-and-spittlegrimed floor.

And that's when Cookie snapped a finger and smiled to himself. He backed toward that rambunctious piano player, off in a darker corner, pounding out his anger or passion, Cookie couldn't tell which. Didn't much care. But he did know of something that would get every living soul in the place motivated — the threat of fire.

Cookie fairly cackled in glee and wore a wide-eyed mask of horror as he looked left, right, then raised his hands to his mouth and bellowed, "Fire! Fire! Oh, God, everyone out! Fire!"

The reaction was as he expected — pure, balls-out pandemonium. And he loved every second of it. It was all he could do to not smile as he continued shouting and threading his way toward the door. He noticed a weasely looking fellow snaking his hand toward a litter of cash on a baize table and reckoned the man wasn't entitled to it.

As he advanced through the howling, stirred-up crowd, Cookie shot out with a sharp, well-placed kick to the side of the man's bent knee — the leg he was using to rest his weight on as he leaned over the table. With a shriek the man folded sideways and collapsed to the floor like a bad hand of cards tossed to a tabletop.

Satisfied he was now one up on his good deed quotient for a few days to come, Cookie worked his way to the door, elbowing past the frenzied crowd. Already he was largely forgotten as the man who'd sounded the alarm. His shouts had done what he hoped for — they stirred up a nest of whirring activity inside the Gem.

It wouldn't take them long to figure out that there was no fire, but by that time Rafe would hopefully have grappled onto the girl and be lugging her out back and toward freedom. Cookie would be hot-footing it toward the same destination.

Thinking of Rafe, Cookie scanned toward the bar, where Rafe had been standing, waiting for him to create that distraction so he could slip back behind the bar, disappear into the guts of the place. Cookie didn't see Rafe, didn't expect he would, neither. So it was enough of a distraction, he guessed. He wondered what else he might be able to do, aside from not being late to the meet-up.

He grinned as he stomped down the front steps to the place. And that's when an ironclad, white-knuckled hand reached right out of nowhere and — *whoomp!* — clamped right onto his shirt collar, balled it up tighter than a fat man's hatband, and nearly succeeded in choking him.

"Why, Cookie McGee. If it ain't you, living and breathing, and right here in my little town."

The voice, or rather the hand that was somehow connected to the voice, loosened its vicious death grip on his neck, but didn't quite let go. Cookie massaged his sore throat and coughed. He peeked up at the vile creature that issued such a balderdash greeting.

"Bullock! You crafty S.O.B.! I ought to . . ." A coughing jag caught Cookie in mid throat, elsewise he was set to lay into the ramrod lawman, give him what-for and why-she-done-it. But Cookie's ardor soon cooled, and reason reasserted itself. He forced a grin as he recalled the real reason they were in Deadwood in the first place.

"Why, Cookie, it's awfully nice to see you, too." Bullock smiled down at him, wide, well-combed mustaches bobbing in time with his candied words.

Cookie did his best to straighten up.

"I ain't never . . ." Another round of coughing muckled onto him.

"Must be all that . . . smoke got to you." Bullock looked briefly toward the open doors of the Gem, where a number of people were clustering and waving their arms and shouting as Bullock's deputies hustled in and out, quizzing everyone and giving others the hard stare. No one was to move. That much was plain.

And yet move they did, still in an uproar, shouting and shoving one another, hoping to get out of the building they had all been convinced, moments before, would soon be an inferno.

Bullock leaned down, still smiling, and spoke close to Cookie's ear. "I wonder what all those hotted-up businessmen and professional gamblers and love-struck miners and oh, all the rest, would think if they found out that maybe, just maybe that was a false alarm."

Cookie returned the man's steel-hard gaze. Was Bullock offering him an excuse, a way out of a fix? For old time's sake, maybe?

As if reading his mind, the lawman sighed and let go of Cookie's collar. The shirt remained peaked and bunched behind the skinny old man's neck. "Now, what brings you to Deadwood, Cookie McGee? Last time we crossed paths it was what, eight, ten years ago? You were running with Rafe then, as I recall."

The tall man rubbed his smooth-shaven chin with a work-hardened hand. "Damn shame about him, his family, and then to end up in Yuma. Not sure how to take that.

Didn't ever seem the type to me. Wouldn't surprise me none if they were to overturn that ruling. He'd be a free man again one day. Nope, wouldn't surprise me in the least." He cocked his eyes to Cookie, who'd been regarding him coolly.

Cookie said nothing.

"Come on," said Bullock. "I'll buy you a beer. But not here." He jerked a thumb over his shoulder at the still-thrumming front porch of the Gem.

Somewhere in the mass of voices Cookie thought he heard Swearengen's voice shouting for calm. He suppressed the urge to smile.

"If you're buying, then okay," said Cookie. He tugged his shirttails down, rammed them into the top of his trousers, and readjusted his belt. "But don't go yarnin' on my gizzard anymore." He rubbed and stretched his reedy neck. "Man gets so he likes to keep what little he has intact — that includes his swallower and his clothes!"

A deputy hustled over to Bullock. "There ain't no fire, sir."

Bullock stopped. "Excuse me a moment, Cookie." He turned back to the deputy. "I know that, Clancy. Tell me something useful."

The young man's brows knitted, clearly

confused. "Okay, then, sir."

Cookie was enjoying this day more and more as time went on. He shifted his gaze to the Gem. It was a tall building, three, maybe four floors. He wondered how Rafe was getting on.

"Go and tell them that it was a false alarm, nothing more. If you need me, I'll be at Bev's. I'm off to have a beer with an old acquaintance. And tell the fire squad to stand down!"

"Already did, sir."

"There's hope for you yet, Clancy."

Back in a forgotten corner of Cookie's mind a tiny brass bell rang and rang and rang. He finally paid attention to it and it seemed to be warning him about something. Mostly that Bullock was a lawman first, an old "acquaintance" second, no matter what he wanted Cookie to believe. The man was fishing for something. And a glass of beer was the bait.

"Naw, you know, sheriff, I reckon I'll mosey on back to the livery and pick up my horse. I only came into town to see the sights, see what all everyone was jawing about. Now I have and I can die happy knowing that Deadwood is a place I do not need to see ever again. No offense, mind you."

"None taken, but it will not sit well with me if you were to refuse to have a beer because you thought I might be up to something."

How in the hell did Bullock do it, thought Cookie. The man was some sort of mesmerizer, that was it. He read minds, or some such. He'd heard about such people. "Naw, naw, I'm busy is all. Got people to see, business to attend to." Not meaning to, Cookie shot a quick glance up at the Gem.

"You worried about something, Cookie? You look a bit raw around the gills."

"Me? Naw." He stuck out a hand. "Well, Bullock, I'm happy to see you again. Guess I'll be riding out."

The lawman took his hand and squeezed hard. "You have yourself a fine gallop on out of town, Cookie McGee." But he held on tight to that hand, tugged the old man in close. "And try to keep those two sticks of dynamite unlit and out of harm's way, you hear?"

Bullock's voice was a low purr. "I know the Gem's a mighty temptation, and in some ways I can't say I'd weep if it caved in, but my job is to make sure no one in this town, good, bad, or otherwise, comes to harm through their own fault or from others. And old acquaintances aside, I will

137

do whatever I have to do to keep the peace."

Cookie canted his jaw to one side. "Yep, I reckon that's what a lawman should do." He knew, sure as shooting, that Bullock knew Rafe was out. Might be a simple explanation, odds are he saw them ride in together. Then why the games? If Rafe wasn't busy, he'd likely enjoy a chinwag with the lawman.

They had been pretty good "acquaintances" back in the day, after all. But after his slip up in the bar in front of Swearengen, Cookie wasn't inclined to tell another living soul about Rafe. Easier that way.

CHAPTER 11:
IN THE MAW OF THE BEAST

Rafe had to admit Cookie's distraction was a whole lot more subdued than he expected from the old rooster. But it had been effective. As soon as Cookie began shouting "Fire!" the burly bartender turned his attention to the commotion across the smoky room. He ducked under the far end of the bar and began rolling up his sleeves, as if he were expecting a fight.

The three leaners, one lone man and a pair chatting heatedly, if red-eyed, at each other, all shifted their wobbly gazes to the throng of patrons crowding the doors. Then two of them slid away from the bar and threaded themselves in that direction. The third shifted his gaze back to the bar and caught sight of Rafe as he slid toward the dark doorway behind the bar. The man looked away, licked his lips, and glanced toward the barkeep, who still faced the shouting clot of patrons.

The leaner reached out, snatched up a half-filled bottle of gargle, and glancing at the barkeep, stuffed it in his coat, holding it there with a trembling hand. He cut his eyes back to Rafe, daring him to say something, Rafe stared back a moment, shook his head, and ducked into the doorway.

Takes all types, he thought. Couldn't condemn the man for stealing when he was trespassing, now could he?

He found himself in a dark, narrow hallway. He felt the wall, knew that Swearengen would likely be along this way any second to investigate the ruckus in the bar. The back of his hand brushed a doorknob. He didn't dare open it, but heard a mumbled oath in a low voice from behind the door, something struck wood, a glass being set down hard in frustration, maybe.

Rafe had a gut feeling it was Swearengen's office. And then he heard bootsteps from within, closing in on the door. He stepped twice more down the dim hall, then backed up to the wall on his right, hugging it, his eyes looking toward the door.

Immediately the door swung inward, light from a window in the room bloomed into the dim hallway. And Swearengen stepped into the hall, less than an arm's length from Rafe. The dark-haired man stood, his left hand holding the doorframe as he leaned into the hall, facing the direction of the bar-room. The commotion grew louder, second after second. The man growled low again in his throat.

Rafe could have reached out and punched the man in the back of the head, laid him low for a spell, that would make the entire operation so much easier. He balled a big fist, not daring to make a sound, when Swearengen growled and leaned back into the room, grabbed the doorknob, and slammed the door shut with a rattling bang.

He pounded down the hall, his boots thudding on the worn runner of carpet.

Rafe wasted no time, his breathing shallowed and he walked as quickly as he could along the hall, feeling his way against the wall. He wanted to stash the bags of gravel, but something told him they might be a useful silent tool. They were only a few pounds each and hung easily about his neck.

His right boot clunked against something, then another — steps. A stairwell rose up in the dark toward a dim glow above, likely a window at a landing. He took the stairs, ratty carpeted and bare in spots, two at a time, keeping an eye above and ahead. He was at a double disadvantage, not knowing where he was going, except upward.

Soon he heard voices, women, maybe a man in the mix. Were they talking? No, more like arguing. Up and down the voices went, like crows squabbling over a carcass. Two women and one man, that much was certain now. He gained the top step. A fly-specked window, painted shut, let dismal light, though no freshness, into the close air of a hallway.

They ought to be able to open the damn window, thought Rafe as he slid along the wall. It was a wallpapered span, poorly applied, with great curls and buckles along the edges. The rose-and-green-leaf pattern drooped in curls that wagged gently with his silent breath. Sweat rolled down Rafe's forehead. He hastily dragged the back of a hand across his eyebrows.

The hall stretched before him the substantial length of the building. Doors lining it on either side every dozen feet or so. This would be easier if he could brace someone, force them to give up the girl's location. He heard other sounds, the false groans and stifled cries of sex in the offing. This was not lovemaking, never would be in a place like this.

And not a one of them seemed to have heard the shouts of fire from downstairs. Maybe they had and no one cared. Seems like someone would have sent a body hustling up the stairs to warn the women and their paying party guests.

The stink of unwashed bodies, men and women, did as much to weigh down the sagging wallpaper as the heavy air. He reached the door behind which the arguing trio was holed up. Their voices grew louder, the man's the loudest. He slurred his words, bellowed something foul, a word Rafe had not heard since Yuma, a word he had never used in all his days in front of a woman, nor would he ever. The utterance of it set his teeth tight together.

The word was followed by a smack, the singular sound of skin striking skin, then another, then a hard thudding. Groans and a piteous wailing seeped through the door. The man had attacked one of the women, the other was shrieking for him to get out.

Rafe heard more smacks, the man growled, then something crashed. Rafe's vision blurred, his jaw ached from clenching his teeth tight, and before he knew what he was doing he snatched at the doorknob. It was locked. He jammed a boot hard against it and drove it home.

The door whipped inward, wood splintered where the lock wrenched free of the frame. The door hit the wall, spasmed, and stood half open.

The scene before him could almost have come out of a stage play, and might have been comical had he not heard its prelude moments before.

"What the hell do you want?" A narrow-shouldered man with a midsection wider than any other part of him, stood without a stitch on in the middle of a small, shabby room. He was covered in wooly red-blond hair, darker at his crotch and armpits, freckles pocked his hide, a skin that bore a look all over as if he'd scrubbed himself raw with river sand.

The man's right hand curled tight around the thin neck of a slender, sunken-eyed woman with lank black hair.

Rafe stepped quickly into the room, shut the door behind him. The man's left hand, closest to Rafe, was a fist set to deliver a tight punch to the woman's other eye. One was already swelling. A trickle of blood leaked from the woman's nose.

Rafe crossed the small room in a stride, grabbed the man's poised fist in one hand, brought the man's arm down hard behind him onto his knee. The satisfying, soft, sliding crunch of what felt like one hundred tiny bones in the man's wrist splintered beneath the skin.

The man almost screamed, but Rafe gave him no time. Instead he wrapped his other hand tight around the man's hideous face, cutting off any noises, save for an odd, piggish sound.

"Grunting like a hog won't do you any good," breathed Rafe into the struggling man's ear.

Red rage pulsed in every bit of Rafe's body and mind, and he squeezed the man's face harder, felt teeth pop and sag beneath his fingertips. The man squirmed against him, grunting out high-pitched mewling sounds.

Tiny spots of light darted before Rafe's eyes, dimming until it seemed he saw nothing but night sky. A strange buzzing sound filled his head like cicadas on a summer evening. It was a sound from long ago, from his youth. So long ago.

Then he heard shouting, felt something hitting him, came back to himself, and light and sound and sensation flooded in on him. Rafe shook his head like a bull annoyed by a bee.

The hitting came courtesy of one of the prostitutes, the one the man had been holding by the neck. She punched and slapped at Rafe with thin, bruised arms. "Mister, you're killing him! Mister!"

The woman who'd been on the floor now stood, if unsteadily, and grabbed weakly at him. It was then that he saw what they were shouting about. The man he'd dragged off the thin woman was sagging and becoming limp in his arms, his struggles weaker with each second that passed.

With a sneer Rafe let go of the man's mouth, and the shaggy red head slumped against Rafe. The big man stepped back and let the naked, hairy beast drop to the floor.

The women stood staring down at him. The man didn't move. Rafe felt a twinge of panic rise up his gorge like a fist. What if he'd killed the damned fool? Likely a drunk miner with a taste for slapping around women when he'd been too much at the juice. What if? Thoughts of Yuma forced Rafe's boot to deliver a quick kick to the man's ribs. "Breathe, damn your hide."

The result was instant and impressive: The naked man gasped and shuddered all over. But he breathed, and continued to do so, slowly moving his good arm and legs as if he were an upended beetle. His left wrist and hand had already begun to swell and purple.

The man's face was taking on much the same hue and character. It looked as if he wore a bright-red hand-shaped brand seared onto his lowly maw, so deep and hard had Rafe's big hand clenched. Blood streamed from each corner of his mouth and from one nostril.

He coughed and gagged alternately, his rheumy, bloodshot eyes blinking slowly, unfocused.

"He'll live." Rafe looked at the two women. "You ladies okay?"

They stared up at the big man, eyes wide, their own recently delivered beatings momentarily forgotten. In unison they nodded.

"Thank you, mister," said the thin woman, her voice forced and raspy.

Rafe nodded, half listening to them, half listening for sounds from the hallway, but heard none. Must be such fight sounds were all too common in this dump. "You want me to drag his foul hide out of here?"

"Who, Charlie? Nah," said the second girl, sallow-complected with knotted hair the color of muddy water. "He's nasty when he's drinking, but when he's sober he's not so bad."

"Not the worst, anyways," said the thin girl.

Both women wore thin cotton shifts cut low and high, top and bottom. They revealed far more than they hid, and what they revealed was sad and hollow-seeming to Rafe.

Still Rafe didn't move, wasn't convinced leaving the bastard with them was the right thing to do. The second woman, definitely the older of the two, said in a soft voice, "It'll be all right. Happens every day, mister."

He nodded once more, touching his hat brim with a finger. At the door he looked at them once more. "You ladies wouldn't happen to know the whereabouts of a young woman, name of Susan, maybe Susie. Last name Pendleton. Supposed to . . . work here."

Though they both looked much the worse for wear, so much so that emotion was difficult to read on their sunken, battered faces, Rafe saw certain recognition flash in their eyes. "What is it? You know something about her." He stepped toward them, his own eyes wide. They flinched, clutched at each other.

"I'm not going to harm you, but I need to know where she is, dammit. I don't have time for this."

The thin one made to speak, cleared her throat, but her partner clamped a hand on the girl's mouth, shook her head. They traded frightened glances, but the young one reached up, pushed the older woman's hand down.

She spoke in a whisper. "Down to the end of the hall, take a left, separate rooms. They're Al's. Only she don't go by the names you said. She's Penny. I reckon it's her, though."

"What makes you so sure?"

She looked down at the floor at the softly groaning naked man at her feet. "Only one in here likely enough to have anyone still give a damn about her."

"Mister?" It was the older woman.

"Yeah?"

"She's chained."

"What?"

"Al's got her chained to the bed. She's the youngest of us, for now, anyways. She's in pretty rough shape. He's got her on the bad stuff, feeds too much of it to her. Only way I reckon he can keep her quiet. Used to be, when she first got here, she was a spitfire." The woman almost smiled. "I remember being like that once." The light in her eyes passed, leaving her dead-eyed and forlorn once more.

"You don't have to stay here," said Rafe. "I could help you get out. What's going on here isn't right."

The young one still stared downward, at

her feet, the floor, the naked man, at nothing.

The older woman shook her head. "We can't never leave here. Not alive, anyways. Al's got the stuff. We leave we ain't never going to get it again."

"You could get shed of the morphine, whatever it is he has you hooked on."

She looked right at Rafe's eyes then, right into him. The gaze chilled him. She shook her head no, and Rafe knew that was that. He touched his hat brim once more, nodded. He had a job to do.

He closed the door softly behind him. The entire episode lasted no more than two, three minutes, but it was time that was precious to him. He was now in this madhouse on borrowed time. And if caught, he knew Swearengen would shoot or stab first, and to hell with the questions.

Rafe strode fast down the hallway, his bootsteps muffled by the thready red-and-blue runner. To the end, then left. The door would no doubt be locked. Swearengen, he guessed, was still below, shouting and cursing at whoever was in sight. He hoped so, anyway.

First — if the women were right, Susie Pendleton was also Penny, which given her surname, was more than likely. Would she be in there? Rafe paused before a white door, paint chipped here and there. He tried the cut-glass, brass-rimmed knob. It rattled but didn't give.

Looking behind him once, Rafe drove a boot heel to the left of the knob. It shuddered but stayed locked. He gave it another. Then one more kick, harder than the first two, and with a long cracking sound, the door whipped inward.

The room was dark. Rafe stepped in and closed the door behind him. The dim hallway would be of no use to him in helping to see in this dank cave. But there was a window on the far wall, a dozen feet away. He edged toward it, nosing his way with his boots, his hand on the hilt of his Bowie knife. He didn't dare raise his boot to step, might slip up and topple over.

The air in the room was the same as that of the hallway, close and stuffy. Rafe kept his teeth tight together and did his best to not breathe through his nose. The air was a foul blend of sweat and pomade and urine and other scents too rank to dwell on. He crossed to the window, parted thick, dusty curtains enough to let the afternoon's westerly light angle in. His gaze followed it and he tried to make sense of the room.

He'd passed a sizable brass bed, a steamer

trunk against the wall opposite, two chairs barely visible beneath mounds of clothes. A chest of drawers with a mirror atop stood off to one side, each drawer open to some degree, its contents hanging out. Again, mostly wearables. Swearengen had a decided taste for clothing.

There were also dozens of whiskey bottles, some upright, a few holding yellow liquid that he bet was middle-of-the-night piss. Though how anyone could manage to aim that true was beyond him. Maybe Swearengen was small enough to do the job.

A corner of Rafe's mouth lifted in a wry smile. That's when he saw the leg. A woman's, sticking out from under what he had assumed was nothing more than a heap of twisted bedding atop the mattress.

He walked over, set two fingers on the leg, it was cold but not ice cold, not dead-body cold. He reached up, parted the bedding with caution. In a place like this, a man never knew what might leap up at him.

What he saw surprised him as much as anything could at that moment. Partly exposed before him lay sprawled, half on her side, a thin, naked woman. Not a scared girl as he had expected. Maybe it wasn't her? Maybe he was too late.

Rafe shook her shoulder, put his face close

to hers. "Hey," he hissed. "Hey, girl." He shook her. Her head lolled, but her eyelids fluttered, once twice, then her eyes opened.

The eyes were yellowed, bloodshot. But even in the dim light, he saw they were a strange color that no amount of abuse could change — deep green with sparks of gold in them. "Hey!"

"What? Al?"

"No, I'm not Al. Are you Susan Pebbleglass?"

"Whaa?"

He shook her again, put his mouth closer to her ear. Her hair was unwashed, and the stink of sweat and other smells rolled off her. "Are you Susan Pebbleglass?"

Her eyes flickered open again. "Name's Pen . . ."

He shook her and slapped her cheek.

Her eyes sprung open that time. "Pendleton." Her eyelids drooped again. "Not . . . Pebble."

Good, he thought, so she's the one. His silly little test had worked. "Come on, girly," he said, scooping her up. "You're coming with me."

"What? No, Al . . . he has my . . . medicine, Al . . ."

"He has nothing you need. Nothing anyone in the world needs. Now help me get you dressed."

He lifted free the last of the blankets. She was thin, covered with bruises along her ribs, her cheekbones, and those along her arms bore what looked like mosquito bites in the center. Needle marks, had to be. He tried to look away from her naked body, still lovely despite the abuse, as he scooted her to a sitting position.

"Ow . . ." Her voice was weak, her eyes flickering. "You're hurting me."

That's when he saw that her right arm was still behind her. He moved more of the chewed wool blanket. She hadn't been propping herself up. She was manacled to the brass bed frame.

He eased her back down and looked at the handcuff. It was typical, forged steel with a thick pin, a wrought lock hanging from it. Swearengen really wanted her to stay put.

Rafe's eyes widened. Swearengen knew exactly who this girl was. Knew that her father was the governor of California, knew what he had in his grimy hands. And from what Rafe had heard about the man, it sounded as if this little excuse for blackmail fell right into Swearengen's lap.

No wonder he didn't leave her out with the others on the service line. He wasn't so gracious, though, as to keep her from being sullied. He kept her for himself. Kept her drugged and chained in here like a beast.

Swearengen didn't want her, though, he wanted the money. He wanted whatever amount he could command from her father. So why hadn't he? Maybe he only recently found out who she was.

"Girl, hold on," he said, and dragged the bed back away from the wall. This would likely cause a few folks down below to look up. Wouldn't be long now before folks came running.

Rafe drove his boot down again and again at the crosspiece of brass tubing that prevented the manacles from slipping down. It soon gave way, only to clunk to a stop at the next piece. Three more times he repeated the kicks, his increasing impatience and unease with the situation making each boot jam more direct and effective the one before.

"Damn . . ." Kick!

"Fancy . . ." Kick!

"Bed!" Kick!

Finally the handcuff slid down to where the wood-and-steel crosspiece joined the upright.

Through all this the girl was no use, lolling and mumbling something about Al. Rafe had to hold her wrist with one hand to prevent crushing her thin wrist beneath his boot sole. With a quick tug upward the frame lifted free and, without pause, Rafe slid the handcuffs to the floor, free of the bed frame at last. The girl protested feebly once more as he jerked her arm, but Rafe didn't care. It was time to move.

As he bent to wrap her in a quilt she slapped his cheek. It was little more than a pat, but he was glad to see she had some sense about her.

"Can't say as I blame you — me being a stranger and all. But you have to trust me, Miss Pendleton. This is for your own good."

"Al!" she wailed, her head still flopping, but her eyes making an effort to stay open.

Rafe flopped her onto a quilt and did his best to bundle her in it. He scooped her off the bed and almost ripped off the sacks of gravel from around his neck, but now that his arms were occupied, he decided he'd have to dispense with them later.

The girl smelled bad, as if she had given up washing and instead doused herself with cheap toilet water. It didn't work. What made the situation worse was the fact that the girl felt like she weighed less than one of his legs.

She was ribby, and definitely not well. Her

eyes looked as if they were set in coal-smoked holes in her face, her cheekbones too defined, her hair, the color of dirty straw, hung as if it hadn't been properly washed for many weeks — or longer.

It was all Rafe could do to keep from busting right down the stairs and back to the barroom to smear Swearengen's smug face into a soppy mess of regret and pain. But that wasn't going to get the girl or him or Cookie out of town any sooner.

He'd almost made it to the door when quick, stomping footsteps hammered down the hall and stopped on the other side.

Heavy breathing, then: "Al? Al, you in there? Wasn't nothing but a scare, some idiot drunk, likely. Al?"

Rafe waited for the man to leave. But he didn't. He stood on the other side of the door — Rafe heard the heavy breathing and floorboards squeak as the man shifted his weight from one foot to the other. Didn't sound like he'd seen the kick-splintered frame yet.

What was the fool waiting for? Rafe was ready to draw a revolver, whip the door open, and force him into the room. Maybe clout him above the ear to shut him up. That's when the girl decided to pipe up.

"Al? That you, Al?"

157

The man on the other side of the door let out a low, animal-like grunt — no mistaking that sound for what it was. "Yeah, girl, let me in."

Rafe heard the man panting like a heated-up dog.

As she tried to respond, Rafe shook her, joggling her head. It interrupted her yammering, and seemed to confuse her.

"Girl? You all right in there? Lucky Dan would like to show you something."

The man's voice had gotten close to the door, and Rafe heard his breath coming in short gasps. Rafe stepped back as the man turned the doorknob slowly. The room was better lit than when Rafe had stumbled in, so he knew he'd soon be seen by the man.

All he needed to do was get Lucky Dan into the room far enough for him to shut the door — before being seen, that is. Rafe held the girl close to himself and hugged the wall behind the door as it opened.

Presently Rafe saw the back of a man — broad shoulders and a wide, bullish head set atop. From the back the man looked as though he were carved from stone. And he wore a white shirt and arm garters. Had to be that large barkeep from downstairs. Great.

One more step into the room, the man

eyed the bent and battered bed, took another cautious step forward . . . and Rafe slammed the door. He held the girl in the crook of one arm as he slipped free his right pistol and thumbed the hammer clean back to half-cock in one smooth motion. All as Lucky Dan turned to face him.

The man's eyes stayed wide open, but recognition bloomed on his face within a second. Rafe lowered the girl to the floor and, staying in a low crouch, barreled into the ornery barkeep.

The move was unexpected and Lucky Dan lost his footing and pitched backward onto the broken bed. Dust and feathers bloomed in the air. Rafe brought the butt of his Colt down hard, aiming for the tender spot behind Dan's temple. But the man turned his head and the blow caught him high on the cheek.

He grunted and drove a knee at Rafe's gut. Rafe felt a rib pop, lost his breath, and felt his vision dim for a moment. It was enough time for Dan to jam an arm across Rafe's chest and push him away. The barkeep rolled out from under Rafe and brought down both his meaty arms like a club, locked tight together in a joined fist, across Rafe's back.

Rafe collapsed, all wind driven from his

body. He was helpless and enraged. He had enough anger in him to grit his teeth and push with whatever reserve of effort he might still have. It helped, and even though he knew it would be too little too late, he'd be damned if he was going to wait for the next stroke. It would likely be a blade buried deep in the center of his back, or a gunshot to his skull.

But they didn't come. Instead he heard Lucky Dan's wheezing, more pronounced than it had sounded earlier by the door. The man might be large, but he was out of shape. Or worse, had an affliction of the lungs. Good. Served the bastard right.

Rafe managed to edge himself up, get one arm under his bulk, and push. In the melee he'd somehow lost grip of his Colt, but it had to be close by. His fingers scrabbled for it as he propped himself up with his left elbow. He fought to breathe through slitted lips and finally managed a whistle of air.

Why was it so difficult to get up off Swearengen's foul, cursed bed? And the reason brushed his chin — the top of a canvas sack filled with gravel. He was still lugging the damnable bags. They didn't weigh but a few pounds each, and were little larger in size than a bag of Arbuckles' coffee beans, but as suddenly weakened as

Lucky Dan's pummeling had made him, they felt to Rafe as if they each weighed a hundred pounds.

Rafe looked up at Dan, saw Lucky Dan's face was a welter of purple and red splotches. But he also saw the man was setting his considerable girth into motion once more. Right at Rafe.

With a grunt and roll, Rafe pitched himself forward, tumbled off the side of the bed, and landed a kneecap directly on a jag of displaced iron from the bed frame he'd savaged minutes before. Hot pain, like a sudden shaft of sunlight through a rocky chasm, flowered up his leg, brought sharp clarity to his mind. He stifled a groan.

No time to indulge in whining, he told himself. Lucky Dan was taking the direct route and crawling at him over the bed. Rafe pushed away, felt a whiskey bottle behind him, knocked others over. A thought skittered in and out of his mind — he hoped it hadn't been urine. He grabbed the neck of a bottle and smacked it hard against he floor.

The thick glass neck held together, but the bottom half of the bottle now lay in wet pieces. Rafe ground the jagged, raw glass into one of the sacks of gravel. With his other hand he grabbed at it, filled his hand from the leaking sack, and with a quick backward motion threw it straight into Lucky Dan's eyes.

Rafe grabbed another handful and raised the jagged bottle with the other hand, but it wasn't necessary. He'd caught Dan, in the dim light, in mid blink with eyes wide, and mouth the same.

The big man screamed, coughing and clawing at his eyes. He managed to get to his feet, howling gibberish words, slavering and raking at this face with meaty hands.

Rafe stood as the man stumbled by him toward the far end of the room, still howling and screaming and gnashing his teeth. "Blind! I'm blind!"

And then Rafe watched Lucky Dan crash straight into the window and right on through it, screaming and yelping the entire way down. Except when he hit the long porch roof.

Dan crashed on through it and, for a blessed, eerie moment there was no sound. Then a woman screamed and men shouted and Rafe bolted upright, ignoring the stabs of pain from his ribs, his back, his knee. He sucked thin ribbons of air he desperately needed into his still-winded lungs. Then he remembered his missing Colt and flat-handed the bed until he found it, still on the half cock. He was grateful it hadn't gone off in the ruckus.

He eased the hammer back down and slid the gun into its holster. Even before he got back to the door he saw that the quilt he'd wrapped around the naked young woman did not contain a naked young woman. She had gone — somewhere.

He snatched up the quilt and ran into the hall. She couldn't have gotten far. And she hadn't.

"You looking for this . . . Rafe Barr?" Al Swearengen stood a dozen feet away in the middle of the hallway, a drawn revolver, peeled all the way back, poked unwavering at Rafe's gut.

Susie Pendleton knelt beside him, also facing Rafe. The Gem's sleazy owner held the girl upright, his left hand knotted in her hair. It had to hurt to be held like that, all her weight, such as it was, pulling down on her hair. And yet the girl seemed unfazed. "Al . . . you promised . . . good stuff this time." Her eyelids fluttered, the rest of her body hanging like her hair, lank and weak.

He jerked her head — the girl whimpered and her face jounced from the pain.

"Shut up, trollop."

"Let go of the girl and mix it up with me, if you're so bent on harming others." Rafe

163

tried to keep his voice steady, but his ribs pained him something fierce, and Swearengen's rough treatment of the girl made him grind his teeth together. It was all he could do to keep from charging the man. That would get him nothing but gut shot.

"Not on your life, Barr. You're a big man, likely you'd kill me with a single blow. That is unless Lucky Dan managed somehow to take some of the steam from your Yuma-hardened engine."

"Lucky Dan got a lot more than he gave." Rafe wished he could believe that, doing his best to ignore the stitch in his side, needling hot and sharp with every breath drawn. While he spoke, Rafe inched the hand clutching the quilt down toward his holster.

"You have taken to thieving, is that it, Barr?" Swearengen shouted over his shoulder at a small but curious crowd of haggard, half-dressed fools looking on. "Hey everyone! A famous war spy is stealing my blankets!"

Rafe nodded, his eyes not leaving Swearengen's. "It's true, seems I can't resist befouled bedding. Odd habit I picked up in Yuma. Which reminds me . . ." Rafe groped for something, anything to say to keep Swearengen preoccupied. Rafe shifted his weight to his left foot. "How do you know who I am?"

Swearengen snorted a laugh. "Are you joking? Everyone knows who Rafe Barr is. Hero turned bad seed. Classic story there, eh?"

Rafe shrugged. "Makes no never mind to me, Swearengen. Why don't you let the girl go? She's nothing to you — you have a house full of them."

"Oh." The man shook his head theatrically, kept his eyes fixed on Rafe. "None of them are quite as special as my Penny here." As he said her name he gave her hair a yank. The girl moaned again.

"At least cover her up, for God's sake." Rafe sneered the words, then lunged low to the right, and forward, driving the wadded-up quilt at Swearengen. The heavy blanket made it nearly to the man before the hallway exploded with the deafening, echoing gunshot, and the stink of cordite and scorched cotton. Doors opened and slammed. Brave or foolish half-clad men and women, eyes wide, a few with guns drawn, peered out.

Rafe's ploy worked. Swearengen released his hold on the girl. She had slumped to the floor as Rafe barreled into Swearengen. The man's revolver flew ten feet down the dark end of the hall. The dive slammed the pimp into the wall. Plaster cracked, and laths snapped as women up and down the hall screamed.

Swearengen lay blinking and stunned beneath Barr, who straddled the foul man's chest.

The Gem's owner came to quickly and growled, bearing his teeth and thrashing beneath Rafe's weight. "You son of a bitch! Get off me! You tried to kill me —"

As he ranted and struggled, spittle flew from his mouth. Rafe glared down at the raging man for all of a second, then drove a big-knuckled hand at the man's jaw.

The head whipped sideways and the ranting stopped. Blood geysered up from the man's mouth. Rafe couldn't be sure, but he thought maybe Swearengen bit off the tip of his tongue.

"That'll make your rot-gut whiskey mighty tasty for a while."

He got to his feet, looked down at the man, deciding what to do with him. Better not do any more than he already had. He was trespassing, stealing, and causing quite a ruckus in the process. Rafe doubted the law would look as kindly on him as it did on Swearengen, at least in this instance. The notion stuck in his craw, but it was something he could fret over later, on the trail.

"Come on," he said, grabbing the girl by the upper arm. "Stand up, will you? We have to go."

He stomped the smoldering blanket, then wrapped it around the girl. He scooped her up, before she collapsed once more, and slung her over his right shoulder. He'd need one arm free, in case this house of horrors had more in store for him.

As he bolted down the hall, back the way he'd come, he shucked a Colt with his left hand. "If he comes around," Rafe shouted to all the folks lining the hallway, still watching in drop-jaw silence, "punch him again in the head."

He didn't expect an answer, but as he passed the last room, the one he'd first entered where the two ladies had been entertaining the hitter, the older of the two women smiled at him. "Gladly, mister. Good luck with that one." She nodded toward his shouldered burden.

"Ma'am," said Rafe, nodding his head as he ran by. "To you, too."

Then he pounded down the stairs and ran straight down the back hallway toward where, he did not know. He had a vague idea it might lead to a kitchen. And if that was the case, it probably led to a back alley. And that meant freedom.

He had precious little time to think his actions through. Between the false fire cries, the scuffle with the likely dead Unlucky Dan, and knocking out the owner of the place, he was sure half the town would be hot on his trail, and soon.

It felt to him like hours had passed since he entered the place with Cookie, led by that Frenchman dandy — and where was he anyway? — but Rafe knew from past fighting experience that in the throes of action, time had a way of writhing and curling in on itself like a stomped snake.

The further down the hall he traveled, the more he smelled onion and the thick odor of fried beefsteaks. It clung to the walls of the passage like stink on a two-day-dead man. His guess was right, then. He only hoped his luck would hold and lead him to a back door. Anywhere but the front of the place.

At the same time he heard rising shouts of men, boots hammering wood floors and stairs in a hurry, and doors slamming upstairs and downstairs.

The girl said something unintelligible and kicked. He gripped her tighter, his big arm wrapped around the top of her legs. "Hush up now. If you can't be useful, be quiet."

It didn't work. She thrashed, hitting his

back with tired, ineffective blows. Finally the effort exhausted her and she slumped once more, her head bouncing against his shoulder blade in counterpoint with his running.

Rafe burst through a dark door and sent it slamming into a stack of dirty pots and pans. They teetered and spilled with gusto across an already heaped table, a number of them clattered to the floor.

"Hey! You can't come in here! What are you doing — what are you doing with that girl? She dead?"

The voice came from a short, fat woman, whose accent sounded Polish to Rafe. He didn't stop for her, but shouted, "How do I get out?"

"Another dead one, huh?" The woman dried her hands on a filthy apron, equally dirty hair hung in her sweaty face as she shook her head. "Best take it to the pig sty, let them have at it. Al won't want to pay for a burial, not with all the questions that brings. I told him to leave off that girl. Like as not he was too rough with her, feeding her all that stuff and . . ."

He'd heard every word, all of it turned his stomach sour, but Rafe had no time to quiz the woman. She thought he was lugging a dead woman, so much the better. From the

169

looks of it, another few days, a week, maybe, and the girl might well have ended up dead.

At last, he came to a door, this one painted light green, as if welcoming him to the outdoors. He reached for the handle, but it swung inward before he could grab the knob. He stood face-to-face with the dandy Frenchman.

"Well, well, *monsieur.* I am so happy to see you again!"

"Out of my way!" barked Rafe.

But the man raised a cocked revolver. "No, I think not. You see, you have saved me the trouble of tracking you down. The other man, I still have to find him, but I am betting, were I a betting man, of course, that he will not travel far from you, wherever it is you might be going with a girl."

He advanced, wagging the pistol. "You are an unusual man, in that most of Monsieur Swearengen's customers prefer to, ah, dance with the girls here in the Gem itself, and not take them off-premises. In fact, I am sure that Monsieur Sweareng—"

Rafe rolled his eyes and grinned theatrically. "Now look," and shook his head as if to disagree with the man, but at the same time he drove his boot upward hard and fast and sent the Schofield spinning. He hoped he wouldn't regret the maneuver with an accidental bullet to his body, but something had to change. The man was talking the day away.

The gun hit the floor somewhere behind him, and wonder of wonders, didn't fire.

The Frenchman squawked and dropped against the narrow doorframe, holding his kicked arm. "You . . . you —"

Rafe nodded as he heard voices behind him, shouting something about how he needed to stop.

"Yep, me. Now, you." He drove his boot into the Frenchman's chest, sent him sprawling backward down a short but steep run of steps. Rafe bulled on through the doorway right after him and slammed the door shut behind him, then looked around as he heard shouts and pounding footsteps in the kitchen.

A ragged hank of rope lay draped over the leaning rail lining one side of the steps. He snagged it and nudged the girl up higher on his shoulder. She groaned and yelled, "Al . . ."

With one free hand and the other somewhat useful, he tied the rope to the railing upright, a sturdier option than the rail itself, and wound the other end around the doorknob several times. Then he tied it back on itself. Might hold them for a few more seconds.

Once more Rafe adjusted the girl and pounded down the steps. The Frenchman lay at the bottom, sprawled on his side and moaning. His eyes searched, focused on Rafe, and through gritted teeth and with no trace of an accent, said, "I knew you weren't miners! Tried to tell Al, but he don't listen to no one."

"And I knew you weren't a Frenchman or a dandy. Neither is quite as boring as you. Well," said Rafe as he stepped over the man and looked down. "Nearly so, anyway."

He reached down, delivered a quick, hard punch to the man's face, much the same as he had done to the man's employer, and ran down the narrow dirt track toward the livery, the girl bouncing and nearly lifeless on his broad shoulders.

The day had not turned out as he had hoped. Not enough planning, too little reliance on the way he used to be. Prison had weakened him, left him careless, angry, bitter. Something has to change. Have to get back to how he and Cookie used to carry themselves in fights.

He grabbed too much false confidence after the fight with those desert rats who attacked in the night. Mostly, though, Rafe knew he was to blame. He knew he was not the same man he was before Yuma, before that . . . time, burying them . . .

No, couldn't let himself think that way. He had a job to do, and if he'd made a hash of it up to now, he could blame himself later, think too much about it. Knowing he'd brood, combing it over and over again until he'd gleaned from it every morsel he could. But for now he had to do a better job of the rest of the day.

"Cookie, you better be there," grunted Rafe. Not the moment nor place to tug out his pocketwatch, he gauged the time by the angle of the sun and the depth of the shadows it cast against the long sides of the buildings.

He risked one look back behind and saw movement from around the barn he'd skirted. Had to be close to the feed depot by now. He wasn't sure how much more of this he could take. Wheezing and lugging this girl, light as she was, annoyed those cracked ribs — he felt certain there was more than one — almost more than he could take. His breath threaded out of his wide-set mouth and steady runnels of sweat trailed down his face, stinging his eyes.

Still, Rafe Barr didn't let up. He even managed a tight grin as he ran.

CHAPTER 12:
PLAN B

Six minutes earlier and two streets over, Cookie was doing his best to make his way back to the depot, doubting the man would have the horses ready yet. He'd seen that oaf flop on out of that window of the Gem, and he knew Rafe had something to do with it — he legged it faster. Soon the depot came into sight, and Cookie was mighty pleased, perspiring as he was those last few hundred feet.

This is why I don't like to get down off a horse if I can help it, he thought. Might be I should give up some bad habit or other, but I can't bear to part with 'em. Ain't like chaw nor a pipe has much to do with a man's wind, anyway. And drink is a way of keeping the pipes clean and the mind free of cobwebs.

He made it to the depot, saw the horses, still unsaddled, munching on something in a well-cribbed trough out back. They looked to have been rubbed down, and despite the long days of travel seemed spry enough. His mustang, Stinky, tried to nudge Rafe's easygoing buckskin out of the way, but the larger horse stood his ground, ears laid back.

"There now," said a voice out of sight, then the old black man stepped into view, a ragged burlap sack in one hand, an old brush in the other, more wood handle than bristle.

As he walked up to the place, Cookie watched as the man clucked and talked in a low voice, moving easy around the horses. Cookie admired folks who had that smooth and easy way with critters, particularly horses. He'd always been little more than a fair hand with them, but he knew he'd never have that bond with ol' Stinky that other folks had with theirs.

Rafe was a good man with horses. Even the ones he'd been given from the warden, horses he didn't know, and he got along with them fine. Might be Cookie needed to have more patience. "Hey there, old-timer," he said, holding up a hand.

The man looked up from his task, over the back of the packhorse, his milky eyes squinting. "Didn't expect an old man to call me old, heh, heh." He shook his head and went back to brushing.

Despite the dig, Cookie smiled, leaned on the edge of the little stable's doorway. He liked this fella, didn't know him from Adam, but there was something about him he liked. "You don't take much guff, do you?"

"If by that you mean I don't suffer fools, then you right. Say, you early, ain't you?"

Cookie nodded. "Yep, that fracas over at the Gem. Got a hankering to head on out of Deadwood while the gettin's good."

"You done got rid of your gold, I see." The man had already moved to racks along a side wall, grabbed the blankets and made his way back to the horses.

"Let me give you a hand," said Cookie, ignoring the comment. "Might be my partner will want to leave early. I'd like to be ready to ride when he shows up."

The two men worked side by side, saddling the horses, tying on the pack saddles to the two other horses, then Cookie stopped in the middle of lashing down the load. "Might be there'll be a third one of us. Then again, she might not be fit to ride."

"Sizable as that horse is," said the black man, nodding toward Rafe's buckskin, "you could ride double and it wouldn't be nothing to the horse."

The old man turned to face Cookie, his head leaned to one side, his eyes squinted.

"You two didn't seem rascals nor thieves to me when you come in."

"And we do now?"

"No, didn't say that. But you look to be in a hurry."

"Well, we are in a hurry, leastwise we will be. And no, we ain't thieves. Had a couple of pieces of business to attend to here in town. I did mine, my partner's finishing up his, I expect, any minute now."

"Ain't no never mind to me." The man shrugged.

"What do we owe you, friend?" said Cookie, finishing off the last of his horse's saddle cinching.

"The money he paid before is plenty. I hope you boys know what you're doing."

"Me, too." Cookie flipped up his stirrups, double-checking while he had the chance. The depot owner handed over Rafe's reins.

Cookie figured he'd wrangle the pack beasts, one tied behind the other. He'd shifted the load on the lead packhorse to accommodate the girl, and figured on rejiggering the loads later, once they were away from Deadwood and camped in safety.

"That partner of yours," said the depot man.

"What about him?" Cookie looked up from tightening the mustang's cinch.

"Only . . . if that's him — and it do look like him — you best get a move on. 'Cause that passel of folks behind him don't look like they is bringing him cake and tea. They giving chase."

Cookie craned his neck to look over the horse's back. Lordy, it was Rafe and he was carrying what looked like a body wrapped in a quilt on his shoulder. Oh hell, he thought as he slid Rafe's carbine from its boot. Was the girl dead? If so, why drag her carcass back with him? Proof for the warden? He'd find out soon enough.

He saw at least three men trailing Rafe. They were still far behind, but coming on strong, not burdened as Rafe was by a body.

Cookie thrust the reins back into the hands of the man. "Hold on to these for a second. Got some cover to throw out there!"

Even as Cookie said it he scooted low to his right, peered out between a wobbly stack of crates and kegs awaiting repair. They wouldn't stop bullets, but they would hide him. Had to stop those men from following. If he rode up to meet Rafe they'd never get out of that alley before the chasers threw down on them.

He shoved the barrel of the long gun between two flimsy boxes and waited one, two, three seconds — there went Rafe, thundering by and making straight for the horses. Cookie heard his big friend's raspy, labored breathing. Didn't sound good — he hoped Rafe hadn't taken lead.

The reedy old man cranked a round and widened the gap between the crates with the rifle barrel. There, the first pursuer was coming, he could hear him. Cookie nearly squeezed the trigger, but couldn't make himself do it. Too dangerous to shoot in the confines of this back street where houses and businesses were packed tighter than a burly woman's corset.

Then he had a better idea. No time for smiling and feeling smug about it yet — he unbuttoned a long, inner vest pocket and tweezered out a paper wad containing a mixture of powders of his own devising, and topped with a wick. It had heft, was roughly half the length and the same brown paper of a stick of his favorite remedy, dynamite, though none of the fun punch.

Still, he kept a few handy for such occasions. He lit the little toothless bomb and lobbed it up and over the crates. The smoking, spark-spitting fuse doing its best to look like what it wasn't — a half stick of dynamite. But no one else knew that.

It did everything Cookie expected it to — and without bullets. The first pursuer nearly ran into it, stopped short, windmilling his arms as if he found himself unexpectedly at the edge of a cliff. He worked his boots hard, digging and spinning and spitting gravel even as the other two men drove into him as if they were shoved from behind.

They ended up in a pile, a couple of feet from the hissing, sparking, smoking paper-wrapped dupe of a bomb.

It was all Cookie could do to strike another match and set the second alight. He wanted to laugh as he sent the concoction whipping and hissing, trailing gray smoke in an arc across the width of the alleyway. It landed about where the three shrieking men had but a second before been piled atop one another.

They had nearly sorted themselves out and were kicking up gravel back the way they came, shouting, "Dynamite! Oh, God!"

Behind them, thick, boiling clouds of gray-black smoke built up like a low wall of storm clouds, filled the narrow roadway between the buildings. People shouted, coughed, ran in all directions, not quite sure what was happening.

Cookie was still howling with laughter as he aimed a smart, two-fingered salute to the livery man, hopped aboard the waiting mustang. He followed Rafe as fast as their horses' legs would carry them, on out of Deadwood proper. Their dust trail and the various commotions they left behind seemed to be doing the trick nicely.

The depot man stood in the street, watching the strangers ride away, then looked to his right at the slowly clearing wall of smoke. He shook his head, then clinked the coins in his hand and chuckled as he walked back inside the barn.

Chapter 13:
When Men Meet

"I never seen a country the like of this, all pretty trees and steep grades one minute, then" — Cookie snapped a finger, bouncing in the saddle as they kicked up a dust trail on a feeder road southward out of Deadwood — "quick as a hot flame through birch bark you got a homely old hole in the ground where some poor soul has been scratching for gold for years!" He shook his head. "Seems to me a man ought to value his time more than that."

Surprised his tirade didn't elicit a response from his companion, Cookie squinted over at him through the dust. Rafe was still giving it all, maintaining their hard pace, and looking down a whole lot at the girl cradled in his lap. It was an awkward arrangement, but the girl was too feeble to set a saddle herself.

"She okay?"

Rafe shouted over to him. "I think so. Her

breathing thins out, but then she'll growl and curse in her sleep."

Cookie smiled. "Good sign — means she's a fighter."

They had set a hard pace out of town miles back, despite the snake-twisty road through mountainous terrain and the burden of the helpless girl. Though neither man said anything, they knew this could prove to be one hell of a short ride if they didn't put a whole lot of miles between them and Deadwood.

As if to challenge their wishes, fifty yards ahead a lone rider emerged from the pines and slid down an embankment, the horse's hooves skittering a small landslide of gravel into the roadway. The horse fidgeted and the rider angled the gleaming black gelding lengthwise across the road.

"Oh boy — Cookie, get set," said Rafe, slowing his pace. He held the girl upright with one arm, and snatched up a revolver with his free hand.

Cookie rode up alongside, packhorses trailing in line. He laid his long gun across his lap, and squinted toward the rider. "Aww, hell, Rafe. It's Bullock. I ain't had a chance to tell you but me and him had a bit of a chat back in town."

Rafe looked quickly at Cookie and whispered, "You didn't tell him anything, did you?"

"What? No, course not. I told you that slip to Swearengen won't never happen again."

"I know, I know. Does he know I'm out?"

"Seemed to. He was mighty secretive, though. He's an odd duck."

"He's a lawman, that's all. His concerns are different than ours."

"I'll say."

Rafe reined up a dozen yards from the motionless rider, but said nothing. For long moments the three men exchanged glances, finally the girl roused from her stupor, shook her head and clunked into Rafe's. She almost knocked off his hat.

"Looks to me like you have your hands full, there . . . Rafe Barr."

Rafe slid his Colt back into its holster. "Good day to you, Seth. Fine afternoon for a ride."

The man in black said nothing, merely nodded, not taking his eyes from Barr. But he was smiling.

He walked his horse toward them slowly, both hands lightly holding the reins before his vest, watch chain swaying with the motion.

"Look, Seth. This isn't what it —"

Bullock cut him off. "I don't want to know, Rafe. I reckon the man I knew a long time ago is still the same man, had a few bad hands dealt him since then." He shifted in his saddle, the leather creaking.

"It's good to see you're out of Yuma. And it's good you have Cookie watching your back, too." He offered a quick smile and nod to Cookie, then looked back to Rafe. "Do what you need to. I'll not molest you."

He rode closer, though, then tugged out a small selection of jangling keys from a pocket inside his coat. "Hold out the girl's wrist."

Rafe did, and on the third key Bullock succeeded in unlocking the heavy manacle. "Damn that Swearengen," he said, before tossing the clanking contraption into the roadside scrub.

He gigged the horse a few steps to the side of the road. "Now ride before my deputies thunder up and cut loose like they know what they're up to. I'll do my best to see they don't fog your trail too hard, or too soon." The ramrod lawman stood smiling in the stirrups a moment, offered a sharp wave, then heeled the horse around and rode back to town.

The men watched him go, then Cookie said, "Well don't that beat all. Can't never figure a lawman, and that's the truth."

"We best take his advice and get while we still have a lead on the others."

And they both knew the others weren't zealous lawmen. They were likely a contingent of gunhands hired by Swearengen.

"Cookie, I believe Swearengen knows who she is. I believe he was looking at her as a fine score."

The older man thrust his bottom lip out, scratched his chin. "You saying he was fixing to blackmail her old man?"

Rafe nodded.

"Then not only did we steal her from his employ, we all but took money — likely a stack of it — from that weasel's coin purse, eh?"

"That's about the size of it."

Cookie grinned. "Good!" He touched heels to his horse's belly and, with the packhorses thundering behind, threaded his way up the trail. "Keep up with me, boy. If you can!"

Despite his cumbersome load and the cracked ribs paining him with each footfall of the horse, Rafe smiled. Right back in the thick of it with Cookie, like all those years ago. And he realized, rusty and off-center as he was nowadays, there were few places he'd rather be.

Chapter 14:
Thurrounded by Idiots

"Thut up! I want anything from you, I'll tell you what it ith I want."

"But . . ."

Al Swearengen jammed a shaking finger in the Frenchman's face, nearly touching the tip of the man's long, slender nose.

"And thtop pretending you're French. You thound like an idiot."

Swearengen was shorter than the man by several inches, but that had never mattered to the brothel owner. In his mind he was at least a head taller and a foot wider at the shoulder than anyone he'd ever met.

"Get you in trouble one day," his father had said. He told the old man he didn't care, as long as trouble was somewhere other than the family farm. That had earned him a hard backhand to the mouth.

Now, all those years later, he ran his sore tongue along the inside of his swollen mouth. Thought maybe he could feel the tiny nub of scar from the old man's smack. Al had taken a lot of beatings in his day, given a good many more, but today's was . . . unexpected.

Should have known something was amiss when that little bird of an old man had let slip the name *Rafe*. That's when a notion quick as a thunderclap went through his mind. He'd only needed a few seconds to work out that the man before him had to be none other than Rafe Barr, war hero turned spy — or was it the other way around?

Still, if the men had gold in those bags, why should he give a spit who they were? Could have been the Queen of France for all he cared. As long as he had that gold under his roof, he could afford to mull over the situation, figure out how to get them to part with it willingly. And if that failed, he'd damn well take it from them.

He'd left them with fresh drinks at the bar, went back to his office to figure out a plan, then that fool had shouted fire. That's when it all fell apart. Swearengen groaned and raised the glass to his lips, forgetting for the moment the bloody ragged tip of his tongue. The whiskey soaked itself into the chewed mess and stung like he'd stuck his face in a bag full of bees.

"Al . . ."

He sighed, leaned back, his eyes closed. "What?"

"I am sorry. I'll ride out with the boys. We'll get her back." The man known as Frenchy winced as he spoke, his breathing whistling through his freshly broken nose.

"I'll give you thith, Frenchy. You're nothing if not perthithtent." He swallowed more whiskey, this time along the side of his mouth, keeping his tongue away from the fiery liquid. Better. "And you're damn right you'll get her back. Or don't come back."

"Oh, I'll get her back, Al. You wait and see."

"You come back without her and I'll gut you with a dull thpoon, you underthtand me?"

Frenchy nodded, holding his side, his arm, his head all at once. He didn't dare touch his nose — it felt like a hot rock hanging off his face and he couldn't keep his eyes from watering. Threats from Al were the least of his concerns. The boss made them every day in some form or another. Sometimes more than once a day.

Frenchy had no intention of ever returning to Deadwood. He knew too much about his own paltry abilities where tracking was concerned. He also knew how the pimp dealt with those who disappointed him. No,

189

Frenchy decided, he'd ride on out — fast — and not look back. Swearengen's reach was only so long, after all.

"What's so all-fired special about that girl anyway, Al?" The man leaned over the desk, winked. "You got a thing for her?"

As bad as he hurt, Al still managed to snatch up the heavy whiskey glass and drive it right into the center of Frenchy's face. The man collapsed to the floor, screaming like a mourning old woman and cradling that swelled-up nose in both hands.

"Now get out," said Swearengen in a low, even voice. "Before I kill you. The only reathon you are thtill alive is because Lucky Dan ithn't. And much as I hate to admit it, I need someone elthe to kick in the ballth. You get the job until I find thomeone more capable." He turned back to his desk. "It thouldn't take long, though, don't get too comfortable."

Frenchy moaned, whimpered. Al stood and walked around the desk. He kicked the man hard, landed two good blows, one square to the man's crotch, before Frenchy, howling and gagging, scrabbled his way through the door and into the hallway.

There is no way the oafs he'd sent out after Barr and the old man were likely to turn up with anything other than excuses.

And though Frenchy was an ignorant fool, he was the brightest of the lot he had left working for him.

Lucky Dan was dead, that would be a hard loss. The man was appropriately named, and so could keep a rowdy barroom quieter than a small man, but he was no fighter. He proved that much today, dropped to the street like a sack of wet cornmeal. And smashed through a porch roof, too.

"Where in the hell ith that damn lawman, Bullock?" Swearengen shouted at the walls of his office, then sat down hard in his chair. As if in answer to his shout, the door opened and a haggard-looking woman poked her head in. "Al? Sheriff Bullock is here. Should I send him in?"

"Yeth, dammit. Why athk?"

The woman nodded and disappeared. Presently she knocked again and the door opened wide. In walked Bullock.

"Looks like I am too late to the ball, Swearengen."

"You are too late and too loud." Al stood, quivering hands holding the edge of his desk. He felt like he'd spent the previous evening swimming in a bottle of whiskey.

"You rather I leave?" said the sheriff.

"I'd rather you find my property and bring back those killerth and thieveth."

191

"Not so sure there was any witness to Lucky Dan's unfortunate demise. Could be he got a bit addled and toppled out of that window all on his own."

"Are you daft? That wath my bedroom window!"

Bullock wore a serious face. "I don't want to know what you get up to in your down-time, Swearengen. I am dead certain little of it is legal anyway."

"But they made off with my property!"

"A human being is not another person's property, Al. That girl was supposed to be free to walk out of here anytime."

"Yeah, only she didn't, did she? Why do you suppothe that ith, Bullock? Could be she liked it here?" Even saying it almost made the bar owner laugh. There wasn't a girl in the place who didn't hate the trollish owner of the Gem, likely all of them wanted him dead. But they stayed around, for the "good stuff," as he promised them.

"Hard to leave when you're chained in place, eh, Swearengen?" Bullock's stare was hard-eyed and without trace of mirth.

The bully pimp ignored the comment. "She cotht me money and now she'th going to cotht more of it with every day that patheth and she ithn't here under my roof, earning her keep. Meanwhile you thtand here doing nothing. I expect your deputieth are as utheleth as ever, can't find their own headth with both handth."

Bullock's grin returned. Much to the proprietor's disgust, the lawman seemed to be enjoying himself.

"Oh, those junior lawdogs lit out right quick, but since they aren't back yet, I'd say the two men they're chasing are experienced in evading the law. You know the type, hardened criminals with all manner of plans and methods of escaping capture."

Swearengen fixed the sheriff with a dull, dead stare. "I will have my property returned, Bullock. Nothing will thtop me." He'd meant his words to sound menacing, but with the tip of his tongue swollen and mangled, he sounded like little more than a whiny, lisping drunk.

"I'll wager there's one thing that will. And I hope to be the one to deliver it. Personally." Bullock touched his hat brim. "Until that day, Swearengen, you will no doubt continue to be a carbuncle on the ass of progress in this otherwise decent town."

The lawman took his leave. Normally the pimp would send him on his way with a litany of choice phrases intended to scald the ears of the pious and pure. But today he was plain tired. Dog tired.

This day had started with so much promise, too. He'd planned on partaking of the pleasures of Penny to break up the long afternoon, knowing he'd have to relinquish her at some point if he intended to follow through on his blackmail plan.

In fact, he'd begun drafting a letter to her old man, none other than the sitting governor of California, one Cuthbert Pendleton. He had been halfway through setting the wording to paper when that damned Frenchy had rushed in babbling about two strangers with bags of gold.

Not for the last time did Swearengen wonder why he surrounded himself with idiots. He grabbed the bottle of rye and drained two deep swallows from it, wincing as the whiskey seared his wounds.

Chapter 15:
A Cave of One's Own

They rode hard through the rest of that day, slowing only for the horses. For a day in mid August, the afternoon had begun to cloud and a scent carried to them on a budding breeze — what was that? Sage? No . . .

Cookie sniffed at the air like a rangy old coonhound. Rafe caught sight of him and nearly smiled, but found himself flexing his nostrils, too.

"Rain," he said.

"Rain? Here and in this dry season?" Cookie seemed skeptical, scratched at an underarm. "Might be you're right."

"Might be we're in for a gully washer, too."

"Uh-oh," said Cookie. "Time for higher ground."

Rafe nodded agreement, not having to say that they needed to be cautious about it — no sense skylining themselves. Rafe knew that old lawdog Bullock would be true to his word and keep his deputies from creeping up on them. But Swearengen's men? They were bound by no laws, at least in their own minds, and Swearengen would be desperate to get the girl back.

"There!" Cookie pointed to a pine-studded rise to their east, not far away. "We get up there we can wait it out, might even be a cozy outcrop we can hunker under."

"Lead the way — and be sure to check for snakes wherever you decide to crawl. I expect they look for high ground, too, when they sense rain coming."

Earlier he'd repositioned the girl so she sat astride the saddle in front of him. The soaking sun on her unwashed hair and the rank old quilt weren't doing his nose any favors, but there was no way he was going to stop and try to clean her up. Time enough for that later.

She was thin. Good, as there wasn't a heck of a lot of room in the saddle. She was far from emaciated, though. She was also older than he'd been led to believe. Maybe even of an age where she might well make up her own mind about her life.

He had to keep an arm around her waist to make certain she didn't topple from the horse, but it made him uncomfortable to do so. Under all the grime and smell, she was a pretty young woman and bouncing along in front of him in the saddle was testing his patience and fortitude. Lucky for him his ribs felt as if the devil were grinding a branding iron into the side of his chest. Still, he'd be glad when she was coherent enough to ride her own horse.

But he knew the real reason he was bothered by her presence so close to him. Maria was dead, and anytime he allowed thoughts of a woman to creep into his mind he felt twinges of disgust with himself. The memories of life with her — and then of her dead in his arms — clung to his mind like spiny ice on the freezing banks of an autumn river.

No doubt, he was a man with a problem. And that problem was riding in front of him in the saddle. He felt the delicate angles of her abused body through the quilt. The soft weight of her breasts pressed on his forearm with each step the horse took, and then there was the smooth line of her neck where her hair parted as she slept.

Her legs hung lank and limp before his and he felt bad about it — she'd have a sore time of walking for a while once they got to wherever it was they were going.

Rafe sighed. There was so much to figure out.

She had been sleeping a whole lot in the

past few hours, and seemed to have less spunk about her than when he'd first found her. He wondered if maybe the pimp had slipped her something when he had her in the hallway before Rafe came out. It was a short time, but if there was a way to dope the girl, Swearengen would know it.

Rafe had gone most of the day without lighting a stub end of a cigar, not wanting to disturb the girl, but now he had a hankering for one. And he figured if they were soon to get wet, he'd lose the chance.

He switched the reins to the hand holding the girl, and tweezered his fingers in his shirt pocket for the partial cigar he kept there. It was a little worse for the wear, the end having been squashed no doubt in the tussle from earlier, but he managed to moisten it with his lips and form it into some sort of smokeable shape.

He flicked the match alight on the thigh of his trousers and waited for the stink to burn off before setting fire to the homely nub. There it was, a mouthful of good old blue smoke. Not the best cigars in the world, but not the worst, either. He'd stocked up at that little mercantile in Camp Joe, a day's ride north of Yuma.

"Those things will kill you."

The voice was quiet, barely more than a

whisper.

Rafe lifted the cigar from his mouth. "Pardon me?"

"I said . . ." A pause gave unintended weight to the words. "Those cigars will kill you."

Rafe chuckled. "Not only are you awake, but you have a sense of humor."

"Been awake a while. Too weak to do much."

"You remember anything of earlier?"

"Some. Mostly I'm worried."

"Why?"

She didn't reply right away, so Rafe thought she might have drifted off. Then she spoke, her voice tighter, grimmer, a pinch louder. "Been this far before . . . it's that quiet time before . . ." Her voice trailed off.

"The calm before the storm, I think you mean." Rafe guessed her intention. "How bad will it get? Will whiskey help?"

Her reply told him all he needed to know. Through the quilt he felt her body stiffen. She sat upright, clenching in on herself. Her head jerked front to back and she shivered so hard he heard her teeth rattle together like castanets.

He took that as a yes and heeled the already trotting horse into a gallop. "Cook," he said, coming up behind his partner. "We have to get there faster."

"It ain't even commenced to rain yet."

"Not the problem." Rafe nodded down at the girl and Cookie's eyes widened. He nodded and snapped the rein ends on his horse's flank.

Soon the girl was quivering with such violence that Rafe had both hands full trying to keep her from thrashing right out of the saddle. "Easy Susan, easy now," he said close to her ear. "We'll make camp soon. Almost there."

Behind, they heard a low, long roll of thunder, like a cannonball set in motion down a long wood floor. It echoed and caromed around the hills. Rafe looked back, saw far-off lightning stitch the day's darkening sky. Vivid white jags lanced through low purple clouds. From beneath the roiling mass, sheets of black rain sliced downward, glinting like silver in the lightning.

"It's coming, Cook! Head to that high ground!"

He didn't have to tell Cookie — the thin man ahead of him bounced in the saddle, sinking boot heels and flapping his arms like a chicken trying to take flight. He whipped the ends of the reins, mostly slapping his saddlebags and himself in the legs. Cookie's sweat-soaked hat had slipped from his wispy pate and hung bouncing on his upper back, the slide of his stampede strap riding on the point of his Adam's apple.

Rafe rode his horse tight behind the second and most-wide-eyed packhorse. The solid beast gave all, lunging upslope, scattering scree, breathing hard, and lathering beneath the shifting load she hauled.

The girl struggled harder than she had since he'd made her acquaintance. It was all Rafe could do to maintain his balance, keep the horse digging hard upslope, and hold on to the thrashing woman. Her quilt was slipping off again and he didn't think she cared. If that was his only garment, he expected he'd be looking to get shed of the smelly rag, too.

Rafe held her tighter about the midsection and hoped he wasn't harming her. It was either that or let her drop — then she'd be in a real world of hurt — naked and fevered and rolling down a scree-slick slope. As suddenly as she had begun stiffening and twitching, her body relaxed and sagged once more against him. For that slight change, he was grateful.

They were nearly to the top when he heard the rain driving behind and closing in fast. Cookie had reached the trees and was nearly lost to view as he threaded his way in. Rafe had experienced enough storms in his time to know that the safest place when the heavens played slash-and-burn was not under a tree, but there would be no way of talking Cookie out of it. Besides, as he recalled, the old hound dog had a way of sniffing out shelter and promising and protective spots in the unlikeliest of locations.

"Here! Rafe, here!"

The big man bent low, feeling the first cold, surprising pelts of hard summer rain pummel his back. It stung like buckshot from the skies, then harder and more insistent, from one blink to the next. Where was that man?

"Rafe!"

There he was, through the thicket of trees and hard by a massive tumbledown of a cave. Perfect. The big man rode up and, still holding the girl by the waist, he slid down out of the saddle and slid her down after him. Her feet smacked the ground as Rafe scooped her up, doing his best to keep his eyes from that damnable parted quilt.

"Cookie — take her, get a fire going. I'll tend the horses."

He handed her off to a stiff-armed Cookie, who stared wide-eyed at anything but the girl's bare skin.

"She won't bite, man. She needs our help, now get on it!"

That seemed to snap Cookie out of his reverie of modesty. Rafe gathered the reins of the two dancing saddle horses, unstrapped the saddlebags and gear, and shoved it all as far inside the rocky lean-to as he was able. Next he dealt with the half-laden pack animals, propping their loads close by the driest side of a boulder and hoping their goods didn't get too wet. He almost made it before the rain began sluicing down with gusto.

Cookie meanwhile had done his best to make the girl comfortable in the rough cave, which he was pleased to find was deeper and more commodious than he'd thought. He dragged the gear in as Rafe brought it to him, and managed to kindle a small fire and got a pot of coffee bubbling in no time. They were all chilled and wet to the bone, and judging from the ugly bruise of a sky, the storm looked to be in no hurry to move on — a real soaker.

Finished with the horses, Rafe ducked into the low overhanging entrance to the cave. "I expect you didn't have time to clear out any critters who might have found this hidey-hole before us."

Cookie set down his coffee cup, smacked his lips. "You expect right. But I figure if we ain't heard from them yet, no sense in going looking for trouble."

"Fair enough."

For long minutes neither man spoke. Rafe crouched bent-backed in the low declivity, the stiff, oiled canvas of his slicker scratching the close rock wall. Rain and lightning lashed and cracked, occasional errant gouts of wind drove pelting rain in on them.

Rafe hunkered down before the fire with his broad back to the cave's mouth, blocking the fire-killing rain. Much of an hour passed before the storm's teeth began to lose their bite. Rafe stood, bent low, and glanced at the rescued young woman, still sleeping fitfully. "I'll take first watch."

"What about the girl?" whispered Cookie, looking askance at the sleeping form as if she were some undiscovered creature.

"What about her?" whispered Rafe, mocking the old man's tone.

Cookie narrowed his eyes. "Now you look here, whelp. She's a girl and we're, well, we're not. You follow me? She ain't but half clothed in some old rag."

"And she's in a poorly way and needs our help. So when she thrashes and shivers and kicks off the clothes and blankets we've laid on her . . ."

Cookie leaned forward, waiting for Rafe to reveal some helpful truth.

"Drape 'em back on her." Rafe scooped up his rifle, draped it over an arm, and groaned lightly as a quick lance of pain ripped through his side.

"Got to bind those ribs, Rafe."

The big man nodded. "In the morning when we can see. I don't want you accidentally wrapping my head instead."

"See if I help you when the time comes."

They both knew he would. Rafe cracked a thin smile.

The big man made his way back outside, straightening gently in the wide open. The rain had lessened, nearly pinched out, but Rafe eyed the dark, starless night with suspicion. Not the usual clear sky he expected after a hard-driving rainstorm like that. Might be they were in for more. Bad for them if they wanted to move on in relative comfort, good for them in that they could stumble along tomorrow in the rain. Only real dedicated and dogged trackers would follow.

He didn't put it past Swearengen to hire experienced men to dog his trail, but he'd have to send for them. Anyone in Deadwood the pimp might persuade to track them would likely be a down-on-his-luck miner with a rusty six-gun, a bone heap of a horse, and a need for cash.

Rafe checked on the horses, saw that though they were droop-eared and wet, they seemed at ease, if not comfort, resting after the pounding ride of earlier. All they put them through that day, he was amazed they were little more than tired. They'd lost flesh lately, but that couldn't be helped. He'd have to hole up somewhere soon, figure out what to do with the girl.

The warden's plan gnawed at him. There was something off about it, and Rafe didn't feel inclined to play a part in anything that might harm others, particularly the girl. Though he didn't see how she could do much worse than what she'd done to herself at the hands of Swearengen.

"Swearengen," he growled in a low whisper only he and the horses could hear. The man's name clogged in his craw like a swallow of rank water.

He plucked out a fresh cigar, sliced it in half with his pocket knife, working the sharp blade in a circle, the meat of his thumb guiding it. It was amazing to him the pleasure he gained from such quiet, everyday acts, moments and tasks that before prison he'd taken for granted.

Now when he prepared a cigar for smoking, he thought about it, enjoyed the process, savored the strong scent of the dry leaves, the pungent wafting smoke as he set fire to the end. Would he forever be so easy to impress? He hoped so, but doubted it would last.

Like everything else in life, even daily life in Yuma, though to a lesser extent in that dank hole, a man got used to routine, to a new way of existing.

What was it Mossback, the ancient prisoner who had befriended him, said in Rafe's first week? "You don't have to like it, but you do have to endure it." That was a harder lesson to learn than it was to hear. Accept that your life is different. Forget what you used to know and you will be more at peace, less at war with yourself and others.

It had taken Rafe much of his time in prison to keep from driving his fist into the face of anyone who tried to bull in on him. And now?

He sniffed the length of the unlit half of the cigar and put it back in his pocket.

Now . . . he was in a dicey situation again.

He moved way from the picketed horses, his boots scuffing lightly on the wet gravel. A rough-worn scoop in a boulder tucked close by a ponderosa pine provided him with a welcome seat. Rafe plunked down with a sigh.

He'd thrown a lot of punches that day and taken his fair share of knocks, as well. And now he felt every one of them. Damn, but that Lucky Dan was a huge man. Just not healthy. Heart trouble and no wind, a bad combination. And then whatever luck he had pinched out.

"Girly, you try to rest now."

From behind him, the faint voice was Cookie's, and he sounded frustrated. Must be the girl was awake and kicking up a fuss.

"I know whiskey can't take the place of whatever it is you are used to, but that there's the measure of the situation right now."

Rafe heard more of the low, mumbling words, then Cookie spoke again. "Don't get surly with me, little miss. I didn't do it to you. There's only one person to blame for all this."

Rafe pushed to his feet, walked quietly back to the cave. "There a problem, Cook?"

"Naw, it's —"

The girl moaned, thrashed, kicked off everything covering her, running her hands up and down her arms, scratching and rubbing at herself as if she were trying to force biting insects from feasting on her. Her moans turned to gritted teeth, then a quick, unexpected scream that seemed to rattle the rock walls of the little hidden chamber.

Rafe rushed in, helped Cookie to subdue her in the near dark.

The fire had struggled thus far through the night, but was now paltry as the rain had soaked through much of their meager store of firewood. The weak flames had done the job of boiling coffee and pan-frying biscuits, but weren't up to the task of drying their wet boots and clothes. Still, the men knew they were fortunate to have the cave's protection from the brunt of the lashing elements.

Now that the girl had begun to lash out with spastic contortions that looked as if they might snap her own bones, the little cave seemed far less cozy. Cookie did his best to keep her from flailing into the fire and trying to hold her down at the same time.

"It's as if she's being controlled by a demon somehow." Cookie stared at her with hangdog pity in his eyes even as she kicked at him and moaned a sobbing shriek that sounded as if she were being peeled apart from the inside out.

"She is," said Rafe, dragging her outside. "Swearengen."

She didn't appear to be aware of them as she thrashed and howled in pain.

"Enough of this, Cookie," said Rafe, "grab her feet." Rafe seized the girl, half wrapped in the old quilt, roughly with an arm around her middle. He wrapped both arms tight around her from behind, holding her arms. Her feet pedaled and kicked without mercy at him, at the air, but he moved her out of the mouth of the cave where she wouldn't hurt herself or them, or scatter the little fire to the dampness.

"Whoa now, girl, hold on there, Susie. You hear me?" He spoke firmly but loudly, straight into her ear and kept it up for a full minute. Eventually he felt her body lessen its thrashings. She subsided into a state where she was rigid as a board, trembling all over, then eventually lessened to a spasm every few seconds before going limp once more.

A smear of blood welled near her mouth. Sometime during the episode she had bitten her lip or scratched herself.

Cookie had rummaged and found his best set of longhandles. He approached with caution, held them up. "We got to get this girl dressed, Rafe. It ain't right, her parading around all nekkid and such."

"I know, but we had no time at the Gem,

no time on the trail, and then the storm hit us. We'll get these on her, then get more of that whiskey inside her. I think it helped."

"Yeah, it did. But by God, she's a fighter." As soon as he said it, the young woman's left foot whipped upward and caught Cookie on the chin.

He rocked back, shook his head like a skunk-sprayed dog, and dove back to the task of keeping her feet somewhat stilled. "My word, but for a slight girl she's a kickin' mule."

Her body relaxed once more and she thrashed her head slowly side to side, moaning low. Even at the far edge of the firelight they saw tears roll from her eyes.

It took a few more minutes but they managed to get the one-piece underwear on her. Even though Cookie was of slight build himself, they were large on her, but a definite improvement.

"That'll do for now," said Rafe. "In the morning, we can scare up more garments for her, maybe strap on those camp moccasins of yours, Cook."

Cookie nodded, though secretly didn't want to give up his camp shoes. They were a gift from an old squaw he'd spent a pleasant long winter with over along the Green River in Wyoming country a few years back.

211

"You'll get them back," said Rafe, smiling. "Now help me figure out how to get her to drink this whiskey. I expect it will soothe her more."

"Let me try to talk with her. I got a way with drunks and women. Children and dogs, too."

"Which am I?"

Rafe and Cookie both stared down at the girl. They had brought her back into the cave and leaned her against the pile of blankets and clothes before the fire.

"Did you speak, girly?" Cookie whispered the question, afraid somehow of the answer.

She reached up and dragged a shaking hand down her chilled, clammy face. "So cold."

Quick as a gunshot, Cookie assembled the blankets and extra clothes about her, tucking them up around her head like a shroud. "We got to build up this fire!" He said it angrily, as if the sight of the weak flames offended him to his core.

"I'll be back with something that will burn, if I have to chop down a tree and peel off the bark!" Cookie stomped off into the night and Rafe let out a long sigh, moved closer to the girl.

He hunkered down before her and popped the cork of the half-full whiskey bottle.

"Here," he said. "You'll need this before too long, I expect. Best take it while you are able. We had a devil of a time getting it in you before."

She looked up at him, narrowed her eyes. "Why? What are you planning on doing to me?"

Rafe regarded her a moment. "Not going to do anything to you but get you out of harm's way. Get you back to your father."

She closed her eyes, let out a long breath. "That's who you are then. Sent by dear Daddy. I should have known."

Rafe handed her the bottle. "Please, it'll help ease what you're going through. It's all we can offer. Trust me, I've seen men go through similar afflictions and it's not going to be pretty for a while."

"Gee thanks, mister. You know how to make a girl feel good."

"I'm trying to be honest." He tossed a damp branch on the sputtering fire. "And my name is Rafe."

They looked at each other. She still regarded him with obvious suspicion. "And the other one." She shivered, closed her eyes, and clamped her teeth tight. It subsided and she said, "Who's he?"

"Why, hell, missy, I am none other than Cookie McGee. I have been all around the world, depending on your worldview. I know a thing or two about one or two things, and I am, among many other titles, a fetcher of firewood that maybe was dry once in its life."

He tossed a jumble of snapped branches to the ground before the fire, and rubbed his hands together. "And you, missy, ought not to ignore Rafe's advice. He's been known to be right once in a blue moon and tonight might be it. So drink up . . . or you'll be in more than a world of hurt."

"You threatening me, old man?" The girl's eyes narrowed, the whiskey had given her face color.

Cookie canted his head sideways, lowered his voice. "Now look, girly. I ain't threatening you or anyone. I am tired and wet and don't much feel like wrasslin' with you anymore. You already kicked me upside the head and . . . you smell like old socks. Now drink or not, but I need some shut-eye."

Silence draped over the little gray cave like a wet wool blanket. Rafe looked at Cookie, who squatted by the fire warming his hands and looking out into the dark night. Rafe extended the bottle once more to the girl, still not looking at her. He felt it leave his hand. Presently he heard the soft sounds of sipping, swallowing, a soft cough.

Tiny victories . . . he'd heard someone say that once in the war, at bloody Sharpsburg. Nothing tiny or victorious about that battle.

A fusillade had missed him and the boys as they squatted in that muddy hole surrounded by the ragged stalks of what were once proud trees, their tops shredded and burnt. He remembered that high above, the near-night sky had turned a raw smatter of blue-black streaked with smoke and filled with the screams and moans and sobbing of the dying.

Small victories, indeed. Be thankful you lived to fight another day. But what if you grew tired of fighting?

Was this girl, Susan Pendleton, that tired? Was it possible to ever want to fight again? Would he find that out himself one day?

He cut his eyes over at the girl and saw she'd done a decent job of knocking back the juice. As slight as she was, it was likely to make her tired enough to take the edge off the tremors.

Rafe knew her mind would be her worst enemy in an instance such as this. She was going to gnaw this bone for the rest of her days. Some win, some lose. He wished her good luck.

"We all need to get rest. I don't think there's a chance anyone will have followed

215

us through that storm. But just in case, I'll hole up out there. Cook, you stay here and keep our guest company."

"Rather swap with you, all the same." Cookie didn't look at him.

"No, Cook. You need your sleep. I'm good." Rafe stood before Cookie could protest, and looked down at the girl.

"Try to sleep. Pull on that bottle if you need to. And yell if you need help. We're not going anywhere." He touched his hat brim, turned to the dark, then leaned back down and in a low voice said, "Trust us. I know it's not easy, but try."

The last the young woman and Cookie heard of him that night were his boots crunching damp gravel as he walked back out toward the trail.

"What storm?" she said in a small voice.

Cookie made a small noise and shook his head. He crawled over to the rock wall and leaned against it, sighed, and lowered his hat over his face.

The girl sat, shivering, wrapped tightly in all their blankets and spare clothes. As she sipped the whiskey, its warming effects draped themselves like a soothing comfrey compress. She sorted through what ragged jags of memory she had of the previous day, or days. What had happened? Who were these people? And where was she? Away from the Gem, that much was certain.

She sipped again and looked at the old man, whose chest rose and fell slowly under his folded arms, a holster with what looked like sticks of dynamite strapped about his waist.

And that big man out there in the dark. What was his story? Sue Pendleton sat musing for a long time, watching the small fire's weak flames gutter, then die. Eventually she dozed.

Next morning found the young woman awake after Rafe. He'd already walked off behind the horses and urinated in a thicket of scrubby juniper. He was buttoning back up when he heard footsteps and clawed a Colt free of its holster.

Sue was still a few feet from the entrance of the cave and walking slowly, as if she'd recently been taught the task. Her thin hands worked at holding the quilt about her shoulders. They were failing at the task and it dragged behind her.

Seconds after he drew the gun, she looked at him, her face puffy-white and red-eyed, looking more like a mask than a woman's face. "What . . . are you doing?"

Rafe slid the revolver back into its holster.

"Too cautious by half," he said, running a hand over his jaw. "Dare I ask how you feel?"

She shrugged, looked around, not really seeing anything.

Rafe folded his arms, looked down at her. "Listen." He cleared his throat. "I wouldn't dare say so in front of that man." He nodded toward the cave, his voice low, hard like gravel grinding between steel wheels and steel tracks. "For fear of embarrassing him. But that cutting remark you sent his way last night? No. I will not stand for anyone badmouthing or accusing him of anything untoward. He is as true as a loyal dog, as smart as a scholar, as straight as an arrow, and the best friend a fool like me could ever hope to find in this long, miserable life."

He poked a finger at her face, close to the tip of her nose, beneath wide-open eyes. "You understand me . . . girl?"

To his surprise, the young woman nodded. Her face more alive and colored than he'd yet seen it. He fancied he saw a blush creep on her cheeks, too. Good, maybe he cut through that tough shell she wore.

"Now, we need to hit the trail hard. We have a long day of riding ahead of us and with each minute the odds of jackals tracking us increase. Swearengen won't take this easy."

"You're right — he won't," said the girl in a whisper, shaking her head.

Rafe regarded her a moment. He had lots of questions, but he hoped she would answer them on her own when the time was right. But there was one he had to know now, might make a difference in what he decided to do with her.

"How old are you? I was led to believe you were a girl. A young girl."

She looked at him. "I'm still young."

"Never said you weren't."

She sighed. "I'm twenty, if that makes any difference."

"You look younger. Well, you would if you were healthy."

"That's a hell of a thing to say."

Rafe shrugged. "Sometimes the truth has teeth."

CHAPTER 16:
WE AGREE TO DISAGREE

"You keep swiveling your neck like that and your head will pop clean off."

Cookie, still leading the procession, spun his head back once more and grazed Rafe with a glare. "Somebody's gotta keep a sharp eye on our back trail, you sure aren't up to the task."

"I'm watching, don't you worry. You concentrate on what's ahead. We don't want to ride into something we can't ride out of because you're more worried than an old maid at a Sunday social."

"Bah." Cookie sputtered to himself and dug his heels into his horse, which only made the placid creature crow hop until his yelping calmed it down again.

"You two fight like this all the time?"

"Pretty much," said Rafe. "How's that horse working for you? The pack saddle might not provide the most elegant ride, but it's bound to be more comfortable than being slung over this saddle."

"It's fine." A few seconds passed, then she said, "Thanks for going to the trouble. All of it. It can't have been easy, with Al and the rest of it. I still don't know why you're doing all this on my behalf."

Cookie muttered something.

Sue said, "What was that?"

Cookie didn't turn around, but shouted, "I said I don't know, either."

The girl looked at Rafe, who shook his head. "Suppose you tell us why you think we're here," he said. "Be a good place to start."

She said nothing, but wrapped Rafe's mackinaw tighter about herself, despite the rising heat of the new day. They all rode in silence for a few more minutes, then in a voice loud enough for them both to hear she said, "I don't want to go back to my father. I'm none of his business, anyway. I'm a grown woman, can make my own choices."

Cookie snorted. "Doing a hell of a job at it, too."

"What do you know about it? About me? About any of it?" She'd reined up and Rafe saw her tense, look as if she were about to jump down and rush on up to Cookie. At least she was showing some spunk, and not the sort caused by a lack of morphine, or whatever the pimp had plied her with.

"I didn't ask you to rescue me."

"Nope, that's true enough," said Rafe, setting a cigar alight. He puffed, got it smoking, blew out a thick cloud. "But we did, just the same. You want to go back there, you say the word."

She stared at him for a long time. Finally she drummed her heels against the horse and walked on, following behind Cookie and ahead of Rafe, who nodded to himself. It was a start.

CHAPTER 17:
OF WHISKEY, WOMEN, AND WATCHES

"What do you suppose Deadwood is like, El Jefe?"

The boss spat out the last of the matchstick he'd been chewing. It was a lifelong habit — he liked chewing on all manner of items. His mother had called him a *perro,* a dog, for his constant biting. But he reasoned that was why he had such strong teeth.

"It won't be like anything, boy. It will be what it is, nothing more or less. You understand me?"

The Kid nodded, the silly crow feather he'd tied to his hat brim flopping lazily with the movement. But El Jefe could tell that the boy did not understand him. El Jefe did not care. He was too bored with riding to begin a lesson. Later, perhaps, when the others had killed the ass-end of their day with liquor.

He ran his tongue over his broad teeth. There were none blackened in his mouth like those of Tepito and Pepe. They preferred soft foods and too much drink, and didn't rinse their mouths with water in the morning like he did. Sometimes he even rubbed his teeth with a nub of snapped branch.

They passed another hour in this manner, the Hell Hounds riding in a straggling line, the three newcomers first, then the rest of the men plodding along in the middle, with the Kid, and finally El Jefe.

He did not trust his Hell Hounds, not even the boy, and rarely rode out front. He would rather watch their back trail than feel the sting of a surprise bullet cranked down at them from a hiding bandito nested in high rocks above a narrow pass. Let the idiots have the honor.

They began to pass more frequent sign of man's activities — sign they were all well acquainted with, having pillaged plenty of mine camps and solitary miners at their diggings over the years.

The rain of two days before was now of the past, only the light green haze of sparse grasses on the hills showing any sign that moisture had visited the place. Otherwise the narrow wagon road into town was a dusty, choking affair. Most of the men had tugged up their bandannas and snugged their hats down low.

224

"It would be something if we could make money from dust, eh, boss?"

El Jefe was about to tell the Kid to shut up and ride, but he had to admit, the fool was not wrong. Not about the dust, but about making money from nothing. He didn't know what that might be, but it should be thought about more. Right now, though, there was too much to do. He had to find this Al Something-or-other, who owned the Gem bar, where the valuable girl was kept. With any luck that bastard, Rafe Barr, and the old man with him would still be in town.

Maybe they were dipping their wicks and found they liked it too much to leave right away? Or better yet, maybe they were killed somehow, maybe in a bar fight. That would solve a problem for El Jefe. Then he remembered what sort of man Barr was and he knew none of those guesses was likely.

"We get into town, you men do what you need to, but be ready to ride in the morning. You hear me, Tepito? Pepe? That means you, too. I know you will drink yourself stupid, but you be ready to ride or I will gut you like the smelly fish you are."

It didn't take him long to stop a man in the street and ask about the location of the Gem, but by then El Jefe had lost most of the men. He didn't much care if the three they'd picked up on the road stayed around or not. He was tired of the gringo cowboy — he complained so much he sounded like a whining child. I'm too hot, I hate to sweat, I need more water.

The fool did not know how close he had come three times to feeling a long, thin blade slide between his ribs and poke holes in something important deep inside him. Even now El Jefe half regretted not doing that.

So it was just as well when he saw those three new Hell Hound recruits trail off in the direction of the others. The only one left with El Jefe was the Kid.

"You should go somewhere, find something to amuse you. Maybe a bottle or a game of cards? Do you even know how to dance with a woman, boy?"

The boss turned in his saddle to face the boy, right there in the middle of the busy, rutted, dung-riddled street of Deadwood, and in a loud voice, continued, "Answer me, have you ever laid with a woman, boy? Ever stuck your poker into the hottest fire of all? Eh?"

El Jefe looked around, a smile on his face. People close by, riding by, walking not but a few feet away on the sidewalks and in the street, tried not to make eye contact with this braying bear of a Mexican who smiled as if he were trying to show off every tooth in his head.

The Kid did not like El Jefe's taunts, but all he could do was turn red. His prominent ears, like nubs off the sides of a saguaro, were as good as sunburned from the shame.

El Jefe saw the shame he had brought on the boy, saw, too, that the fine people of Deadwood did not appreciate the joke he had offered them to share in.

"Bastards," he said. "They are all idiots. Come on, boy, I will buy you a drink. Take your mind off your useless wick, eh?" El Jefe kept up his braying all the way down the street and around the corner, right on up to the front steps of the Gem.

He slid down out of the saddle, and the boy did the same. The boss bent over, rested his hands on his knees and groaned low. "One of these days I will own a railroad car and not have to worry about all this riding, riding, riding. Boy!" El Jefe straightened, slid his rifle from its sheath on the saddle.

"On second thoughts, you take these horses to that stable there. Here is money to get them tended." He held the coins above the young man's outstretched hand. "Don't waste this money on women or card games or liquor, you understand me?" Again he laughed, wiped his eyes with the back of a hand.

The Kid, with renewed redness on his face and ears, led the two horses down the street, more confused than ever. The boss was a difficult man to understand. And the Kid had felt for some time that he was no longer learning anything from him. Perhaps it was time to leave him, or kill him and take over the Hell Hounds himself. Now there was a thought.

Up the broad steps to the Gem strode El Jefe. At the top a man leaned against a round pillar. He wore a blue serge jacket with a gold chain swinging from beneath. That led, no doubt, to a fine engraved gold watch that worked like magic. Maybe it would spring open to reveal the pretty face of a long-ago lover, all white skin and hair the color of ground corn.

But no, thought El Jefe when he saw the man's homely face. This was the face no fine woman could love, pocked and lined as it was. And that nose! It looked to have been recently dealt a hard blow or two. It was bent and swollen and had more in common with a clot of chewed meat than a nose.

The man regarded El Jefe through eyes

ringed with heavy purple and black bruises. "You're a long way from home, ain't you, Mexican?"

El Jefe set a heavy foot down on the top step, perhaps three feet from the homely man with the promise of a fine watch. He looked at the man from under his wide-brimmed sombrero. "Sí, sí, that is true. But then again, wherever I go I am home, you see?"

He spread his arms wide, facing the man, let him see the full complement of black leather draping him, and weaponry stippling his person. "And today I feel as though I have come home. At least for the afternoon."

El Jefe kept a wide smile on his face, but his eyes were not the sort to do so. They remained fixed on the man, whose casual brashness had slipped considerably in the few seconds it took him to figure out this was not a man with whom he should toy.

"And you are?" said El Jefe, letting his arms drop.

"I . . ."

"Sí, sí, sí, yes, you."

"I am . . ." The homely man licked his lips. "Well, that is, they call me Frenchy."

"Ah, then you, too, are a long way from home, no?" El Jefe's laugh jabbed at the man. He turned once more toward the front doors, then looked back. "By the way, do you happen to know the time?" El Jefe cut his eyes to the fine chain.

"No, no, I don't."

"That is a shame." He sighed. "I hope one day to have a fine watch, then I will not have to annoy people with my questions." He looked back at the chain, then at Frenchy's eyes. "One day, perhaps. With luck, maybe sooner than I think." Then he stepped inside and left Frenchy as he found him, though decidedly flustered.

"Hey, greaser, you gonna have to leave."

El Jefe sighed once more, but to the dozens of eyes now focused on him, he raised his eyebrows. "I hope you do not think, mister bartender, that I am like any other Mexican. No, no, you are mistaken. I am an agent for the government of the United States of America."

The bald man behind the bar chewed his tobacco slower, his eyebrows drawn close together. A few folks in the sparse afternoon crowd tittered before turning back to their games.

The bartender was about to speak but El Jefe leaned over the bar and in a low voice said, "I know it may be difficult to understand, but I need to speak with the proprietor of this establishment. It is an emergency."

"Oh . . . Al ain't here."

"Where is he?"

The man behind the bar shrugged.

"Relax, Tom. I'll take over."

The bald barkeep spun. "Oh, hey, Al, thought you were out."

"I was." The man who'd come up behind him was of medium height, with dark, slicked-back hair and sharp eyes that looked to take in everything all at once. Like a ravenous hawk.

"You sound better, Al," said the barkeep. "Tongue on the mend?"

"Shut the hell up, and go tell that damned piano player if he keeps on pounding the keys like that he's going to wake up dead." Then he turned to El Jefe. "Now, what can I do for you?" He looked El Jefe up and down.

Unlike most other folks the Hell Hound boss met, this man showed no signs of hesitation or outright fear. El Jefe liked that. This must be the boss man he came here to see. If he is not, he should be.

"Are you the boss of this place?"

The new man behind the counter tilted his head to one side. "I thought I asked a question. See, how it works is one person asks a question, the other answers, then he asks one, and on and on. You follow?"

This one thinks he is a clever fellow, but he doesn't look so good, thought El Jefe. He is all bruised around the eyes and the side of his face. And his mouth looks puffy. What is the trouble with these gringos? Did he fight with that French idiot out front holding up the post?

"Okay, then," said El Jefe, pulling on his toothy smile. "I am El Jefe of the Hell Hounds. Maybe you have heard about us?"

The dark-haired man slowly shook his head.

His eyes are like snake eyes, thought El Jefe. All dead inside. No, no, not dead . . . cold. Cold as stone.

"Why don't you tell me why you are here and maybe I can save us both more wasted time."

"Okay, okay." El Jefe lost the smile, returned the gaze with his own hard stare. "I am wondering if you have had a visit by a big man who travels with an old man? This would have been . . . oh, several days ago, perhaps."

The man behind the bar ran his tongue over his lower lip. El Jefe saw that his tongue had been hurt, cut somehow. What sort of a fighter is this fellow? Or maybe it was a devil woman who did it to him in a feeling of passion, eh?

"Why?"

"I am beginning to think my guess is correct. I am also beginning to think you like to ask questions but you are not so quick to answer them."

The man behind the bar poured El Jefe a glass of beer, almost without looking at what he did. He dragged a knife across the top to cut the foam, then nudged the beer toward El Jefe.

"Fair enough. I'm Al Swearengen. I own this place. Now, about the two men . . ."

"Oh, yes, yes, let me see. They were riding this way to steal from the man who owns this place. That would be you! It was something about a girl." El Jefe hoisted the glass. "But then when is it not, eh?" He laughed and offered a quick nod, then quaffed deeply, smacking his foam-covered lips. "That hits all the spots. My thanks."

"That'll be two bits."

El Jefe paused, wiped his mouth with the back of a gloved hand. "Certainly." He was disappointed the man was such a difficult walnut to crack. And he had hoped to cadge a free drink or two. Maybe later, once they had discussed business.

But Swearengen surprised him.

"They were here and they did steal from me. How do you know them?"

"Let's say that me and my men, the Hell Hounds —"

"Yeah, yeah, you said."

"We are in the business of tracking those two outlaws for an important man. What he has stolen from you does not concern us, but if we happen to bring it back to you, I expect that would be worth something to you, eh?" El Jefe sipped his beer, eyed this Swearengen fellow over the foamy rim.

"Could be. What are you planning on doing with the two men?"

"I have been told I may kill them if I like. I only need proof for the man who hired us." El Jefe leaned heavily on the bar, spoke in a low tone, as if conspiring with the man behind the bar. "Those two, oh ho ho." He shook his head. "They have caused me no end of grief in our quest for them, so it will be a pleasure to do so."

El Jefe felt clever thinking up a little twist on the story like that. He should be richer for all the fine ideas he has. It must be the Hell Hounds who hold him back.

Swearengen jerked his head toward a table in a corner by the back wall. "Take a seat over there, we'll talk. I'll bring the whiskey." He shouted, "Tom! Back to the bar."

A minute later he set a bottle and two glasses on the sticky tabletop. "Damn women can't clean," he said, shooing away a fly. To El Jefe he said, "Breaking in a new barkeep and he isn't worth a dry spit."

"Why do you not find someone else?"

"Sadly enough, he's the most promising candidate so far. It's the same reason I haven't been able to find anyone to track those men who stole my property." Swearengen poured two drinks.

El Jefe hoisted a glass and said, "I beg your pardon, but I think you have found them."

"Maybe," said Swearengen. "But there are one or two little items we'll need to clear up first."

"Oh?" El Jefe liked the whiskey. He hoped the bastard wasn't going to make him pay for that, too.

"The . . . item they stole from me needs to be returned, unharmed and alive."

"Alive, eh? Then it is a person? Ah, sí, the girl, as I suspected."

"If she is harmed . . ." Swearengen leaned over the table and fixed those stone-cold brown-black eyes on El Jefe's. "I promise you here and now, you and your Blood-hounds —"

"Hell Hounds."

"Fine. You and your Hell Hounds will all pay. Dearly."

"Mr. Swearengen, I am not a piano player. You can threaten me, but I am not afraid of you. You see, I, too, am a businessman. But unlike you I do not have to worry about taking care of my staff. If they do something I do not like, I kill them. I go through a lot of Hell Hounds this way. But I sleep better at night. I will get you this girl. Alive and not harmed."

Swearengen nodded, sipped his whiskey, and winced. "I also want those two men brought back here alive."

"Oh, now, now, that is something I cannot promise. They maybe deserve something from the Hell Hounds, you see?"

Swearengen stared at him. El Jefe relented and nodded. "Sí, sí, okay, we will do our best. But that is all I can promise."

"How will you find them?"

"It could be I know where they are going."

Swearengen crossed his arms over his chest and narrowed his eyes. "How do you know that?"

"You ask a lot of questions for a man who needs me more than I need him."

Swearengen ignored the statement and

asked another question. "When can you leave?"

El Jefe pooched out his lips, looked up as if there might be an answer clinging to the cobwebbed rafters overhead. "Tomorrow morning. Yes, that is it. My boys deserve some time to explore your town."

"No later than that. The trail's already cold."

"We are the Hell Hounds, and we can sniff those two bad men from very far." He tapped his nose and chuckled.

"See that you do." Swearengen rose. "Enjoy the whiskey. On the house."

"Thank you, Mr. Swearengen," said El Jefe. "But there is one more point to discuss — my price. I will need two hundred fifty dollars now and the same when we bring her back here."

"You'll get a hundred now and two hundred when you bring her back."

El Jefe sighed. "We shall see, we shall see."

He could have sworn that Swearengen was smiling as he turned away from the table. But inside El Jefe was pleased. That would be the easiest money he had made in a long time. Too bad he would not somehow be able to collect the remaining amount.

But he would make far more than that by selling the girl to Warden Timmons, whoever paid more money for the wretch. And if she turned out to be pretty, he might wait a little longer before selling her back.

CHAPTER 18:
TROUBLE COMES UP SHORT

"Buford, you take the top end of the street, up along the deadline. I'll be down around the south end. Saw a pile of bad seeds ride in today, so keep your ears and eyes wide. Likely we'll not see the trouble until its hot and ready."

"Sheriff?"

"Yeah, Clancy." Sheriff Bullock looked up from the latest copy of the *Black Hills Pioneer* to see his other deputy poke his head through the open doorway.

"Bunch of strangers are kicking up a right fuss down at Dink's place. They are a tough-looking lot. Mexicans, mostly, and they are armed plenty, with knives, guns, hatchets, you name it."

"Well, hell," said Bullock, pushing his chair squawking back across the floor. "I believe it's already started." He plopped his black hat atop his head and tapped the crown. "And here we weren't invited."

239

The young deputies were never quite sure when their boss was joshing with them, but they grinned and followed him anyway. If he were walking through the gateway of Hell itself, they'd tag along.

Bullock knew it was going to be a long night even before Dink's bar came into view. He heard a gunshot, frightened shouts of men and women, then a high-pitched *yi-yi-yi-yi-yi* right before another shot.

"Hurry up, boys!" bellowed the sheriff over his shoulder as he drew his sidearm. To the staring men and women who'd come out on the sidewalks he pointed a long finger, waving them back. "Get back, back inside. You'll catch a stray bullet!"

A few folks shuffled their feet, made to step back, but none went anywhere. He didn't think they would, but he tried.

Dead ahead, a huge window blasted outward, glass erupting around a heavy, airborne chair. It landed in the street, and following it through the jagged hole flew a skinny miner Bullock knew as One-Eye Pete. He gained the name not because he had one eye but because he was poor in the hearing department.

Pete had an odd way of cocking his head to one side and leaning toward whoever he was chatting with, squinting one eye and opening wide the foremost eye. The sheriff found it unsettling, but Pete was a good egg. The man came into town frequently, as his claim was not far off, to the north. He didn't cause much commotion, but he did like to drink and socialize.

And now here he was, gasping and sprawled on his back, half on the boardwalk, half in the dirt. "Clancy, get someone to tend to Pete. Buford, follow me."

Bullock hustled up to one side of the establishment's open door and with revolver chin high, peered around the frame. He saw a dozen or so folks plastered to the walls, most standing, a few in chairs. All had their hands up. Many he knew by sight, most by name. And most were not troublemakers any more than Pete was.

The objects of their wide-eyed stares were clustered in the center of the room, three hard cases, leather-wearing strangers he'd seen earlier in the day. They'd ridden in with a young, skinny drink of water, a few more Mexicans, maybe five, six, and a gringo who then peeled off from the group with two of the Mexicans. And then there was the burly man who looked the part of a leader. None of them impressed him as being on the level.

"You three in the middle of the room. This is Sheriff Bullock and a passel of deputies.

Raise those hands high and keep 'em there. You are surrounded."

They reacted about like he expected drunks to — he'd been through this many times. The one closest to him, a squat, bowlegged man with a fleshy face, bad teeth, and a bent nose that had likely been broken recently, began to laugh. "Show yourself then, lawman. I will treat you with the same respect as I showed that old man who stared at me funny."

"I said to put those hands up. I will count to five and then I am going to shoot one, two, or all three of you. One. Two. Three."

At the moment two of the men raised their hands, one still holding a sawed-off gut shredder. The third, the one he'd spoken with, shook his head and kept his hands right where they were, waist-high, each gripping a revolver.

"Drop those guns, you!" Bullock side-stepped into the room as he said it, moving away from the folks hugging the wall, his revolver aimed above the man's breadbasket.

The drunk giggled and stepped toward Bullock, raising his weapons. Ten feet separated the two men, and Bullock closed them fast. The Mexican's thumbs groped upward for the hammers, a motion that would have taken a sober man but a second. This man was far from sober.

"No!" bellowed Bullock, eyeing those thumbs as if time had been slowed. Bullock squeezed the trigger on his Colt and the dumb drunk caught the bullet high in the chest. It jerked him backward as if a rope had been tied around his neck and yanked hard.

His arms flew upward like raised wings, the revolvers gripped in each hand whipped from his grasp and spun toward the back of the room, thudding where they landed.

The blast was close enough that the Mexican's dirty green tunic beneath a ragged fringe-and-concho-riddled black vest caught fire around the entry hole. It smoked as he lay gasping and twitching on the floor between his two friends.

"You shot Tepito!" shouted the thinner of the two, the sawed-off shotgun weighing down his skinny arm. He appeared unaware that his face and the front of his shirt, vest, and trousers dripped with gore from the exit wound on his friend's back.

"Yep," said the lawman. "And you're next if you don't keep those hands high."

"No, no I don't want no bullets in me."

"Wise man, now lay down that gut shredder and back off."

The man complied, then stood again, slowly, with his hands raised.

"I am warning you, I see a bead of sweat quiver on you, or a single hair on the back of your hand so much as move in a breeze, and I will drill you where you stand. Comprende?"

Apparently the man understood him, for a high-pitched "sí!" squeaked out of his otherwise unmoving mouth. Bullock approached. The only sounds in the smoky, well-lit room were the lawman's polished boots stepping across the sawdust-flecked plank floor, and the gasps and moans of the man he shot.

Bullock looked down at the dying man. "Pipe down. You've one last job to do, now do it well." He addressed his deputy without looking at him. "Buford, get somebody to scout up the boss fella who rode in with these clowns."

"He's at the Gem. Or was earlier. Looked like he knew Swearengen."

"Doesn't surprise me. Trash seeks its own kind." Bullock laid the shotgun on the bar top. "On second thought, leave him there. I'll fetch him later."

"What are you going to do with us?"

Bullock faced the up-to-now-silent third man. The speaker weaved slightly, the only

244

indication he was drunk.

"I'm going to escort you to tea. What in hell do you think is going to happen? You're all going to jail. Well, not him." Bullock nodded toward the man on the floor. The hole still smoking in his chest, his lips popping like the mouth of a beached fish.

"What for?" The man took a step forward, his hands lowering. "We didn't do nothing."

"No, but you will." Even as he said it Bullock covered the six feet between them in two quick strides and leveled the heavy revolver snug against the man's forehead. Sweaty, oily skin dimpled around the snout of the gun. "Keep up with your shenanigans and I will pull this trigger. I have done it before and don't doubt it will happen a few more times before I hang up my spurs."

"Hey, hey," said the man, looking surprisingly comfortable with the situation. "There is no need for this."

"Shut up and raise them." Bullock pushed the gun harder into the man's forehead, forcing the sweaty man's head backward with a jerk. "Higher."

Later, in the jailhouse, the sheriff sighed and looked up from his paperwork. He regarded the mouthier of the two drunks he'd brought in a half hour before. "There is little I want from you, save for you to shut your mouth and provide us with peace and quiet. Your friend, I am duty bound to report, has died, and you drunken sots are going to be in here for as long as I determine you need to be."

"But that is not fair."

"Fair?" Bullock pushed back from his desk and walked to the cell. "Wasn't fair that I had to shoot a man who was so drunk he was going to shoot me, now was it? Wasn't fair that you tossed old Pete through that window."

"That was Tepito who done that."

"Don't care. You all were there, terrorizing that barroom full of patrons out to enjoy their evening. Now we're stuck with a mess to clean up. The money in your pockets didn't amount to a hill of dirt, not enough to pay for that window nor to help ol' Pete make it through until his shoulder heals up. Then there's the busted chair, the bloody floor — all of it has to be paid for, repaired, cleaned up. You didn't think of that when you drank yourselves stupid, now, did you?"

The two men looked through hangdog eyes at the sheriff, who stood glowering at them outside the bars. They looked away and sank further into the hard cots on which they sat.

Boots and a sudden flurry of angry oaths sounded through the open door, drawing closer. Bullock shucked a Colt, with the other hand he raised the wick on an oil lamp and walked to the door, peered out along the frame.

"Sheriff?"

Bullock relaxed. "That you, Clancy? Buford find you?"

"Yep, good thing, too." The thin young man came into view behind two surly, bedraggled men whom he nudged with the business end of his carbine.

Bullock eyed them, then before he could step out of the way, he heard Buford's voice, then bootsteps on the boardwalk somewhere behind Clancy. In came Bullock's second part-time deputy, also prodding a pair of similar-looking rascals.

The newly arrested men were of Mexican descent. Beyond that they bore a look similar to the men they'd hauled in earlier from the fracas at Dink's. That is to say they all stank of campfires, dung, sweat, and looked like they'd kill a man for a penny.

And they sported those odd black leather vests draped over sweaty paunches and hairy chests. Their arms sported leather wrist gauntlets, some wore black chaps over patched peasant trousers or worn-through leathers. And each sported the words "Hell Hounds," in English, stitched, carved, or scratched across the backs of their vests.

"Hell Hounds," said Clancy. "New to me."

"Me, too," said Bullock, standing back and covering the scene with his Colt.

"Same here," said Buford, not wanting to seem inattentive to the proceedings.

"So what happened?" said the sheriff, shifting his gaze to Clancy.

"You know that tussle I went to check out?"

Bullock nodded toward the four sorry-looking critters arrayed before him. "Let me guess — they were it."

"Yeah," said Buford, unlocking the second cell. "Them and a few of the boys from the Snakepit diggings."

"And where are they?" said Bullock, hiding a smirk behind his thick moustaches.

"Oh," said Clancy, whose brother and two cousins worked at the Snakepit. "They were kind enough to help us subdue these gents. Figured the least we could do is leave 'em be. They weren't near as bad as these hombres."

"Uh-huh. Where did all this take place?"

"Effie's, where else?" Buford grinned. "They got the prettiest lassies and a line out the door. That was the problem, I guess.

Fellas from the Snakepit claim this lot here cut the line, so they commenced to whomping on 'em, and back and forth it went. I reckon they didn't take kindly to being one-upped by these drunken banditos —"

"Now, now," said Bullock, winking and holding up a hand. "We don't know that these fine fellows, visitors to our town are bad men with evil on their minds. Hell, they might well be investors come to boost Deadwood's livelihood."

Both deputies stared at him as if he'd pulled a goose egg out of his drawers. Bullock sighed. "They still have a few weapons on themselves, I see."

Buford nodded. "Heck, Sheriff, they each are carrying so many ways to kill a man I figured it would be easier to handcuff them and empty their pockets once we marched them back here."

"Fair enough. Feel them over and dump whatever dangerous items you find in that pile over there." He nodded toward a small arsenal of skinning knives, tomahawks, boot knives, a pocket pistol, revolvers, one scattergun, a steel-studded bullwhip, a rusty-but-serviceable carbine, and sun-puckered ammunition belts, half of the loops empty.

The two deputies did as Bullock instructed, tossing atop the mound the newest additions, including an array of knives and guns, plus two lengths of chain, a crude steel file, and a small leg-hold trap such as a man might catch a critter in. The jaws' edges were honed sharp. But it was the last item they all had to look at twice to get the full measure of — some sort of leather-and-steel contraption that looked to be made to muzzle a man.

Bullock wanted to ask why the ruffian felt it necessary to carry such a bizarre item on his person, but the man they'd taken it from was so drunk he couldn't even focus his gaze. He was the one, it was now plain to see, that Clancy said had pissed himself while stumbling over to the jail.

Bullock's two deputies had rounds yet to finish, so the sheriff bade them well and turned to eye the short stack of paperwork still awaiting him in a neat pile on his desk. He'd rather rove the streets than push papers. He sighed and looked at the collection of curios instead.

"My word, gentlemen," said the sheriff, breaking his gaze from the pile of weaponry and strolling over to stand in front of the two cells. "I never have seen so many bits and pieces of tools used for taking something from someone else by force. I've a good mind to look up in the statutes, see if there isn't some law being broken by toting all this junk around with you."

To his little speech he received no reply, not that he expected one from this sad-looking bunch. Two of the six men were snoring, one slumped on the stone floor, having missed the cot altogether. Other of the men rested with their heads in their arms.

Bullock almost felt bad for them. Show up in town looking to blow off steam, have a little fun, and end up in the clink. He almost felt bad . . . but not quite.

The lawman poured himself another cup of coffee and settled his long legs up on his desk. He hoped this lot represented the lion's share of the evening's trouble. Having to kill a man wasn't a task he took lightly, and though he recalled the events over and over in his mind, he ended up with the same result — he'd had no choice.

And he'd do it again a hundred-fold if need be. He blew across the top of the stoneware mug and sipped. Good and hot, the way coffee should be. Now, to that paperwork.

Hours later, with dawn having come and gone, and with a couple of uncomfortable hours of catlike shut-eye at his maple desk,

Seth Bullock was on his second cup of coffee when the door of the jailhouse thrust open.

The sheriff spun, hand on his gun, and angled away from the stove, closer to his desk. He recognized the visitor as the burly Mexican who rode in with these fools the day before.

The stranger spoke. "I am El Jefe. I was told I would find my men here, and I see I was told right." The man took in the room at a glance, then strode in and stood before the cells. He settled his eyes on the men in each cell in turn. "I do not see Tepito. What I was told must also be true. He is dead, then. And what of the Kid? And those other three? Is this what I told you not to let happen? Eh?"

He looked at the men in silence, then shook his head. "Bah." He spat at them through the bars and turned away.

"That'll be enough of that filth, mister. Or you'll be in there with them."

The Mexican turned to face the sheriff, a smile already wide on his face, teeth gleaming beneath an oily moustache. "There must be some mistake. My men are maybe a little rowdy, but they are not harmful men. Besides, I have need of them. We are late for business. They work for me and when they are locked up like this I lose money."

"What sort of business would that be?"

The man's smile stayed in place, but his eyes narrowed. "Now, sheriff, I hope I do not offend you by saying so, but that is my business and no one else's."

"If it's in my town, then it is my business. If it has anything to do with Al Swearengen, then it is likely illegal, which definitely makes it my business."

How did this man know he had talked with Swearengen the evening before? No matter, El Jefe would win him over — or kill him trying.

"I was told you could be a hard man. But I do not think that is the case, eh? If you will let my men go I will promise you to be out of your town within an hour. Long enough for us to get our horses."

Bullock stared the man down, slowly shaking his head.

"Oh . . ." El Jefe's eyes widened. "I see, I see. You want money, yes, yes, to pay for the damaged goods of their fun times last night."

"Fun times? You call one man dead and a whole heap of mess and injuries a fun time?"

"It is true they might have gone a little bit" — he circled a grimy finger beside his head — "loco, sí, but they are not bad men."

"So you keep telling me. My experience tells me otherwise."

El Jefe's smile slid from his face as fast as it appeared. "How long are you going to keep them here, Sheriff?"

"I haven't decided. But you can bet your boots they'll be here all day today. Now, you can go collect your dead man at Horton's Livery and Coffinworks. That's where he was brought last night. Pay him or pay me. But you will pay."

"Tepito was nothing to me. He was a grown man, the same as these idiots. And so they are all responsible for their own actions and for any money they owe. I am not their mama."

"Fair enough. But you are their boss. And since they didn't have enough cash on them to buy a slice of pie, I hold you responsible for cost of damages sustained. Fair or not, that's how I'm viewing this sad situation."

The Mexican stepped through the door.

Behind him Bullock said, "And don't leave town without telling me first. Or paying your new debts."

El Jefe walked out into bright glare of an early morning in Deadwood.

CHAPTER 19:
CHOOSE YOUR PATH WISELY

"We'll drift southwestward on down to the North Platte. Should be a settlement there where we can get reoutfitted." Rafe blew on the spoonful of beans, tested them with his top lip. Cool enough — he could eat a wolf whole, he was so hungry.

There was no response to his statement, which would normally suit him right down to the ground, but this was different. He set down his plate of beans on a campfire rock. "Now look, you two."

The girl and Cookie both looked up at him from their own plates of steaming beans.

"I know you got off on the wrong foot, but a couple of days of this? On top of everything else? I won't have it. I understand if you don't much like each other. Heck, I don't like everyone I meet."

Again, they regarded him as one would a curiosity. He smacked his hands on his legs.

255

"Tell you what, either of you find the other's presence so intolerable that you can't take it another minute, then you are free to go. But one way or another, this situation has to change."

"Go where?" Cookie said.

"Anywhere you like."

"You have to be joking," said the girl, chewing slower. "Just like that?"

Rafe snapped his fingers. "Just like that."

Sue dragged her hand over her lips, did not quite suppress an unladylike belch, and stood, patting the legs of the denims Cookie had loaned her. "I believe I'll take you up on that offer and get while the getting's good."

Rafe didn't want to appear nosey, but he was curious. "Where will you go, if you don't mind me asking?"

"Not at all. Thought I'd mosey on back to Deadwood. This has been fun and all, and you two are obviously nice gents, but . . ."

The clatter of Cookie's tin plate pinging off a rock, the spoon clattering to the ground, caused them both, Rafe and Sue, to stop talking and stare at the little man.

"Now don't that beat all? The young lady here can't wait to skedaddle back to that nest of filth and set up housekeeping again with the Demon of Deadwood, likely be-

256

cause he was so kind to her!" By that time Cookie had gained his feet and was digging in his pocket for his knob of plug chaw.

"Now, Cook," said Rafe, eyeing the codger with a knowing glance. "Makes no never mind to me. As I said, she's free to go. I've about given up on keeping my word, especially since it's caused so much strife. And no one, least of all me, seems happy with the situation."

Sue hugged herself, wrapped the coat tighter about her. "Well fine, then. I guess I will go. At first light in the morning."

"Fine," said Rafe as he settled back against his saddle.

Cookie, bushy eyebrows drawn together, cut off a plug of chaw with his pocketknife and stuffed it in his mouth.

A quiet minute passed, then Rafe said, "Course, I can't part with that packhorse. Travel out here without a spare mount is a death knell." The girl said nothing as he lit a cigar. "And I'll need the duds I loaned you. I don't have much in this world and I'll need to keep what I have."

Cookie cleared his throat. "My moccasins, they was a gift to me . . ."

The girl set her jaw and swiveled her gaze at each of them. "You don't think I won't go back there under my own steam? And naked, too? I don't care. It's how I came into this world and I don't mind going out that way, I can tell you that for certain."

Rafe said nothing, merely puffed and nodded in quiet agreement. He let her comments hang in the air, hoped she understood what it was she said. That she was most certainly naked and nearly dead when he found her.

Then she did something neither of them had seen her do in the short time they had been around her. She sat down, leaned her arms on her knees, lowered her head. A few seconds later they heard slight squeaks and snuffling noises.

Wide-eyed, Cookie looked at Rafe as if expecting an answer to an unspoken question. Rafe shrugged, looked back to the girl sitting a few feet away. Twice in the next few minutes he was about to ask if she was all right when she snuffled or her shoulders shuddered with an unseen sob.

Finally, in a whisper, she said, "I'm so tired. So very tired."

And then, before either of them could think of something to do next, Susan Pendleton spoke. At first she talked into her arms, facedown, as if speaking to herself, for herself. Presently she lifted her head, dragged the back of her hand beneath her eyes, and kept talking.

"My father is not a bad man. I don't want anyone to think that. He's . . . a man who is more concerned with his career than he is with his family. No, no, that's not quite right. There was a time when he was nearly the opposite of that. I was seven years old when my mother died. A fever of some sort, I never knew. She was a wonderful woman. My father doted on her, but she was frail, a thin woman with long, beautiful, dark-brown hair."

Susie touched her own lank hair, pulled back and tied with a rawhide thong Rafe had given her. Her hand dropped. "Papa used to say I reminded him of her. I took it as a compliment for the longest time. Then he married a thoroughly . . ."

Rafe saw her cheek muscles work, concealing tight-set teeth, as if she were chewing the words before she spoke.

"My stepmother, as she insisted I call her, is . . . unpleasant. And consumed by greed and power. She will do anything to make certain my father one day becomes president of the United States."

"Why on earth would a man want to do that?" said Cookie.

Rafe scowled at him, shook his head, and Cookie simmered down. His outburst didn't stop Sue.

"I came to realize as a young girl that yes, I made him think of my mother, but not in a good way. I was a living reminder that the woman he loved was dead and gone." She spoke the last quietly, then was silent for long moments. It was only by the gleam of tears sliding down her cheeks that the two men realized she was still awake.

Rafe lifted out a clean, neatly folded bandanna and set it beside her.

She flashed a quick look at him, used it to dab her eyes, and muttered, "Thanks." She breathed deeply. "I was twelve when he remarried. After that he changed. I had lived with him for five years or so after Mama died. In all that time he rarely spoke, but walked through his life as if he was in a sleeping trance."

She shrugged. "I suppose any change would have been welcome. But the woman he married, oh, the changes she brought about were not good ones. He did come alive again, but only to her interests. It's as if they share a passion for power." She looked quickly at the two men, then back down at her feet.

"And that's when Papa became obsessed, because of her, no doubt, with marrying me off to someone wealthy. Someone, as he said, 'well connected,' preferably from 'back East. Where the power lies.' "

"And that's not what you want." Rafe relit his cigar, puffed thoughtfully.

Susie turned on him. "Of course not. I love the West. I don't want to be anywhere else."

Cookie spat discreetly off in the shadows. "How on earth did you wind up in that godawful place?"

For the first time since they met her she truly smiled. It was brief, and not full, but it was a smile. "You'll think me foolish."

"Naw, me? Half the words I say are foolish and half the things I do are the same."

"My secret desire ever since I was a little girl was to act in stage plays. To sing, to dance, perform in a traveling troupe across the nation. Perhaps one day to tour Europe. I was told I had promise, but that was years ago. Then Papa married again and . . . life was never quite the same. There was precious little time for anything but boarding schools, finishing school, the stifling whirl of society balls and being forced to sit for hour after hour with awkward young men who rambled on about how much money their families had."

She shook her head. "My father and I argued often, something we never used to do. And, of course, I argued with her, the stepmother. And then he informed me that I was a petulant child, a fool, and at seventeen I was far too old to be of any use to anyone." She looked at them, her voice shaking in anger. "He actually told me he was going to marry me off so I could give him grandsons — no doubt to make up for the sons he never had."

Her voice rose even higher as she spoke. "And then he informed me he had found me the perfect mate. Can you believe that? He actually told me who I was going to marry. A man from Boston, of all places, whose family was well placed and who would provide me with all the finery I could ever want. Ha!"

She sneered, thrusting at the fire with a length of branch. Rafe and Cookie looked at each other.

"I said, 'What about what I want?' " She looked at Rafe, then Cookie. "Do you know what he said to that? He said, 'You're a woman, dear. What you want is not important here.' I'm a woman, yes, but I'm also a person. What I want in life is as important to me as what anything anyone else in life wants, especially men."

She nodded with finality and Cookie and Rafe both looked away from her for the moment, not sure how they measured up to such a stern claim.

"I left him in his study, went upstairs, and packed a carpetbag. That night I left his house, vowing never to live under his or any man's roof ever again."

The situation they found her in went unspoken, but lay over the little group like a scrim of dark cloud.

"I had little money, but I had ambition. And what's more, I was desperate to prove my father wrong. I found work on the stage, in San Francisco, but then the troupe moved on and I was not considered seasoned enough to go with them. I worked at food halls, in a dress shop, but all the time I yearned for the stage more than ever. The costumes, the bright lights, the crowds, all those people quiet, waiting on your every word . . ."

"Like now," said Cookie, smiling at her.

She smiled slightly again, became somber once more. "I found an advertisement in an entertainment circular. 'Wanted: Experienced female thespians with the ability to sing, dance, and move crowds with word and actions. High-paying work in elegant surroundings, stage plays and musical revues daily. Now actively hiring women for all positions of entertainment.' You see, I even memorized the advertisement, so stirring, so important such a lifeline was it to me when I found it. Of course I wrote away immediately, enclosing a photograph as required."

She fell silent again, then as abruptly said, "Would that I never saw the wretched ad. I am a fool of the highest order. Al Swearengen is . . . oh, I tried to get away from him, immediately when I got there. But he had paid my fare there. He insisted I work it off, or he would have me arrested. But you saw the place, the people. The only work there was as you can imagine. It was all lies.

"I ran away once." She wiped her eyes, nodding at Rafe. "I did, really. I got three, maybe four or five miles from Deadwood, but his man, Frenchy, he came after me and . . . let's say it took us longer to get back to town than it ought to." She wrapped her arms around herself tight.

"And the drugs. He keeps all the girls addicted. It's the only way to get through the days. Some girls can't take it. If disease doesn't get them, they kill themselves, if they're lucky. Or Al beats them to death. I saw him hit a girl so hard when he was in a rage that her nose broke and she lost three teeth. The next minute she was on her knees begging him to forgive her. I have seen so much worse. Have done . . ."

She shook her head, looked down at her lap. "But then he found out who my father was, somehow. It never came from me, that much I can tell you. I don't know how he found out, but in a way it saved my life. I was one of those girls who was ready to kill herself."

She didn't look at them, but kept sobbing as she spoke. "I had the razor blade ready when he took me off the line, as they call it. Brought me to his rooms, and chained me there. He injected drugs into me, did . . . things to me, I don't know what. But I know he was planning on ransoming me back to Papa. He told me as much. I think he was getting ready to when you showed up."

Silence once again descended on the little group. The fire cracked and snapped and Cookie tossed on a couple of sticks.

Sue looked at Rafe. "I still don't know who you are or what you do. I mean really, who you are."

Rafe stare at her a moment, said nothing.

She shrugged. "No matter. Nothing matters now anyway. I can't sink lower, unless it's six feet down. The only place a fool like me deserves to be anyway. But I tell you this, these past couple of days I have decided

I might live. But only because if I don't, then Al Swearengen and my father and all the other men . . . from there . . . will have won. And I cannot let that happen."

"I'm pleased to hear that, Sue," said Rafe. "I truly am. You're still facing some tough times where the drugs are concerned. You'll have to fight them hard. I've seen grown men cry and curl up like newborns at the pain."

"But we're here," interrupted Cookie, with a harsh look at Rafe. "And we still have a little whiskey left." He smiled at her.

"I know what's in store for me. But I have to quit this sickness and I know it won't be easy. But once I make up my mind, that's all there is to it."

It was a long time before any of them spoke again. They stared at the coals as they dwindled slowly to embers. It had been a long few days, and there were more rough ones ahead, but this fester of anger among them had torn open and drained. Maybe she had begun to heal.

"One more thing, girly," said Cookie, breaking the quiet. "You keep those moccasins."

"Oh, no, Cookie. I can't do that. They're yours, they were a gift to you."

He nodded. "Yep, and now I'm giving

them to you."

"I . . . I'll buy shoes as soon as I can and give them back."

He shrugged, turned away. "Do as you want with them moccasins, but they're a gift, you can't give them back. That's a genuine Injun law. They're yours now."

"Oh . . . oh, Cookie . . ." Before the little man knew what was happening she knee-walked over to him and wrapped her arms around him, hugging him tight.

After a few seconds in which he turned red and made sounds that weren't words, she seemed to realize what she was doing and let him go, and sat down back at her place by the fire.

Rafe cleared his throat. "I hope you know we weren't really going to let you wander off on your own, naked and afoot. You will need our help. Being independent is all well and good, but friends are mighty thin on the ground out here."

No one said anything, so he continued. "And besides, we aren't out of danger yet. Given who your father is, and given the sort of man Swearengen is, I bet good money he'll send a few trackers after us. We have to be ready when they come. And they will come — we haven't exactly been traveling fast nor taking great pains to cover our back trail."

"I'm sorry I've slowed you down," she said.

"You haven't. You're the reason we're here, so in a sense, we're right where we need to be. But make no mistake, they will find us and when they do we have to be ready."

Cookie patted his peculiar holster. "Ol' Cookie will be ready, don't you worry none. All I need is a handful of lucifers, or my flint and steel. Hee hee! Those boys won't know what hit 'em when you turn ol' Cookie loose!"

"We're likely safe enough tonight. But we'll need to keep watch. Cook, you want the first? We have to rise early tomorrow."

Cookie was already on his feet and squaring his hat. "I'll check the horses, then find a spot by that boulder yonder. Good night, girly. And remember, you're among friends." He winked and ambled off.

In a low voice, Rafe said, "Told you he was a good man."

"You were right. But so are you." Susie offered a weak smile, then curled up and closed her eyes.

Soon, Rafe saw her features relax, her breathing even out. He watched her for a long time, watched the glow of the low coals reflect on her clean, thin face, listened to the slight sound she made as she breathed deeply in sleep. He hoped the worst was over. But he doubted it. He'd never had much reason to believe in hope.

Chapter 20:
Cometh the Quaker

Later the next day, having made decent time despite stopping twice for Sue to "visit a bush," as Cookie called it — the drugs and whiskey were playing havoc with her system — the trio rode down onto a wide, open river-bottom stretch of grassland.

Rafe, in his usual quiet manner, had only nodded vaguely ahead of them when Sue inquired as to where they were traveling. Cookie, who had been as quiet as he could most of the day, could take it no longer.

They were walking the horses side by side, letting them get their wind back, when he tapped his nose. "I know a thing or three about this country, girly. And what's more, I know a story about it. A true one, too." He nodded, a catty smile on his face, and commenced to tell them a windy, as Rafe called the old man's yarns, true or no.

It seems that somewhere ahead there had once been a dugout built along the bank of the North Platte River. But that was twenty or more years ago. By the time its third owner came along, it had been host to much raw behavior.

The first and second owners, or both firsts, depending on how you considered them, had been brothers and partners in the business, being the ones who built it. They were also the only participants in a knife fight that went wrong. Horace, the older and dumber brother, accused Timbo, his younger brother by six years, of short-changing him of his evening ration of whiskey.

Timbo, possessed of a fiery disposition, was not inclined to take the insult lightly. He palmed the stocky handle of a poor-quality trade knife, its ilk suitable, it was widely considered, only for Indians. The particular Bowie replica he chose from the "for sale" bin had a severe flaw in the blade, a hairline crack that ran the length of the poorly forged tool.

Unaware of its shoddy construct, Timbo shucked it and lunged, caught Horace smack on the thigh bone. The blade snapped clean along its length and Timbo's momentum, halted by the abruptness of the bone and blade meeting, caused him to continue his angry lunge forward. This resulted in the handle snapping off at the top of the blade.

At the same time, Horace, who had his back to his brother, mostly as a show of sulking defiance, understandably screamed at the pain the knife caused. He swung around, adding his own unintentional complication to the dustup.

In his pain and rage, Horace upset Timbo's balance. Timbo fell forward onto Horace, knocking him to his backside, no mean feat considering Horace weighed close to three hundred pounds and was wide enough at the shoulder that he often entered doorways at an angle.

Timbo, on the other hand, was of slight build and moderate stature. Nonetheless, the pair of brothers went down. The maneuver winded Timbo who had sort of flopped on top of his brother momentarily.

In his pain and rage, Horace had enough mental wherewithal to slide his own blade, a fine-quality Green River skinner he'd had custom made some years before by a traveling smith, free of its sheath. He wasted no effort in driving it deep into Timbo's breadbox.

The two brothers lay gasping for quite some time. Timbo, however, bled out soon enough and Horace, sprawled beneath him, lost blood and consciousness. When he came to, he was horrified when he realized what he'd done. He also knew he might be in danger of dying if he didn't get his leg tended to. It was blood-sticky and swollen far beyond normal size.

"What happened then?" said Sue.

Even Rafe had no idea where Cookie was taking this odd tale. But since it wasn't slowing them down, and since he hadn't heard this particular story from the old coot before, he said nothing.

"Well now, since Horace was found dead not but twenty feet from his brother — half in, half out the door — and not but a few days, maybe a week after the two had fought, it can only be guessed at, mind you, that Horace's leg was in worse shape than he first thought. Course, when he was found he was also mighty chewed over by the pigs them brothers kept. When their regular meals stopped coming, those pigs escaped from their pen around back of the place, commenced to snacking on the first tasty treat they found — that was Horace." Cookie let loose with a stream of chaw juice and continued with the story.

"As the dugout trading post was a new business, it wasn't much known among the whites, though the Indians in the area all knew of it. To them it was a place they could get firewater and cheap guns, knives, axes. Then along come the Crazy Quaker."

Cookie looked at his companions for a reaction. Getting none he continued. "He was a tall, thin Quaker making his way from one coast to the other. He about had enough of legging it across the country, so by the time he made it to the North Platte, he vowed to set down roots, at least for a spell. He heard rumor the trading post was for sale, so he set down his cash and bought the business, complete with a couple of frightening feral pigs roving the flats around the place, and one old nasty stain on the floor that never did wash clean."

Cookie spit again. "At least not until the flood took the place out. That was, oh, eight, ten years ago. By the time anyone thought to check on the Crazy Quaker, at least that's what they called him — still do — he had managed to pull himself free of the pile of debris he woke up in some ways downriver. He crawled up out of the mud, spluttering sand and water and spitting grime, only to find he was standing not anywheres he recognized.

"See, that flood had up and ferried him ten mile down the river! I kid you not. He looked around him and found that most of his possessions were lodged in the mud and tangles of branches and rocks and sand bars. So he commenced to unearth them all. Place looked like a prairie dog colony after a fashion. But he scrounged enough to set up shop again. He also found that he liked the spot where he ended up better than he liked where he'd been. So he stayed put. And that's where he is to this day."

Cookie nodded, as if conversing with himself. "Course, it's all built up now. Got himself a brisk business trade with the river folk, traders and trappers and injuns and all them fools traveling west when they have no business uprooting themselves and traveling anywhere but to their barn in Missourah to milk their old bossy cows."

Cookie stopped talking and shook his head, as if he'd heard something he couldn't help but disagree with.

Sue cleared her throat. "Cookie, as fascinating as that story is, I will admit I'm confused. What does that have to do with us?"

"Why, girly, that's where we're aiming right now. To pay a visit to the Crazy Quaker. He's the one to see in these parts. Knows everyone, sees everything, doesn't tell tales out of school. He's a right trustworthy fella, is the Quaker."

They rode on in silence for a few more miles, then Sue said, "Cookie, you are, without doubt, the most amazing raconteur I have ever encountered."

Cookie narrowed his eyes. "I don't know what to say to that, girly. Could be I might take offense to that word, racko— whatever you said."

Sue laughed. "It's a nice way of saying you're a good storyteller."

"I'd say you're a leg-puller from way back," said Rafe.

"All true, I tell you!" Cookie crowed. "Every last word. You don't believe me, you up and ask that Crazy Quaker, 'cause there's his trading post yonder."

They looked toward where he nodded and sure enough, on a rise overlooking the river — high above any conceivable flood line — sat a long, low, log-and-sod structure that looked as if it had been carved out of a pile of dirt by someone who lost interest halfway through.

"Now I know it don't look like much, but the man has all manner of inventory, I promise you. And he's a hell of a —" Cookie reddened. "Pardon me, girly. He's a right fine cook. Food's filling and all, but if I had one complaint, it's that it's a mite bland. I expect that's on account of him being a

Quaker. Those religious types often don't hold with spice."

"What about all those churchgoing Mexicans?"

"Rafe Barr, you keep stepping on my conversational toes and we're going to have a knock-down-drag-out." Cookie held up a wide, bony knuckled fist. "Now, let me do the talking when we get in there, 'cause he's an odd duck."

"No wonder you two get along so well." This time it was Sue.

Cookie looked at both of them. "Oh, I see how it is, then. I see."

It turned out that Cookie was correct. The Crazy Quaker was every bit as tall and as odd as he had described. He spoke little, though did engage in a hushed conversation with Cookie on their arrival. And his cooking, while better by far than Cookie's, which Rafe felt wasn't saying much, was palatable and plentiful. They each ate more than their share.

The interior of the homely, crude structure was a sight to behold, at least for trail-weary travelers such as themselves. It was uncommonly well lit by oil lamps that vented their sooty fumes up and out three odd chimneys of the Quaker's own design. They were cut into the roof at intervals along the one long, narrow front room that served as dining hall, mercantile, and bunk space for travelers.

The floor, though packed dirt, was swept clean and a random pattern had been carved into the earth to mimic a plank floor. The shelves holding the goods were supported by clean-stripped poles. The boards held an impressive and ample supply of goods ranging from tins of milk and peaches to smoked meats and fabrics to sweets and harness leather.

The more expensive items, hardware, weaponry, tools, firearms, bullets, and bullet-making supplies were chained and padlocked behind the long polished-wood counter.

Rafe set about immediately calculating what he figured they needed for whatever distance he had in mind for them to travel next. Sue and Cookie and the Quaker watched as he licked a nub of pencil and tallied in a small notebook he kept in an inner vest pocket. Finally he conferred with Cookie, and a stack of goods mounded up on the long, low countertop.

Later, Rafe walked over to the girl, who had settled into a chair before a slow-burning fire in a fireplace. She shivered every few seconds and her face was pocked with droplets of sweat.

"You feeling it again?"

She nodded, said nothing.

"Cookie's chatting with the Quaker. Turns out the man's also some sort of herbal specialist, learned skills from a local tribesman, said they call him a shaman. He'll be coming over here in a few minutes to offer you some of his tincture. Cookie trusts the fellow, likes him, I can tell. So that's good enough for me. The decision, though, is yours."

Rafe sat down opposite her and leaned in. She looked at him.

"I'm telling you this because it might be a whole lot better for you later on than the laudanum you took off that shelf."

Her eyes went wide.

"I know you did, I saw it. Don't worry. I paid for it so the man doesn't think we're thieves."

"Oh, God, I'm so sorry. I feel desperate." She said this last bit through clenched teeth.

"Tell me next time. I'll buy it for you. I were you, though, I'd give the Quaker's tincture a try. Bound to be less harmful than a laudanum habit. That's sort of like trading one evil for a lesser evil. Down the road, evil's still likely to win out."

"I haven't opened it yet."

"I know," he said. "Keep it, in case you feel you need it."

"No," she said. "I want to be strong, but I don't believe I am that strong. I don't trust myself yet. Not sure if I ever will again."

"You will," Rafe smiled. "It'll take time."

She handed him the bottle and he slipped it into his vest pocket. Her eyes didn't leave it for a moment. He stood and stretched. "We'll sleep here tonight," he said. "Ride out at first light. We've a lot of ground to cover."

"Rafe." She looked up at him. "I . . . thank you."

He nodded, offered a small smile, and walked to the door, biting the end off a newly purchased cigar.

CHAPTER 21:
RAGE OF THE BULLY PIMP

"I'm not in the least bit concerned about problems you're having with your Coonhounds or whatever they're called. You are as I suspected — a two-bit idiot. The only bigger fool in the room is me for wasting my time on you." Swearengen cut his eyes past El Jefe. Something he saw caused a sneer that tightened his features.

He hustled down to the far end of the bar and around it. Instead of making for El Jefe, he set his jaw and made straight for a bruise-faced brown-haired woman moving stiffly and mopping the floor where someone had vomited the night before.

The bully pimp didn't slow his pace, but barreled straight into her, landing a hard, tight belly punch. It doubled her over and a wash of bile burst from her mouth, spattering the floor and wall. The few people close by ceased conversation and stared wide-eyed at the scene.

Swearengen bent close by the heaving woman's head. He hooked a finger through her lank, hanging hair and lifted strands of it gently back over her ear. "The next time you and your friend let a stranger beat one of my customers," he said, his voice a rasping purr, velvet dragged over rusted metal, "you'll be cleaning this place with your tongue." He smoothed her hair and patted her head. "Nod if you understand me."

The woman nodded, not looking up.

"Good. Now hurry up. The afternoon rush will be in soon and you're worth more to me on your back than cleaning the floors. Barely."

Swearengen straightened, clapped his hands together and let his eyes settle on El Jefe. "Still here? You don't take a hint well, do you?"

El Jefe pushed away from the bar, squared off before the calm proprietor. "You know something, Mr. Swearengen —"

"As it happens, I know a lot of things, though few of them seem relevant right about now." He unrolled his cuffs, buttoned them, smoothing the sleeves.

El Jefe continued as if he hadn't been interrupted. "You are a bully. Me, too, sometimes. But hitting a woman? That is bad business. The mark of a weak man. I don't think I will bring that girl back to you now. I think I will figure out why she is so important to you. Then we will see what is what, eh?"

Swearengen smiled. "That, my friend, is a moot point. That means not worth talking about."

"Oh, why is that?"

"Because, as it happens, I hired three men to do the job that proved to be too much for you and your pups." He slipped back behind the bar. "You might be interested to know they were three of your own men. Two Mexicans and a white. More cowboys than Bloodhounds, though, from the looks of them. Seemed to be glad to get away from you. In fact, they didn't have much of anything nice to say about you — something about you trying to kill them? Then forcing them to ride with you? But they felt certain they could bring the girl back to me." He opened the door behind the bar. "Oh, by the way . . . I paid them well, very well, up front."

El Jefe knew his blood was up, his face red, his jaw muscles clenched. But he stood and listened. Even after that vile man scurried off into his building somewhere, El Jefe stood staring at the closed door, imagining the smug look on the face of that bastard.

He muttered, "It's Hell Hounds, damn you."

Chapter 22:
Cometh the Gambler

Something in the dark night awakened Sue Pendleton. She had begun to think of herself as Sue again, allowing the slimmest sliver of hope — a feeling long foreign to her — to wheedle its way into her mind once more, all because of these two strange men who had rescued her.

But the noise, what had that been? She felt groggy, but knew immediately where she was. In the odd Quaker's trading post along the North Platte River, somewhere in Nebraska. And he had given her a tonic of some sort he'd made from tinctures of his own devising. Its effects had been quick and pleasant — she felt a strange sort of light feeling, as if she were floating, then she slipped into a restful sleep. Though this strange noise had awakened her, she felt good, much better than she knew she had a right to feel.

There it was again. She looked toward

where she knew the front door stood, but it was too black to see anything more than the dimmest of shapes in the room.

Where were the sounds of the others sleeping? She knew she should at least be able to hear Cookie. He snored like a locomotive grinding away on an uphill grade.

"Sue?" came a whispered voice. It was Cookie.

"Here."

"Good, you're awake." He moved closer. "Somebody's out there. Rafe's checking on it. Might be nothing at all. But you keep low and stay put."

Rafe must already be out back, maybe the Quaker, too, for she only heard the slightest scuffing noises as Cookie cat-walked over to one of two windows on the front of the place.

Then she heard noises outside the sod walls. Horses stamping, drawing closer, men speaking in low voices. They were rude in their loudness at this hour, not taking any pains to disguise their presence. She heard two distinct voices, a quick round of laughter from one, the other voice shushing him.

Chains clinked, leather creaked, and a horse snorted.

"Two men," whispered Cookie. "No,

there's a third, riding behind. Don't look too happy about it, neither."

"What do you think they want?"

Cookie glanced her way, then back to the crack in the wooden shutter. "Same as anyone wants here. Food, supplies."

"What about Rafe?"

"What about him?"

"Well, there are three of them and he's out there."

Cookie grinned. "I know. He'll follow them on in, you wait and see."

The men walked to the door and tried the latch, but it was barred from the inside. The Quaker by then had lit an oil lamp, turned down low, and set it on the bar top. He looked much the same to Sue as he had earlier, save for a flannel dressing down. His eyes passed over her to Cookie.

"Let 'em in," said Cookie. "Rafe'll be along."

The Quaker nodded once, slid to the left the halved pole that served as the door's bar, and stood back in time. The door slammed inward and bounced off a tidy stack of sacked feed.

A tall, fat man wrapped in a fur cloak waddled in. " 'Bout time, Crazy Man! We been out here near on two hour —"

The man's bluster ceased immediately as

his eyes fell on Cookie, who wore his gut shredder of a shotgun slung across a crook in his arm. Cookie nodded, said nothing. Then the man's gaze fell on Sue and his tongue slid out of his mouth like a lazy pink slug. He took time licking his lips.

A second man stomped in behind him, considerably shorter and wearing spectacles that reflected the dull glow of the oil lamp. "Well, lookee that!" said the second man. "We got us some company."

Sue saw he was not only shorter, he was much thinner and, if possible, even uglier than his fat companion. His face was a gathering place for badness, laced as it was with welted scars, pock marks, boils, and scabs that had recently been boils.

"Quaker, ain't you going to introduce us to your friends?"

But the proprietor only turned, went behind the counter, and donned a white apron. The fat man clapped grimy hands together and strode to the counter. "That's more like it. We need rye whiskey and biscuits and some of them eggs you make. And throw on a couple of steaks. We been riding hard, worked up a appetite, we did."

The Quaker nodded, and turned unhurried to the stove, in which he kept a low fire banked.

Outside, boots sounded, and another man stepped in through the door. All eyes went to him. Out of the shadows came Rafe, his rifle angled downward, but a second from being jerked into action.

"Now who in the hell is this?" said the fur-wearing brute. "Another no-talkin' son of a bitch?"

The second man found this humorous and brayed like a sick donkey.

"Aren't you forgetting someone?" said Rafe.

"Huh?"

Rafe repeated his question.

"Oh, our shadow."

Again, the smaller man guffawed.

The fat man leaned on the countertop. "Ain't no cause to get riled. He ain't going nowheres. He's chained. Couldn't run if he had a mind to."

"Like the animal he is," said the second man.

The first, meanwhile, had parted his cloak to reveal a sizable jigged-bone handle skinning knife and a scar-gripped revolver, both strapped across his ample paunch, cross-draw style.

Rafe stepped in and motioned to someone behind him. From out of the shadows behind Rafe they heard a sliding, clinking sound. A lean, black man stepped into the dim room. His face, puffed and cut from some manner of fight, was a stony mask, but Sue saw sharp, clear eyes.

The man wore manacles linked by a foot of chain on his wrists. The cuffs of a once-white, finely made shirt had been snugged under the steel bands in an effort to lessen the chafing, but that had been some time before. They were now threadbare and worn through in spots.

His black vest, ripped and mud-spattered, matched well-cut black trousers with what Sue thought might be a fine blue line of piping running up the outside seams. About his ankles were a matching set of shackles with a length of chain between, forcing the man to shuffle in quarter strides. His black boots of soft leather were those of a dandy, a gentrified man, though they, too, as with the rest of him, had long since seen better days.

Despite his abused appearance, the man held himself straight. He was not as tall as Rafe, nor as broad, but he was a well-muscled fellow who took in everything with those sharp eyes.

"Git your ass out of here, slave boy!" Pock-face sneered, making a motion as if he were shooing a pesky fly.

The fat man cut in. "You got horses to tend. Get on it or you will wish you died back on that Missouri riverboat."

The chained man regarded him a moment, then turned toward the door, but Rafe laid a big hand on the man's upper arm, staying him.

Rafe fished a stub of cigar from his pocket, slid it in a corner of his mouth. "Now that is no way to talk to another man."

"Huh?"

Rafe sighed. "I may be older than I once was, and my hearing may well have grown poorer over time, but I do not recall hearing you inviting him in for a meal."

Sue heard Cookie mumble, "Oh, here we go."

The fat man's face pinched in the center, then he chewed furiously for a moment on his quid of tobacco, turned and spit toward Cookie's boots. It spattered. Cookie didn't move. The fat man nodded at Sue as he dragged a dimpled hand across his mouth.

From behind him, a cast-iron skillet slammed the stovetop. Apparently the Quaker was not happy that the man had spit on his clean floor.

Fatty ignored the sound. "Mister, I don't know who you think you are, but that . . . animal right yonder is my property. Me and

291

his." He nodded to his pock-faced cohort.

"You bounty men?"

"Might be," said the fat man. "Might not be."

The smaller man spit out an answer. "Taking this uppity rascal to Denver for a proper trial."

"Why Denver?" said Rafe.

"Because that's where our employer is at," said the fat man. "What's it to you?" He eyed Rafe up and down.

"Nothing to me. Odd that the man isn't tried where the crime was committed."

"Yeah, well, mister I don't make the damn laws, but I sure as hell enforce 'em."

"Oh, so you're a lawman, then?" said Cookie, still standing by the bar, the shotgun's business end jutting from his folded arms.

The shorter of the two men regarded Cookie a moment. "Never said that."

"Could be what I heard got misconstrued in my bean. Been known to happen before."

"Could be. Where's that Quaker bastard with our food?"

Seated at a round table large enough for three men at most, Sue realized too late the fat man was walking her way. He stopped in front of her.

"Show me them titties of yours, I'll give

you a dollar."

"That's enough of that talk," said Rafe, squaring off and sliding his rifle to bear on the man's gut.

"What for? She's got the look of a whore on her, that's plain as sin. I only want a look-see."

He grinned and Sue saw a mouthful of tiny, blackened jags where once, long ago, white teeth had been. The hole that was his mouth was made more repugnant by the dribble of chaw juice leaking from it, disappearing into his sparse, curly brown beard.

She had known plenty of such men in the recent past. Large, angry oafs who enjoy hitting and biting and slapping. Making a woman cry and beg gave them a feeling of strength. Seeing this pudding of a man stare down at her made her not ever want to beg anyone for anything ever again.

Rafe Barr moved with the suddenness of a snake strike, clearing in eye-blink speed the six feet separating himself from the fat stranger. He led with a meaty fist, driving straight into the man's haired, leering face.

Sue heard the dull crack of bone separating, saw the fat man turn, spittle, blood, and teeth spraying, spattering a dozen feet away. He spun around once, his fur cloak whipping outward before slamming into the wall behind. His head snapped backward and caromed off the edge of a shelf. Tins of axle grease and a jar filled with bolts and pins bucked into the air before raining down on him.

"Waaah!" The fat man cried like an enormous grumpy baby as he sat slumped against the wall, blood pumping out of his nose and mouth. He barely noticed as Rafe relieved him of the revolver and the knife. Rafe patted the man's boots, but found there was precious little room in them for the man's fat legs, let alone a hide-out gun or short knife.

"What you done?" Pock-face whimpered, sliding a hand into his open moth-chewed wool coat.

"Don't you do that," snapped Cookie, thumbing back the hammers on the double-snouted shotgun.

It appeared the man was hard of hearing because he continued reaching for whatever weapon he felt was about to solve all his problems. But he forgot who he'd turned his back on. Quick as a lynx the black man clanked one, two steps forward and snapped the chain between his wrists over the small man's head. He yanked back hard, his teeth set tight as his muscles bulged beneath his shirtsleeves.

Pock-face thrashed like a spiny river fish on a hook. He clawed at the chain pressing into his throat and made sounds as if he were trying to spit and growl through a mouthful of cotton batting.

"Hey!" shouted Cookie. "Stop that!"

Rafe crossed the room in two strides and stood before the prisoner. "I appreciate your assistance, and I don't know what you're in trouble for, but killing a man can't help matters."

The only sounds in the room were the fat man blubbering, his begrimed hands flopped palms up on the floor to either side of him, and the ebbing croakings of the still-flailing Pock-face.

The chained man's grip relaxed, and as quickly as he'd descended on the homely man, he lifted his arms and let him drop. The little man folded every way possible from the ankles up, collapsing in a gasping heap.

"Well, now," said Cookie. "What'll we do with them?"

Rafe leaned his rifle against the front wall and looked at the two wounded bounty hunters. "I can't imagine they are going to be inclined toward civility where our friend here is concerned." He nodded toward the shackled man. "I am of a mind to send them on their way without him."

"Rafe!"

Sue's sudden shout spun the big man, low and coiled like a cornered viper, one hand already clawing free a well-used Colt. Rafe took in the fat man's changed posture, the sharp stare through blood-rimmed eyes, the half grin of a man convinced of imminent victory. Rafe also saw, looped on a rawhide thong, the six-shot pepperbox the fat man retrieved from between his flabby breasts, a thick finger already squeezing the slight trigger.

Rafe dropped down out of his coil, rolled, and fanned his revolver's worn hammer, once, twice, thrice. The fat man jerked with the impact of each shot delivered at such close range. And with each spasm his fat finger jerked on the little gun's trigger. Only the first fired the pepperbox, but it was enough.

The bullet found its mark, coring a clean hole in the left temple of the fat man's trail mate. The pock-scarred man flopped once, his head wagged as if he were working out a neck kink, then sagged to his chest.

Smoke and the stink of burned cloth curdled with the raw tang of man sweat and fresh blood. The hollow, ringing sound following gunplay in a small, enclosed space filled the ears and minds of the five living occupants. No one spoke for long moments. The Quaker was the only one to move. He swung wide the door and two windows, and levered open the chimneys. Soon the room was free of smoke, and the clean chill of early morning air crept in, driving away much of the foul smells.

In the silence, the black man stepped into the middle of the room. He addressed Rafe, not looking at anyone else.

"Sir." He offered a curt, quick nod, as if he were bowing with his head. "I can assure you, I am no man's slave. I am my own man, a free man, and I know my mind."

"Well, I'll be," said Cookie.

A sideways glance from Rafe stoppered Cookie's speechifying before it gained traction.

Rafe slid a cigar from his pocket and lit a match, rotating the cigar in the flame until the end glowed like a setting sun, then said, "Never doubted it. But you didn't deny being a cheat."

The chained man's face remained emotionless. "No, I never did."

"How much?"

Finally his features reacted. "Pardon?"

Rafe blew out a cloud of blue-gray smoke.

"How much did you take their employer for?"

"First, a small point of fact: I do not need to cheat. I am good at what I do."

"Humble, too." Cookie winked at Sue, then caught a glance from Rafe and looked down at his boots as if he'd been caught snoring in church.

The black man continued. "I merely used the same off-hand techniques the man had been using on others. Now, as to how much . . ." The man smiled.

Sue thought the smile brought youth to his face, though she still had no idea of his age. One moment the newcomer looked as though he might be well experienced in life's travails, the next he could as easily be wet behind the ears.

"Nearly the exact amount he stole from six people belowdecks who could scarcely afford to lose it — and who should have known better than to gamble it."

"And you turned it over to them."

The man's eyebrows rose. "Naturally."

Rafe puffed his cigar, squinted one eye against the smoke, and regarded the shackled man. Then he bent, patted beneath the dead fat man's parted cloak, fished in a vest pocket, and tossed the man a key. "Unlock those and give me and Cookie a hand." He

298

looked around the room. "We have to take out the garbage."

The man caught the tossed keys between his palms, and in seconds had himself freed from the shackles. He rubbed his wrists and ankles tenderly, then walked over to Rafe and stuck out his hand. "Jack Smith. But some folks call me Black Jack."

Rafe nodded and shook. "Mr. Smith, I'm Rafe Barr. These are my associates, Cookie McGee and Susan Pendleton."

Jack shook Cookie's hand, then turned to Sue and nodded at the waist. "A pleasure, ma'am."

"And that," said Rafe, nodding toward the proprietor of the place, busily sweeping up the spilled contents of a sack of oats, "is the owner of this establishment. We best stop with the palaver and lend a hand."

As if a cork had been yanked from a bottle, Cookie began yammering, recounting the bizarre events for all, in case any of them hadn't been paying attention.

Sue helped the silent owner of the place clean the mess. She fetched water and a rounded knob of lye soap, a rag, and a brush, and scrubbed free the blood spatters from the floor and walls.

The Quaker, impassive as ever, merely nodded, but she fancied she saw a gleam of appreciation in his eyes. She owed him much for sharing his tincture. She felt sure its impressive effects would soon wane, but it had given her the first hours of clarity she had had in a long, long time.

Cookie, Rafe, and Jack wrapped the two bounty hunters in canvas and buried them in a small cemetery the Quaker had set up for anyone unfortunate enough to meet his or her demise near his place.

Should the law or family decide to unearth them, Rafe made sure to show the Quaker who was buried where. Jack was unsure of their names, so they rummaged and found the identities of the dead men in their traps — the fat man was one Sal Judd, his small friend, Eldon Winslow.

Found paperwork also revealed the name of their employer, one Byron Tibbets, Esq. "We'll need to get notice of their deaths to him," said Rafe.

"Fancy Dan, I'd say," Cookie sniffed. "Hire the likes of these two, he ain't got much in the way of common sense."

"Maybe not, but their deaths are our responsibility," said Rafe, "in a manner of speaking, and I don't want any further troubles."

Sue stopped herself before she said what was on her mind. But she dearly wanted to ask what troubles he might be in. That they involved her was obvious, but how much woe had she caused these two men? More than she knew? And now Rafe had taken on responsibility for a man who had been apprehended by bounty hunters. What further trouble had he brought on himself?

Chapter 23:
Bullets in the Sky

"We was going to track down those two rascals anyway, so now we get to do it and get paid. That is what I call the smiling face of good fortune."

"Yes, you did a good turn, Carl. But that man Swearengen, I don't know if I want to see him again. He is trouble."

"So was that El Jefe and his men. Bad seeds all around."

Manny nodded and sighed, but said nothing.

Carl shifted slightly in the saddle so he could see his two companions. "That's why this plan is working out fine as frog hair. We get shed of them both, you see?"

Manny nodded. "Sí, still, we don't know what to think of this job you have committed us to."

"Then don't think about it, Manny. You, me, and Miguel, we're about to be rich. Prepare yourself for it!" The white man howled and shucked a pistol, cranked off a shot into the air. It echoed across the long, low tree-studded vale before them. "And best of all, we get our vengeance on those two bastards who lost us those railroad jobs."

The man's two companions, Manny and Miguel, both smaller in stature and more skittish in nature — and less prone to wasting good bullets on the sky — exchanged grimaces, but kept on their plodding path behind Carl, their crazy gringo friend. They were beginning to wonder if following him was best for their health.

"I figure we are at least three days ahead of that Heifer fella and his Hell Hounds. We keep riding hard, we'll get somewhere faster than them. Trick now is to make sure we get to the right place."

"Carl, sometimes I don't understand you so well," said Manny. "You talk in circles, like a butterfly flies, you know?"

The white cowboy chuckled. "Yeah, but them butterflies get to where they need to be, don't they?"

The two men following him shrugged. It was no use trying to understand him. Besides, though they hated to admit it, Carl was right at least on one score — they had to be somewhere, and he had shown them

quite an adventure since they took to the
trail.

CHAPTER 24:
WHEN FRIENDS PART WAYS

Rafe held up a hand and halted his growing train of trail mates. He'd been mulling over the situation with the girl and he still had no sound answer. She was a headstrong young woman, that much had become plain, but she was also still sick. The Quaker's tonic had helped her, but it was not a cure-all solution.

She was game, he'd give her that, but if he didn't stop as frequently as he had, he was afraid she'd fall out of the saddle, so pale and shaky did she seem at times.

Cookie rode up beside him, a questioning look on his face.

"Cook, what say we pass the canteen around, work over some of that tasty jerky your man sold us."

"What? Why we ain't hardly rode but three hours . . ."

Rafe glared at Cookie, and widened his eyes enough to shut him up. Sometimes

Cookie could be thick.

"You got a headache, boy? You keep buggin' those eyes out like that they'll likely stay that way all your days. Didn't anybody tell you that as a youngster?"

"It's okay, Cookie. He's stopping for my benefit."

"Why would . . . ? Ohhh." The old rooster of a man nodded, poked Rafe in the arm. "Why didn't you say so?"

He slid down from his horse and rubbed his backside. "Jack, you up for a wad of the Crazy Quaker's spiced jerky? Now, that is some good eatin'."

"Thank you, Cookie. Don't mind if I do. I'm glad we stopped. Good a time as any to get down to it."

"Get down to what, Jack?" Sue said.

"I expect Mr. Barr knows."

Rafe nodded. "Been wondering when it would come up."

"Well, don't you tell ol' Cookie all at once. Wouldn't want to drag it to death, now would we?"

Jack smiled. "Okay, okay, keep your hat on, Cookie. I'm curious as to what your plans are for me, Mr. Barr? You know, after all, that I was captured and accused of being a cardsharp."

Rafe shrugged. "All I know is we stopped

at a trading post to resupply and a couple of hard cases came in and made life tough. A fight ensued. We lived, they didn't."

"And that's it?" said Jack.

"Unless Cookie and Sue can recall anything more."

Both shrugged and shook their heads.

"There's an answer to your question, I think."

Jack nodded. "Thank you, Rafe. And Cookie and Sue — for everything. Question remains, I don't have money enough on me to pay you for this horse, nor the rig, nor any of it."

"It's not mine to sell. Seems like a fella who's been through what you've been through has earned that fine Palouse. The rig, too."

Jack Smith turned away a moment, hands on his hips, reins held in one hand then he turned back. "You're a good lot, all of you. If you ever make it to Kansas City, ask around for Black Jack Smith. Won't be hard to find. I expect I'll be the only black man wearing bespoke finery."

Rafe smiled. "I don't doubt it. When do you expect to light out?"

"As someone once said, 'No better time than now.' "

"I said that once, maybe it was me you're

307

thinking of. Course it was to a lovely se-
ñorita down Sonora way. She was a large
girl, had the kindest eyes. My Spanish
wasn't so good then as it is now, and I
mistook her question. She come at me like
a dragon from a kiddy story!" Cookie
slapped a thigh, then straightened. "By the
way, what's 'beskpoke'?"

"Tell you later," said Sue. She walked over
and hugged Jack. "I am sorry you had to
see me like this, all . . ." She fluttered her
hands up and down before her body clad in
cinched men's denims, a much-gathered
chambray shirt, and moccasins. On her
head she wore a decent used brown felt
slouch hat, a gift from the Quaker.

"You are a beautiful woman, Sue. Never
doubt that."

Rafe swigged from a canteen. "What will
you do when you get to Kansas City, Jack?"

The man smiled and straightened his
arms, smoothing the sleeves as if he'd
donned a fine new shirt. "There's a gent
there who owes me money. That'll put
enough cash in my poke for new duds."

"New clothes?" Cookie looked as if he'd
been slapped. "I can think of a whole lot of
goods I'd rather have than new clothes, I
tell you, mister."

"I'm sure you would, Cookie, but in my

game, appearances are everything. And I do mean everything. I show up at a table looking like this, they'll show me the door — headfirst. Hard enough time nosing my way in as it is."

Rafe rummaged in the supplies, pulled out a satchel, and began filling it for Jack. As for gear, before they departed the trading post they had done the same with the traps of Jack's captors, outfitting him as best they could, including a decent revolver and holster rig, and a knife. The rest of the gear and the two remaining horses they left with the Quaker as partial compensation for the ruckus.

While Rafe and Sue assembled whatever he felt they could spare and what Jack might find useful, Cookie corralled the young gambler and chatted with him in a shady spot a dozen yards away. Rafe glanced over and saw Cookie palm Jack a folded piece of paper.

Rafe gave them a few moments more, then walked over. "Here you go," he said, handing over the sack of food.

"What's this?"

"You have at least a week's worth of riding between here and Kansas City." He shoved it into the man's arms. "It's not much, so make it last." He turned and pointed a hand. "Thataway, I suspect. Let me double-check." Rafe flipped open a brass compass, oriented himself. "Yep. If you get lost, ride north until you hit the Platte. Keep it on your left and ride east until it meets the Missouri, then south to Kansas City."

"That was my plan." Jack hoisted the bulging canvas satchel, secured it to the saddlehorn. "I can't thank you enough."

"You don't have to. Just don't get caught again," said Rafe. "Best way to do that is to deal from the top of the deck."

Jack smiled. "I will bear that in mind, Mr. Barr."

"And for the last time, it's Rafe."

Black Jack Smith swung up into the saddle, "I know." He glanced at each of them in turn, gave them a smile and a quick salute, then nudged the Palouse into a steady gallop southeastward.

They watched his dust trail for a few minutes, and Sue dabbed her eyes with a shirt cuff.

Cookie turned away, coughed. "Well that's at least one person who knows where he's going."

"Okay, Cook. I hear you."

"You want me to heave out a few guesses? Or are we riding all this way to exercise our horses?"

Rafe slowly shook his head, fired up a fresh cigar, then walked away from them a dozen yards or so. Every once in a while he sent up blue clouds into the air.

Cookie squinted toward him, said to Sue, "We best leave him be. I pushed him too far. Don't know when to shut my own maw sometimes."

A good ten minutes later Rafe turned back to them. "Believe it or not I do have a destination in mind. More like a stop off. But it's not only up to me. Have you decided what you would like to do with yourself, Sue?"

"You mean you're not going to bring me back to my father?"

"No, from the sound of it, he has enough possessions. And besides, I'm not in the habit of kidnapping grown people."

"Nor kiddies, neither," said Cookie.

"That's true," said Rafe.

Sue swung up into the saddle. "I think we'd better talk about this as we ride toward wherever it is we're riding."

Rafe nodded, mounted up. "You've been spending too much time with Cookie."

"What's that supposed to mean?" said Cookie, jaw thrust out.

"Means she's getting bossy."

Rafe and Sue chuckled and guided their horses back into a trot. Behind, they heard Cookie shouting, "I ain't bossy, neither!"

Cookie caught up with them and the three rode abreast, the packhorse trailing behind Cookie. Rafe said, "You both deserve to know what I had in mind, in case you have a better idea." He paused, looked out over the wide plains before them. "We're well into Colorado by now. Cookie can guess where I was thinking of making for, but you wouldn't know, Sue."

She waited for him to continue, not sure what to say.

"I used to own a ranch, oh, a few days' ride southwest of here. A pretty place snug up against the mountains. Actually, it was more or less in the mountains. At its heart was a lovely valley, as green and fertile as you can imagine. Good water. I ran cattle there, had a full setup, corrals, a barn, bunkhouse for seasonal help, and a fine house." He stopped talking.

After a quiet minute, Sue said, "May I ask why you refer to it as something that no longer exists?"

"Because it doesn't. It's all gone. Burned five years ago. I don't know who owns it now."

Cookie rasped a bony hand across his

unshaven chin. "He'd be near enough a young man by now." He glanced at Rafe.

"Yeah," said the big man, his voice hoarse. He heaved up a sigh, then said, "My wife and son are there. I'd . . . like to visit them."

Sue caught Cookie's eye and kept her questions to herself.

CHAPTER 25:
COMETH THE MATRON

The summer weather treated the trio well and they made good time cutting southwestward across Colorado, though it seemed to Sue they never drew any closer to the mammoth spine of the Rockies.

"You think you can remember how to get there, boy?"

"Better than you . . . old-timer."

"Now, now," said Cookie, surprisingly unruffled by the dig at his age, "you might be surprised at my tracking abilities. Not to mention my near-perfect ability to fix a place in my mind. Why, I'm like a trained dog on the scent when I need to get somewhere. Them old coots in the fur trade? They relied on maps and compasses and who knows what else, and then they still got all turned around and kilt off by the Blackfeet. But me?" He tapped the end of his long nose. "Me, I got a special something."

"You certainly do," said Rafe. "Nothing a

bar of soap wouldn't fix."

They went on and on like that, and it pleased Sue to see this, to hear Rafe chuckle now and again, to see Cookie perk up like a happy puppy when he'd done or said something that pleased the big, quiet man.

She decided you couldn't call Rafe's silence brooding, necessarily, but you could think of it as the presence of a man too buried in his own mind, his own past. It was this aspect of Rafe with which she felt a kinship. She had much to think about and much to get "a leg up and over," as Cookie would say.

They rode hard, though not risking injury to the horses. After long hours when no one spoke, Sue began to sense something different about each of the men, particularly Rafe. He sat straighter, seemed more tense, more alert somehow. Cookie, too, who usually slouched in the saddle and was prone to dozing from time to time, carried a new sense of coiled energy about him.

Still a half mile from an escarpment that jutted from a red-stone hill like the prow of a ship, Cookie pointed and Rafe nodded as if he'd seen the same sight at the same time. They rode toward it, the land seeming to converge in upon itself. The trail, which was not really a trail at all, curved and descended sharply.

What amazed Sue most was the sense that she was not aware there was anything beyond the jutting rocks, so much a part of the hillside did they seem. She got the sense a person could ride within ten feet of the entrance and never know it was there.

And then, as if the sudden result of a roving conjurer's trick, they were there, with a pretty green valley spread below them, and she knew it was Rafe's cherished ranch. And she knew why he seemed so wistful when he talked of it.

Rafe reined up, flanked by Cookie and Sue. No one spoke for long moments. Far into the distance, for the length of the valley and beyond, the Rocky Mountains rose high on both sides, reaching to a pale blue sky streaked with sparse white fingers of clouds.

The peaks, jagging and curving taller in some spots than others, gentled on their slopes before flowing outward along the valley, their purpled flanks creased like a rumpled blanket. A river bisected the lowest curve of the valley floor, silvering now and then as sunlight touched its flowing surface.

Rafe breathed in a deep breath of clean mountain air and said, "Okay, then." And he led the way down a long-unused switchback trail. The breeze they'd felt riding higher up was replaced with a lingering coolness, perfect on a high summer day.

Soon enough they came upon another rocky pile, this time a tumbledown of massive weathered boulders that appeared to block the narrow trail. Rafe slowed, then urged the horse forward straight at the boulders. Much to Sue's surprise, the big man and his horse disappeared, inch by inch, from view.

Sue was about to say something when Cookie, leading the packhorse, followed Rafe. At the last moment, he looked over his shoulder and jerked his head as if to say, "Come on, then."

And when Sue's horse carried her through the crevice, she faced open grassy ground, but unlike the earlier view from high above, she now overlooked a broad, lush meadow stretching below and away from the gentle rise atop which they sat. Ponderosa pine grew thick and tall around them and peppered the gentle slopes to both sides, thicker to their left. She rode up beside the two men.

"Looks about as I remember last time I was here," said Cookie.

Sue followed their gaze down toward a pretty swell off to their right, northwest of them, and saw burnt timbers and the remains of log walls jutting from tall grasses.

Before she could stop herself, Sue said, "Did they . . . was it the fire?"

Cookie cut her a sharp look, gave one quick head shake, but Rafe acted as if he hadn't heard and urged his horse into a trot. Down they went along the slope below, then up again atop the next, and that's when Cookie and Sue saw the reason Rafe had ridden ahead.

There was one building left whole, for the most part, and a thread of gray smoke made its slow journey upward from a solid little chimney anchoring one end of the low structure.

Rafe's jaw muscles flexed.

"Who on earth —" said Cookie, but Rafe was already in motion, setting his horse into a run downslope. Cookie shouted, "Hey!" after him, but the big man kept riding away from them and toward the smoking chimney.

"Damn fool's going to get that horse killed he comes on a chuckhole."

"Who's there, Cookie?" said Sue.

"No idea, but we'd best get on down there, too."

By the time they reached him, Rafe had made it to the structure. Up close it was a tidy, though much-abused building, the west end had suffered from burns at some point, but looked to have come through it well. The rest of the building, a log-and-plank affair, looked to have been well built and bore sign of recent repairs.

A pole ramada stood a few feet away from the house, brittle pine branches laid atop for shade. From one corner of the building, back behind the chimney, wash lines were strung to a pole with a T crosspiece. From the lines stirred faded blue, green, and red sleeves of shirts, a dress, an apron, and a number of other white items belonging to a woman. There were a few that might have been those of a man.

Both halves of a Dutch half door were closed. To its left, a thin curtain in a glass pane parted slightly, but no face appeared.

"Come out of there!"

The voice was big, almost a bellow, and if Sue and Cookie hadn't seen Rafe's mouth move in time with the words, they might not have guessed he spoke them.

He stood by his horse, hands resting lightly at his waist.

After what seemed like hours, a sound of sliding wood, then a quick metallic click, and the top of the Dutch door opened inward an inch or so.

The shadow of a face appeared in the dark of the crack. Rafe repeated his order, but with more restraint in his voice.

The door opened wider, then the business end of a shotgun, single barrel, slid forward on the bottom half of the door. "Who are you?"

It was a woman's voice, older, but firm, not tremulous or timid.

"That's my question," said Rafe.

"Rafe," said Cookie. "You got no call —"

"I know what you're going to say and I don't care."

Cookie let his hands drop to his sides, shook his head.

The voice from the house said, "I'll come out if you keep your hands in sight. All of you!"

Cookie and Sue held up their hands at shoulder height, but Rafe kept his hands on his waist. "Let's get to it," he said, not moving.

Another long moment passed before the person inside made a move. She slid a door bolt open and the rest of the door swung slowly inward. The shotgun barrel disappeared and reappeared, outlined against a white apron over a blue dress.

A face was the next to appear out of the shadows. "What do you want with me . . .

with us?" she said, gesturing behind her with a lift of her chin.

"What are you doing here?"

"What's it look like? Now, are you going to answer my question or not?" The woman raised the shotgun, trained it on Rafe's chest. She stood outside the door on a cobbled path, swept clean. "You . . . you own this place?"

"Not the point," said Rafe, folding his arms across his wide chest. "But from your answer I'd say you don't."

The woman's hard gaze slipped. She took a step forward and the afternoon sun lit her face, slants of shadow prevented the trio from getting a read of her age.

Cookie waved his hands. "Why don't you put down that gut shredder, ma'am. Ain't nothing going on here can't be solved with some friendly jawboning."

But she didn't lower the gun, nor did she take her eyes from Rafe for more than a quick glance at Cookie and Sue.

"How long have you been here?" said Rafe. "What are you doing here?"

"You sound as if you own the place." Her tone was softer, defeated.

Rafe sighed, and some of the indignant starch seemed to slip out of him. "I did."

"Still do," said Cookie.

It took a few seconds before his two simple words sunk in and puzzled the others.

"How's that?" said Rafe.

Now it was Cookie's turn to sigh. "Knew you'd give up on it when you . . . well, when everything happened." Cookie raised a finger in front of his face, pointed it at Rafe. "But I also know you love this place."

"But . . . how?"

Cookie shrugged. "Kept up with the bank payments whilst you were . . . away."

Rafe's face reddened, he looked at the ground before him, said nothing.

Silently the woman lowered the shotgun. "I'm Arlene. Arlene Tewksbury. You'll forgive me for taking precautions. It's been a while since I've seen anyone else here."

The odd silence continued and she said, "I'll need a little while to get my possessions together. I've a wagon, and two mules grazing yonder." She inclined her head beyond the remains of a barn, a crude corral had been pitched together beside it, and a water trough cobbled together in the same fashion.

Rafe cleared his throat. "No need for that. I'm the one who should apologize. It's been a long time since I was here. I never planned on coming back." He stalked off toward a thick copse of trees climbing a slope to the east of the charred skeleton of the house.

"Don't mind him, ma'am," said Cookie. "He's carrying a whole lot of freight. I ain't sure he ever will be himself again."

"What does a man like that have to worry about?"

"You'd be surprised, ma'am."

Later, Cookie, Sue, and the older woman gathered before the little shack that once had been Rafe's bunkhouse. It had housed the seasonal hands — and Cookie, when he was around.

Arlene, as she insisted they all refer to her, had them sit around a table she'd coerced Cookie into helping her bring outside. They set it up under the ramada, the branches providing slight shade for them as they got to know one another.

She heated cold biscuits and made coffee, served in a pretty set of china cups and saucers — a wedding gift, she told them. Cookie tried once to raise the entire affair to his lips, but rattled the cup and saucer so much it sounded like castanets.

Arlene laughed at him and retrieved a stoneware mug from the house, much to his relief. He slurped with gusto and tucked into the stack of biscuits, talking and dribbling crumbs on his chin, and didn't care a whit.

He chewed, marveling at the cooking talents of this woman from nowhere.

"I'm a widow," she said. "My husband was Ronald, Ronald Tewksbury. A good man with an incurable case of itchy feet." She half smiled, looked at Sue, then Cookie, who nodded and kept eating and slurping.

"We were on our way . . . West." She waved a hand in the general direction of the late afternoon sun. "Anywhere west of where we've ever been is where Ronald wanted to be. Anywhere different. I followed. Because I loved him."

Sue sniffed, wiped her eyes with the back of a hand.

"What's the matter?" said Cookie.

"Haven't you been listening?" she said.

"Yes, till you started blubberin'!"

Arlene pretended she hadn't heard, but kept on talking. It was as if she had wanted to tell her story to someone for a long time.

"We made it this far, somehow stumbled on this pretty place, and I thought maybe we could settle here, but Ronald wasn't satisfied, I could tell. Soon enough, none of that mattered. He came down with something. To this day I don't know what struck him, but it rolled in on him like a summer thunderstorm, and within days he was gone from me. I tried everything, but he took chills, then became feverish, wouldn't eat. It was all I could do to get water in him. At the end he was covered with red blotches."

Cookie stopped chewing and stared at her wide-eyed. He looked toward the house, then back.

"Don't worry. That was nearly two years ago."

"You've been here since?" said Sue. "All alone?"

Arlene nodded, sipped her coffee. "It's a lovely place to be. So peaceful. And not many people know it's here."

"What about supplies and such?" said Cookie.

"Oh, I've managed to stretch our savings. I rumble to Mullenberg now and again in my old wagon. My mules are still with me, though they are about as long in the tooth as I am."

"Oh, pish posh," said Cookie. "You ain't a day over . . ." His cheeks reddened. He shut his mouth and only opened it again to cram in more biscuit.

A few awkward moments passed, then Cookie began explaining their own story. He weighed his words carefully against what he felt Rafe wouldn't mind him telling.

Though with Rafe the way he was these days, Cookie wasn't sure of the big man's reaction to anything.

Arlene sat still, her hands wrapped around the now-cold cup of coffee. Some minutes after Cookie finished, they both heard a slight coughing sound and looked over to see Sue sitting upright, stiff as if holding her breath in terror. Her eyelids fluttered and her hands trembled more with each second.

"What on earth —" Arlene stood, unsure of what was happening.

Cookie scrambled around the end of the table. "Sue, Sue . . . aw, I thought we was past all this. Sue!" He held her shoulders, looked at her face, and all but shouted at her. "You got any more of the Quaker's tincture in your saddlebag?"

But Sue's tremors grew more violent, and her right arm thrashed outward, sending a cup and saucer to the ground, where each cracked into a dozen pieces.

"Arlene!" Cookie shouted. "I need you to hold onto her. I have to get her medicine."

"Yes, go!" she said. The older woman seemed to know what to do. She hugged Sue tight from behind, keeping clear of Sue's jerking head, and all the while spoke in a calm, firm voice, telling her she would be fine, that it would soon pass.

Cookie returned in moments. He uncorked the little bottle and with Arlene's help managed to get most of the last of the liquid into Sue's mouth. Long minutes passed when it seemed the girl's body thrashed with more power, a wild beast trying to break out of an unseen cage. Arlene held tighter than ever, speaking calmly to the girl, her own face a taut mask of resolution.

Cookie fidgeted a few feet away, his hands working open and closed by his sides. Then the girl's legs kicked the table leg and rattled the cups, threatening to upend them, and he grappled with the table and shifted it out of Sue's reach. Arlene offered him a slight smile of thanks that quickly faded as sobbing moans rose from Sue's clenched mouth.

Eventually the girl's violent spasms subsided to trembles, then evened out and stopped. She sagged backward into Arlene's arms.

"Help me get her to bed, Cookie."

They lugged the unconscious girl into the cabin, and laid her in the double bed in the little room at the west end. Cookie stood by the foot of the bed, looking down at her. "She'll be okay, I'm sure of it. Been down this road with her before. She'll be okay."

The worry Arlene saw on the man's face was anything but reassuring.

"Is there anything I should know, Cookie?"

"No, no. She's had a rough run of it is all. Bad times." He looked at her. "It's not my place, Miss Tewksbury. Keep her comfortable, she'll come around." He stalked quickly out of the room.

A few seconds later, Arlene heard the cups rattle lightly outside and she knew he was cleaning up. Arlene smiled. An odd man is that one, she thought, then turned her attention to dabbing the sleeping girl's sweat-stippled brow.

"What in the world ever happened to you, girl. You're too thin," whispered Arlene. "We need to get you healthy. Whatever happened before, Arlene's here now."

A couple of hours later, Cookie saw Arlene step outside the little house and hug her arms about herself in the late day's sun. He hustled over from the trees where he'd picketed the horses. "Sue okay?"

The woman nodded, offering a reassuring smile. "She's sleeping soundly now."

"I reckon I should have told you —"

"She explained it all to me."

Cookie narrowed his eyes and regarded her. "She's a good one, you know. A good girl there."

Arlene stiffened as if he'd insulted her. "I know that. I try not to judge people, Cookie McGee."

He felt his face heat up, words bounced around his mouth like pebbles, though nothing but silly sounds came out.

Arlene patted his arm. "I'm glad to see she has a champion in you, Mr. McGee."

Cookie nodded. "You betcha. Rafe, too."

Her smiled faded. "Yes, well. I thought I'd make stew." With that, Arlene turned and went back into the little house.

Cookie's bushy eyebrows came together. "Huh, okay then," he said, scratching his chin whiskers as he walked away, wondering what it was he said that changed the woman's tone. He was forever receiving that sort of reaction from womenfolk. Must be why he rode alone for so long.

Rafe came back as Arlene set the stewpot and fresh biscuits on the table.

"Hoping you'd make it back for grub, Rafe." Cookie leaned close to him. "You got to try them biscuits. Best I ever ate, I swear it."

Rafe smiled stiffly, nodded to the woman.

"Very kind of you, ma'am." He rested a hand on the back of a chair, then noticed there were only three plates. "Where's Sue?" He looked at Cookie.

"She's asleep inside, Rafe. Had herself another spell."

"Oh, no." Rafe walked around the table, then inside. He stopped in the doorway and looked at the ground. "Ma'am?"

Arlene realized he was asking her permission to enter the little abode. "Of course, of course, Mr. Barr. She's in the bed —"

But Rafe was already inside.

Cookie and Arlene sat across from each other, not eating, not saying anything. After a minute, Rafe came back out.

"She's sleeping," he said, and looked at Arlene. "Thank you."

Arlene offered a weak smile and dished out stew. "Help yourself to the biscuits."

The meal was a long, quiet one. If it hadn't been so tasty, Cookie felt sure he was going to burst from all the words no one was saying.

He could take no more and he jumped up and cleared the table, taking care to haul in the plates gently, lest he break them. When he came back out, he looked at them. "Confound it . . . I reckon I'll tend the horses." Before either could speak, he

330

stalked off into the dark.

Rafe stood, walked to the edge of the oil lamp's low glow.

"You . . . ," said Rafe. He folded his arms across his chest and bit his lip. He looked at her and started over. "You tended the grave?"

"Of course," she said, moving to the end of the table, a few feet from him. "It was overgrown, needed prettying up. I only did what I hope someone will do for me one day." Then she took a step away from him, her eyes wide. "I hope me burying Ronald up there didn't offend you."

Rafe looked at her for a long moment, unsmiling. Then his features softened. "Of course not. It's my wife and son . . . together. I think they'd be glad of the company."

They were quiet for a long while, each in their own thoughts. Arlene sighed. "I will be leaving this place in the morning. It's not right that I stay, now that you're here. And besides, I have places to see."

"Mrs. Tewksbury, I can tell you like this place as much as I do. Maybe more. You don't mind me saying so, you're rooted here, and that's as it should be. The place has that sort of hold on people."

She began to speak, but he beat her to it.

"We'd all be honored if you'd stay on, Mrs. Tewksbury. It's as much your place as ours."

His voice grew quiet and he stared out into the night. "Besides, you've as much reason as I do to stay around." He nodded in the dark toward the spot where the graves stood.

When she spoke, her voice was thin, controlled. "I don't know what to say, Mr. Barr."

"Say you'll stay on. Consider this your home for as long as you like. Besides" — he turned to her, smiling — "if we're going to round up all those wild beeves I hope are still roaming the hills, and build up this ranch again, we sure could use someone who can cook as good as you can."

From the dark to their right, Cookie's voice chimed in. "If you don't say yes, Miss Tewskbury, why, I don't know what we'll do. I can't live with the thought of not having biscuits like them again, I tell you."

"Cookie McGee," she said, beaming. "You are a piece of work."

"Why thank you, ma'am. I think."

"One last thing," said Rafe, holding out his hand. "It's Rafe, not Mr. Barr."

"Fair enough, Rafe," she said, muckling onto his mitt with a fair grip of her own. "And I'm Arlene. None of this 'Mrs.

Tewskbury' business."

Two chilly nights later found Cookie and Rafe seated on stumps around a fine fire, encamped as they were off the east end of the bunkhouse. Arlene's wagon stood close by, and they used it to lay their gear in.

"Tried to see you, Rafe. Went down to Yuma three times, but those rascals never let me in. Might not have helped that the second time I lit into 'em. One fella, a burly brute with more pig-eyed mean about him than any man alive, looked like he wanted to twist my head off and guzzle my gizzards for breakfast."

"That would be Feeney. The warden's pet. Good job you didn't tangle with him. He's a bad apple. You read him right." Rafe was silent a moment, then said, "Cook?"

"Yeah."

"I'm obliged."

"Any man would want to visit a chum in prison."

"No, not just for that. For everything," said Rafe. "And that makes us partners."

"Always have been, I reckon," said Cookie.

"No, I mean business partners. You and me, we own this ranch together. Fifty-fifty."

"What?" Cookie stiffened. "Rafe, that ain't why I —"

The big man held up a hand. "I know that, but it's the way it has to be. The way it should be. It's that way or no way at all."

Each man stared into the coals, then Cookie cleared his throat. "Rafe, I'll tell you something," he said softly. "We've been chums for a long time, right? And right or wrong I've always thought of you as my pard. Truth be told, I'm enough years older than you to think of you as something like a son."

He nodded, not looking at Rafe. "Yes, sir, a son I could have had if I'd have settled down all them years ago and not had such a wild hair about jumping in the thick of the action."

"That's about the nicest thing you've ever said to me, Cookie. I appreciate it more than you know."

"Don't go getting all swell-headed. I can still give you a lickin' with both hands tied behind me, no mistake."

"And you're still as old as dirt . . . old man."

They both smiled and stared into the pulsing coals.

"I walk up and you're both busy lobbing insults at each other. And yet you're still smiling? As long as I live I will never understand men." Arlene set down a tin plate between them. Cookie lifted a corner of the linen towel to reveal a steaming stack of buttered biscuits.

"Hoo-doggy, Miss Tewskbury, but you beat all. I was telling myself earlier, 'Cookie' I said. I call myself by my name. 'Cookie, you need to whip up a batch of biscuits.' But that's where the dream ended, see because I can't make a biscuit to save my backside." He wrapped a gnarled hand around the topmost fluffy creation and jammed it into his mouth. "But you can, Miss Tewksbury. By God, you can make a biscuit."

Rafe smiled and lifted a biscuit from the stack. "I think he likes them, ma'am. Thank you."

The stout woman rested her work-reddened hands on her wide hips. "You're welcome. But I tell you, we need to stop with this 'Mrs Tewksbury' and 'ma'am' business. I am Arlene, first, last, and forever. Been Arlene long before I was a Tewksbury. Now, how's the coffee situation? As I recall, men seem to need a powerful lot of coffee when they're sitting around conspiring and confabulating."

Cookie's mouth, full of his second biscuit, fell open. "I ain't never conf— conbal— whatever it is you said, I ain't never done that in my life!"

Rafe snorted a laugh. "Cookie, you have confabulated more than any man alive."

"What?" Cookie lowered his head and whispered, "Rafe, you don't tell such secrets in front of a lady."

"It means to talk, maybe have a conversation. You're the only person I know of who will hold a conversation with himself if there's no other ear around to bend."

Arlene turned to leave, then said, "In my experience, you meet a better class of person when you chat with yourself. Good night, gentlemen."

"Good night, Mrs. . . . ah, Arlene."

"Good night, ma'am."

After she left, Cookie leaned over, cuffed Rafe on the knee. "You hear that? She talks to herself, too." He looked toward the bunkhouse, a dim candle glow in the window. "She's something, is that one."

Rafe plucked another biscuit from the plate. "You best be careful, Cook."

"What? Why?"

"I can't bear the thought of her running off on us."

"Why would she do that?"

"You know how moon-eyed you get when you're in love. Liable to frighten the poor woman."

"Love! What in tarna—"

"Shhh, you're also liable to spook the cattle."

"What cattle? Rafe Barr, you are making less sense with each day that passes."

Imitating his chum, Rafe tapped a finger against his nose and nodded knowingly.

CHAPTER 26:
THAT BOY AIN'T RIGHT

"Kid. Hey, Kid!" El Jefe stretched his brawny arms wide and yawned like a bear, low and long. He scuffed over to the beanpole half-breed. "You're taking too long with that rabbit. Gut it out and cut it up."

The Kid eyed him briefly, then looked back to his task.

"What you doing, anyway?" El Jefe looked over the Kid's shoulder and almost wished he hadn't. The youth's long, bony brown fingers were gloved in red, as if painted. They probed the innards of the dead animal, picking and pulling at the small coils of glistening gut.

He held the heart and lungs on his left palm and palpated them gently with his thumb, then mashed down hard and black-red juice leaked out, spraying the Kid's shirt front. Before he turned away, the gang leader noticed the animal's eyeballs were gone, but not plucked out. They'd been squashed deep into the critter's tiny skull.

El Jefe stared back at the camp, biting back the bubble rising in his gorge to gag and cough up whatever was in his own gut. "Is this what you do every time I ask you to make stew?"

The Kid nodded, said nothing, his lean face unreadable. Long ago El Jefe had given up on trying to figure out what the boy was thinking. He figured it was the Apache in him. But over the past three or four months the Kid's quiet behavior had become more troubling.

It was as if they had a slow, quiet sidewinder in camp, flicking its tongue and staring each of the men down, El Jefe included, but never biting anyone. It was unnerving.

"You know that's not right, don't you? Killing an animal for food is good, but you don't make some game out of it, eh?"

The Kid regarded him, a sweat droplet quivering at the end of his long, beaky bent nose, sparse black hairs of moustache and beard curling above his lip and on his bony chin. Eventually he nodded his head even as his fingers groped and fondled the sticky red mess, now abuzz with flies.

El Jefe set his teeth tight and turned away.

"What about killing men?" The Kid's voice was a high-pitched, gravelly whisper.

El Jefe stopped. "Eh?"

But the Kid didn't repeat himself.

"Make the stew. Those idiots whimper like old toothless women if they don't get their food, and I don't want to hear it no more." El Jefe stalked off, knowing he himself would not eat a single bite the rest of the day.

At one time he had had thoughts that the Kid would be something more to him, something like a son, but now the skinny snake of a boy was too odd, too worrisome. He would have to deal with him. And that was something he could ask no one else to do.

The filthy little scene he had witnessed reminded him of a creature he himself had killed as a boy. That slow, relaxing death the frog had gone through when he'd pierced it through the head with a long mesquite thorn.

He'd held tight around the body to keep it still while he stabbed. Still it thrashed and writhed, even after the needle-like barb had punctured its head. The worst and best part had been the sounds the frog had made, tiny bubbly yelps. Frog screams, he had told himself. That's what a frog sounds like when it screams.

It had been the first life El Jefe had ever

taken, that he was aware of, anyway. He was a boy then, but he still remembered how he felt all those years ago. He remembered looking at the frog as it died, twitching its little arms and legs, its white belly upturned, its hands and legs like a person's.

But that was different, he told himself. The Kid was much older now than he had been. The Kid would not outgrow this ritual he did now. Had the boy always been this way?

El Jefe strode among the other men. He smacked his meaty brown hands together. "If I can get you old ladies to ride harder than you have been, we will catch up with those foul dogs tomorrow. Then we will teach them three lessons, one bullet each. That will be that. I should have done so when we first met them, but I was being nice to you fools, giving you more playmates. Now look what I get for my troubles."

CHAPTER 27:
SOMETHING'S OUT THERE

A couple of weeks after their arrival at the ranch, Cookie woke in the night to a rustling sound close by. Keeping low, he spun on his backside on the straw-ticked mattress he'd fixed up for himself. "Rafe?" he whispered.

"Here. By the wagon."

"What's doing?"

"Heard something."

Cookie knew Rafe wouldn't be referring to a stray coyote prowling the ranch yard. Then Cookie heard it, too. "There," he whispered, pointing in the dark, though neither of them could see his hand. A scuffing sound, closer. Cookie knee-walked over to Rafe, strapping on his knife.

Rafe knelt by the front wheel of the work wagon, staring into the dark, a Colt poised in his right hand. He wore a loosely buttoned shirt and his trousers, as was his habit, since the ladies slept close in the bunkhouse.

They heard the unmistakable *tink* of steel on stone.

"Horse," whispered Rafe.

"With a rider," finished Cookie.

Rafe nodded, straining to see into the near dark.

"There," said Cookie again.

They saw a dim shape pass ghostlike by the low line of juniper loosely encircling the outer edge of the ranch yard. Gone again. And there . . .

They heard one of their own horses whicker from the corral.

Rafe sat down and snatched up a boot, tugged it on, then the other.

"Where you going?"

"Where do you think?"

"Wait for me."

"Take care of the women, in case."

Cookie began to protest but held his tongue. He knew Rafe was right.

The sound of footsteps came close out of the dark behind them. "We don't need taking care of," came a whispered voice. It was Arlene and her shotgun, with Sue close behind.

"What's happening?" she said. "We heard you whispering."

Rafe nodded. "Cookie can't keep quiet." With that he was gone, catfooting into the dark toward where they saw the shape walking.

Cookie sighed. "Heard a noise out yonder. Sounded like a horse with a rider."

"How can you tell?" said Sue.

Cookie touched his nose as if that would explain everything. "Now shush. You heard the man. Oh heck's bells, I can't sit here. You two ladies stay put while I protect that boy's foolhardy hide."

Cookie low-walked off after Rafe, his boots making a soft clumping sound in the dirt. In the moonlight, the women saw the faded pink of his longhandles long after the sound of his boots faded.

Not far off in the night they heard a scuffling, then Rafe's voice commanding a horse. "Whoa, whoa now." He soon came into view, holding a horse's reins tight to the bit. Cookie flanked the beast, steadying something on the horse's back. Or someone.

"Sue, please fire up some light for us," said the big man. "And the stove. We have a man here who needs doctoring."

"Or an undertaker," said Cookie.

"Oh my stars," said Arlene, handing the shotgun to Sue.

The younger woman cradled the heavy weapon as she hurried to the house. She returned with an oil lamp, struck a match, and raised the lamp's bail.

"Slide him down, easy now, easy," said Rafe.

"Don't you think I know that?" said Cookie. "I been tending to busted up cowpokes longer than . . ."

"Time enough for grousing later, Cook," said Rafe, the only one of the group moving slow and sure. "He's alive. Please hold the lamp close, Sue."

She moved the light from boots to head over the man, who they'd laid out on the hardpack walkway to the bunkhouse.

"Yes, he's taken a beating all right, plenty of cuts, but I don't see bullet wounds."

"Oh my word," said Sue, with a gasp.

And Rafe and Cookie knew why at the same time.

"Jack Smith."

"You know this man?" said Arlene absently, not waiting for an answer, her hands already tearing strips from the bottom of her nightgown. "Here," she handed a long strip to Cookie. "Cut that into two-foot lengths."

"But it's your bed clothes," he said, gulping and looking at the cloth in his hand as if it might coil and bite.

"It's old, due for the ragbag anyway," she said. "Now get busy, Cookie." Arlene dabbed at the unconscious man's bloodied face. "This blood is dry. Sue, please poke the fire to life. We'll need plenty of hot water. Rafe, Cookie please bring him inside, lay him on the table. Help me with his clothes."

Rafe nodded, bending to gently scoop up the man. "It's been a while since he's been beaten. Days, maybe." He walked backward toward the open door. "How on earth did he know to find us?"

Cookie said nothing as he jockeyed the man's legs through the door. Rafe noticed. He noticed everything.

The men helped shuck off Jack's boots, tried to ease off his once-fine trousers.

"No time for niceties," said Arlene. "Slit them up the side. We have to get him undressed, see what we're faced with."

That's when the man moaned, followed it with a low mumble. Rafe bent over him. "What's that you say, Jack?"

Again the man mumbled something, moved his head slowly from side to side, wincing, bloodied, swollen eyelids twitching.

"I believe he said, 'No.' "

"You're among friends, Jack. You'll be fine now."

"No, no . . . pants."

346

"Are you joshing me, fella's all stove in and he's worried about his dandy-man trousers?"

"I'll sew them up good as new," said Arlene, gripping the fabric on each side of the slit she'd made, tearing the trouser leg. Jack yelped as if he were being skinned alive.

"Oh, simmer down," she said.

Though her words were tough, Rafe saw that she worked as gently as possible.

"Hard to believe it's them trousers he's whimpering about."

"Cookie." Arlene's tone was harsh. "Make yourself useful and fetch my sewing basket from beside the chair by the window. I'll have to sew those gashes on his head and side. Another on his arm."

He set up a low level of mumbling himself, a couple of words — "bossy woman" — were recognizable. Arlene smirked at Rafe.

Cookie set the basket by her on the table. "Anything else I can do for you, ma'am?"

"Yes," said Arlene. "I do wish you'd pull on a pair of britches. Your backside in those long johns is all but bare and not conducive to doctoring a sick man."

Cookie reddened, stammered, ended up saying nothing, and stalked out into the night, his boots clumping across the dooryard.

It took Arlene half an hour before she tossed a wad of bloody rags into a bucket on the floor. She pulled Rafe and Sue to one side. "That's all I can do. I can pretty much tend to anything on the outside, but if a body is bleeding somehow inside." She patted her middle. "In here. Then I have no notion of what to do."

"You think he's bleeding inside?"

"Hard to tell. Best we can do is watch him for a few days."

"Is that all we can do?" said Sue, her arms folded across her chest.

Rafe nodded. "We'll see how he fares. If he doesn't get better, we'll get a doctor."

"Out here?" Cookie reappeared, fully dressed and readying a pot of coffee. "Well, Mullenberg might have a pill roller at that."

Rafe looked down at the wounded man, now swaddled in bandages and looking to be sleeping peaceably. "I'd say he never even made it to Kansas City."

"Ambushed along the way?" said Cookie.

"He is one amazing tracker to find us here," said Sue, no sarcasm in her voice.

"Yeah," said Rafe, looking at Cookie. "Amazing."

CHAPTER 28:
CLEAR AS MUD

"What I want to know," Rafe cocked an eye at Cookie as they lathered up at the washstand Arlene insisted they use before she'd feed them. "Is how Jack Smith found this place."

Cookie used the soap on his face as an excuse not to look at Rafe. "Oh, you know them gamblin' dandies. Shrewd as all get out. Might be as Sue said, might be Jack's an expert tracker." He ran a clean scrap of sacking over his sunburned face.

"Might also be that someone gave him directions."

"Well, what would you have done? He's a good kid, needs a guiding hand is all."

"So you told him how to get here, should he ever find himself riding in the middle of rangeland in southern Colorado Territory, huh?"

"Something like that. Might be a map changed hands." Cookie grinned and smoothed his sparse silver hair against the sides of his head.

"Uh-huh." Rafe shook his head, then looking quickly around him, shucked his long-handle shirt, and began washing his wide, sweaty torso.

From behind, he and Cookie heard a gasp. Rafe spun to see Sue staring wide-eyed at him, a hand covering her mouth.

He snatched up his chambray workshirt and tugged it on. "What are you doing sneaking around here?"

The surprise in the girl's eyes turned to anger. She set her jaw. "I was not sneaking around. I came to tell you supper's on the table." But instead of turning back to the shack, she crossed her arms.

Rafe sighed. "Prison."

"What?" she said.

"Yuma," said Rafe. "The scars on my back came from there. I was in prison. That's what you want to know, isn't it?"

Her face reddened, and she nodded.

"You know what prison is, don't you?" Rafe continued, his eyes narrowed, his words tight and stabbing.

Cookie laid a hand on his arm, but he shrugged it off and walked toward Sue. Her eyes widened but she stood still.

"It's a place where people who've done

350

stupid things for a long time go when all their stupidity finally catches up with them. Then you earn yourself scars, one for each stupid thing you've done. Been working on a set for yourself, eh, girl?"

She stared up at him, her eyes glistening, her jaw set firm. Finally she turned and walked off toward the green hills behind the spot they'd laid out for the new cabin.

Rafe didn't watch her go. He looked at the hard-packed, dry earth, his big hands flexing and unflexing. He lifted a cigar from his shirt pocket and lit it.

"None of us is perfect, Rafe." Cookie's voice was low, his gaze stern.

"I know that," Rafe bellowed, his voice hoarse. "Hell, don't you think I know that?" The big man stalked toward the trees, his cigar sending blue plumes behind him like a belching stack on a locomotive.

Cookie wandered down to the bunkhouse to find the outdoor table under the ramada all set for the nightly feed. He rubbed his little belly and smacked his lips. Arlene bustled out of the house, her face shining red, gray-brown hair wisping in stray strands as she carried food to the table.

"Where is everyone?"

"Oh, Rafe and Sue got in a tussle, each of them stamped off in different directions.

Looks like it's you and me, Miss Tewksbury. That is, unless Jack is fit enough to get up out of that bed."

"No, that boy needs to heal up a few more days yet. I already fed him and he's sleeping like a child."

"I wish he'd hurry up with all this healing. We could use the help."

Arlene ignored his comment and set down a steaming platter of thick-cut fried potatoes and slabbed venison.

"Rafe's been almighty tense of late." Cookie ran a hand over his stubbled chin.

"That's because he's afraid."

Without taking his eyes from the steaming food, Cookie said, "Rafe? Afraid? Ha, shows what you know. Man don't know the meaning of the word."

"Shows what you know," said Arlene, smirking as she parroted him. "He's afraid of Sue."

"What? Now why would he be . . . ohhh." Cookie looked off toward the treeline, then in the opposite direction toward the hill behind the laid-out foundation of the house. "Huh. You think?"

"Plain as that last hair on your head, Cookie McGee." She winked at him.

CHAPTER 29:
COMETH THE HEALER

The buckboard rumbled up, squawking and slowing. Cookie stood braced against the spring seat, tugging on the lines to bring the two stamping mules to a halt.

Rafe hung the bow saw on an arm of the sawbuck and walked on over. "You made good time. Thought it might take three days, here you are in two." He gripped the edge of the laden wagon and looked in. "You buy out the entire mercantile?"

"Ha, just about." Cookie set the brake, looped the lines, and jumped down, groaning as he landed. He straightened with a grimace. "This wagon business ain't good for a man's constitution."

"You'd rather carry all this on your back?"

"Not a prayer of that happening, wiseacre."

Rafe perused the carefully packed crates, various-size sacks bulging with meal and flour, and oddly shaped, canvas-wrapped

353

items. He also noticed a few softer-looking packages carefully wrapped in brown paper and tied in string he'd squirreled up front. "What's in those?"

"You never mind. Some bits in life ain't your business, you know."

Rafe saw the rosy hue of blush creep up from the man's collar and decided to let that sleeping dog well enough alone. Then a sort of snoring sound greeted him. Cookie looked at him, eyes wide.

"Cook . . . what's that noise?" Rafe didn't wait for an answer but leaned deeper into the wagon, shifting sacks and kegs and boxes. Soon he saw a knee clad in black serge trousers, then the rest of the leg, north and south of the knee. It twitched.

"Cook?"

"Yeah?"

"Who's that?"

"Oh him? Oh, well . . ." Cookie crossed his arms. "Whilst I was in town I figured I should see about finding a doctor to see what's ailing Jack. We talked about it, remember?"

"Well, that's true. But Jack's getting better every day. I didn't think you needed to bring one back here. Maybe make a few inquiries."

"Well, now, I did that. Come to find out, the one and only doctor in this patch of country is off on a mercy run somewhere north of town delivering the Hagstrom Twins' babies?"

"You mean . . . ?"

"That's right, them two little apple-face girls used to tag around with their folks at the get-togethers up on Duchesne Creek? They're all growed now, married off, and whelping babies of their own!"

Rafe whistled. "Now that's something."

"Ain't it, though." Cookie nodded.

"So, Cook?"

"Yeah."

A snore crawled up from somewhere in the depths of the wagon. A lone blowfly circled the spot.

"Who's this?"

"Oh, him. He's a doctor, too. Least that's what they said in Dead Eye's Saloon. You remember ol' Dead Eye, don't you? Anyway, found this fella out back. His name is Jones." Cookie seemed unimpressed, but looked as if he had more to say.

"Doctor Jones, then?" said Rafe, hoping for more information from his crotchety sidekick. The old buck had an infuriating way of withholding information for dramatic punch.

"I reckon. But he's more known by another name."

Rafe sighed. "And that would be?"

"Deathbed. They call him Deathbed Jones."

Rafe's eyebrows rose. "Now that is . . . an unusual name for a doctor. Dare I ask how he got it?"

Before Cookie could reply, a croaking voice from beneath sacks and crates in the wagon said, "Typhus."

Rafe and Cookie exchanged wide-eyed looks, and backed away from the wagon a step. Rafe said, "What's that you said?"

A rumbling, wet cough was followed by a rank, drawing nasal sound, then a mashed gray bowler emerged, shoving aside a sack of flour. Two bleary eyes peered out from beneath the sagged brim. A mouth opened in the midst of a doughy face bristling with salt-and-pepper whiskers. "Years back, in Dacotah Territory . . . there was . . . a typhus outbreak." His words came out as a whispered wheeze. "The entire settlement, save me and two others, became afflicted. Alas, I could not save them."

"That's how you come by that name, then," said Cookie.

Jones nodded. "One of the survivors lost his entire family. Alas, the poor wretch blamed me, spread the name."

There was a silence, then Rafe said,

"From what little I know of typhus, not much could have saved them."

"Perhaps, perhaps. I do not know anymore." Jones closed his eyes and slowly wagged his head.

"What happened to the other survivor?" said Cookie. "You said there was two, besides you."

Jones nodded shakily. "A half-breed girl. Kindly lass, helped us through the entire ordeal, never once spoke, let alone complain. Less than a month after we buried the last of the typhus victims, she was crushed to death by an ox that up and died in the traces. Fell smack dab on her."

"Oh, my word," said Cookie, his hand over his mouth. "Ain't that the way of life, though. Ain't it, Rafe? One minute you're curing ills, the next you're . . ."

"Dead. I think the word you're looking for is 'dead,' Cookie." Rafe studied the man in the wagon and chewed the inside of his lip.

"So you see, gentlemen." Jones pulled his arms free and clawed weakly about himself, trying to figure out how to emerge from the pile of goods. "I am not so much a doctor as a talisman of bad luck. You would do well to drag me back to where you found me."

Rafe eyed Cookie, but addressed the

357

forlorn doctor. "I expect we can at least furnish you with a meal and a . . . a place to clean up. Seeing as how you made the trip out here, we might ask you to take a look at a friend of ours. He's a bit under the weather."

"Oh, well," said the man, pushing feebly to his feet. "I do not know. I am not much of a hand at doctoring of late. But I suppose . . . say . . ." He rasped a shaking hand along his stubbly beard. "You gents wouldn't happen to have a sip of . . ." He looked hopefully at them through wet, hangdog eyes.

"Needin' you some hair of the dog, eh, Doc?" said Cookie, grinning.

"Yes, yes, that's it in a nutshell."

Rafe shook his head. "I'm sure Cookie can help you on that score. And while you're at it, why don't you help our guest here over to the shade tree. I'll talk with Mrs. Tewksbury, see if she can't set another place for dinner." He squinted up at the late afternoon sun. "I expect we're all peckish."

A short time later, with the new arrival seated at the table in the kitchen, Arlene made small talk, smiled at him, and made sure his water glass was filled. When her back was turned, Cookie splashed it with sneaked doses of white liquor. He also

358

helped himself to a few random nips.

The doctor's features had blossomed remarkably from clammy and pasty white to pink, and his weak demeanor was on its way to becoming hopeful, perhaps even chipper.

"Cookie," said Arlene, without turning from inducing mouthwatering aromas from her fry pan, "I'll thank you kindly to leave off the inebriants and make yourself useful. Doctor Jones here will require bathwater."

"What? What? Now it's bathwater I'm hauling?" Cookie looked from Rafe to Sue to Arlene to the doc.

"And keep your voice down," said the cook. "Jack is resting in the other room."

"What?"

Cookie's look of surprise made Sue snort and suppress a giggle. She grabbed a water pail and made for the door. "I'll help."

Doc Jones, his approaching grin now among the missing, said, "Oh, oh, please don't go to any trouble on my behalf."

Arlene spun from the stove, a massive wooden spoon wagging at him in counterpoint with her words. "Nonsense, Cookie can do it. He's forever telling me he's as strong as an ox. But learned man or no, I'll not have anyone smelling like a hog let loose in a distillery while he's in my kitchen." Her eyes cut to Rafe and she looked down, suddenly red.

Rafe nodded. "I have to agree, Doc," he said, leaning over and talking in a lowered tone. "You're a bit on the ripe side, and only a hot bath will cure it. I'm afraid Mrs. Tewksbury's word is law in her kitchen."

She glanced at him, smiled like a schoolgirl, and looked back to her stove.

"Come on, Cookie, let's get to it," said Rafe, rising from his chair and escorting the old rooster out the door before he said something that riled the place all over again.

Outside, a giggling Sue joined them. Cookie sputtered, but she threw an arm around his shoulders and chided him until he grinned.

CHAPTER 30:
LONER IN A CROWD

"That Jack, he sits a horse mighty well." Cookie watched the young man on his horse, loping along in the distance. "Still in rough shape, though. Small wonder, considering that beating he took. Said it wasn't nothin' new, more folks who don't like losin' at cards to a black man."

Rafe nodded.

"You notice no matter how much work he does, he ends up looking spiffed and pretty? I ain't never seen the like." Cookie shook his head in amazement.

"He is particular about his appearance. Can't fault a man for that."

Cookie nodded, then said, "You reckon he'll stick around?"

Rafe looked at his old chum. "I doubt it. Man has heat in his veins. That's from youth, certainly, but there's something more, something you and I won't likely get a handle on."

Cookie nodded. "It's that blamed war. Too much one way, not enough another. Afore you knew it, everywhere you went folks were in a kerfuffle."

"It was a volatile time. Still is."

"Got a good spot here, though. Safe for folks like Sue, you know, still sort of fragile-like. She's coming along, though. Gets to wear dresses again. I reckon Miss Tewks-bury's good for her."

"And vice versa."

"Yep, I imagine so," said Cookie.

"Even Doc's looking pinker every day."

"Yeah, that one."

"What's that mean?" said Rafe.

Cookie shrugged, said nothing.

"Ah," Rafe nodded. "Competition at the biscuit plate, eh?"

"Don't know what you're talking about." Cookie patted his pockets for his chaw. "You reckon any of them will stick here? You know, help us build up the place?"

Rafe suppressed a smile. "Why, Cookie it sounds to me as if you're gathering a right crowd to tend your needs in your dotage."

"What?"

"And while we're on the subject, that was a nice gesture, bringing the ladies those fine gifts from town. Arlene is mighty pleased with that nightgown and Sue with her hair comb."

A low groan came from Cookie. Rafe saw the redness on his friend's cheeks.

"Ain't no reason folks have to make such a ruckus," Cookie mumbled. "Ain't no reason at all. They was items I knew they could use, that's all. That's all there is to it."

Rafe fell silent, aware he'd toed over a line with Cookie. Best leave that topic alone, he decided, puffing on his cigar.

The two men were silent for long minutes. Rafe gazed toward the dug trench and stone foundation for the new ranch house. He was having a difficult time imagining how it would look.

"You thinking about Warden Timmons?" said Cookie, as if reading Rafe's mind.

"Yep, and Swearengen and whoever took everything from me five years ago. All of them, all the time."

"You ain't about to hightail on me, are you?" said Cookie.

Rafe took the cigar from his mouth. "You know me better than that, Cook. But when the time comes, I will deal with them all, one at a time. Man to man, me and them." He looked at Cookie. "Alone."

"As long as alone includes me." Cookie

crossed his arms. "And I ain't confabulatin' no more about it."

CHAPTER 31:
GIT UP AND GO!

"We have been chasing our own tails for nigh on three weeks now, gone clear down to Ogalalla and east to Kearney, then up and over again. I reckon we about circled those rascals." Carl stood shaking his head in disbelief, staring at the wide-open landscape behind them, and the bold mountain peaks before them.

"Unless they have vanished into the air we're breathing, why, we ought to be about on top of them." His speechifying winding down, Carl poured himself a second cup of coffee and blew across the top, even though the tin pot's handle was cool to the touch.

One of the other two men, Manny, watched him. "Why do you do that?"

"What?"

"Blow on your coffee that way."

"Could be hot."

"It has not been hot for a long time. The fire is nearly out and we are ready to leave."

The cowboy knocked back the coffee and rapped the cup on his knee, then stood. "Never pays to take chances."

"Is not that what we are doing out here?" Miguel picked at a frayed hole as round as a double eagle in his striped trousers.

"Aw, are you on about this again? I told you, you got to break some eggs you want to make yourself a tasty breakfast."

"There you go again, talking about things that don't make no sense!" Miguel rose, smacking the dust from his seat.

"Don't you want to catch up with them fellas that cost us our jobs?" Carl looked at both men in turn. Manny shrugged and Miguel looked away, squinting into the distance.

"It don't seem so important no more," said Manny, finally. "It was not a good job anyway. Those railroad men, they are — what is that word? — assholes."

"Hey, hey," said Miguel, pointing. "Riders. And I think I know who they are."

Carl and Manny both had learned in three years of riding the trail as a trio not to doubt Miguel's impressive knack for seeing great distances. It was a trait that helped sand smooth the burrs his whining raised.

Carl visored his eyes, though his hat brim did the job amply, and squinted, too. He saw nothing but nodded slowly. "Yeh, okay, then. Tell me who you think it is and we'll compare our thoughts."

Miguel rolled his eyes and made for his saddle. "It is that *diablo,* El Jefe, and his gang of killers."

Carl jumped over the nearly dead fire and scooped up his saddle, whacking the dusty red-and-black woven blanket against his leg. He followed his dancing horse until the animal simmered down. "No time to waste, boys!" he said. "That man ain't right in the head, and them that follow him are even more tetched. Let's git gone!"

CHAPTER 32:
TROUBLE, RIDING
IN LIKE THUNDER

A single, far-off gunshot echoed from the north like a distant handclap. Cookie, Rafe, and Jack, gaining more mobility with each day, paused in their labors and traded looks. Four quick shots volleyed from the same direction, the last giving off the rogue whining sound a bullet makes when it hits rock.

The men jumped down from the pile of logs that would one day be the house, and ran for the paddock where their horses grazed, strapping on gun belts as they jogged.

Rafe had no idea who'd made the shots, but Rafe doubted it was Sue or Arlene, as they were out of sight, but busy splitting shakes for the roof, and Doc was doing his best to help them. As if in response to the thought, the two women met the men as they rounded the corner of the bunkhouse.

"Who's shooting?" said Sue, visoring her eyes and looking northward.

"No idea," said Rafe, "but we aim to find out."

"All of you?"

"What do you mean by that?" said Cookie, but Rafe knew and looked at Jack.

"You aren't fit enough yet, Jack. Do yourself a favor. Stay here and" — he looked at Sue, who'd begun to scowl — "help hold down the fort. We'll be back directly. Likely it's a hunter after some of those antelope we saw yesterday along the flats above."

"Yeah, that's right. That's all it is," said Cookie, nodding with vigor.

Jack was about to pitch an argument when fresh gunfire volleyed and echoed, closer than before.

Rafe was already halfway to the corral, with Cookie and Jack on his heels. Jack ran with a hand to his still-bandaged side, but didn't slow. Each man saddled his horse, with Cookie helping Jack heave the bulky saddle up onto his horse's back. Soon the three were thundering out of the yard. They spread out, riding toward the mouth of the lane that wound its way through a mass of house-size boulders toward the top of the valley.

Rafe reached the top first, slid from his buckskin, and looped the reins around a sun-withered nub of juniper branch. He chose his footholds carefully but managed to send rocks caroming down the graveled slope.

"Watch what you're doing," growled Cookie from below.

"Shhh!" Rafe didn't bother turning around, but by the time Cookie scrambled up the slope beside him, Rafe had his Colt drawn and cocked. Jack came up last, noting their lowered, hatless heads.

Yards apart, the three men peered around wedges of fawn-and-pink-tinged sandstone, scanning for sign of a shooter.

"There," whispered Rafe not moving his head. But the others saw it, too. A man on horseback, then two more, riding hell-for-leather. The man in the lead rode in a switchback fashion, cutting left, then right, with erratic jerks of his reins. The two behind followed. As they watched, one of those two men yanked too hard and his horse went down fast, right shoulder sledging into the sparse green clumps of grass and sage studding the plateau.

Horse and rider rolled down, making a series of soft, smacking sounds, tumbling as if time had slowed. The legs of horse and rider arching up, then down. Finally they came to a stop, and the horse wasted no time in lurching to its feet. The man, however, didn't rise. His two companions didn't ride back for him.

The horse, with a slight limp, ambled off, reins dragging. It kept walking, not looking behind, as if confused but resolute in its intent to escape from the situation bubbling around it.

"What the . . . ?" But that was all Cookie uttered, for more than a half dozen horsemen rode up, cresting a rise before them, obviously following the first three. They howled and rode hard, rifles and revolvers snapping and popping in all directions.

"Doesn't appear to be an Indian among them," said Rafe. "Should have brought my spyglass."

"Don't need no spyglass to tell me that one out front is a angry-looking fella, got a Mexican look. But what sort of getup are they all wearing? Looks like more leather than you'd find on those turkeys who ride those duded-up parade-ground horses. Only not near so purty."

Rafe looked a while longer, then slid back down, and eyed Cookie and Jack. "Cook, those men giving chase, they're the ones who attacked us in the night. Remember? Before Deadwood."

"Oh, boy," said Cookie, his eyes widening. Before he could say more, Rafe said, "And those two being chased look familiar as well."

Cookie edged back up, squinting at the two advancing shapes. The crow's-feet around his eyes softened. "Oh, God, Rafe." He slid back down. "It's them that I worked with on the railroad. Carlton Wickerson, he's the blond-lookin' fella, and the other two, well, one now, since that tumble, he's either Manuel Romera or Miguel Juan-Carlos, can't see which is which from here. That Carl is a right talker. Full of beans half the time — if there's something I can't abide is a man who don't know when to shut his yapper. But them two Mexican fellas he rides with, good cowboys. I'll give them that. But none of them could hold a drop of their liquor."

"No," said Rafe. "But they sure as hell can hold a grudge."

Cookie grunted. "Looks like all our chickens are coming home to roost."

"What are you two on about?" said Jack.

"We'll explain later, Jack," said Rafe. "But I can tell you they aren't hunters or old friends."

Cookie looked at him. "And if they stay their course, they'll land in our laps, sure enough."

"That's why I'm going to divert them."

Cookie nodded.

"You know that trail that cuts over to the northwest?" said Rafe, gesturing with a nod. "That should keep them from finding the valley entrance."

"Then what?" said Cookie, bushy eyebrows arched in question.

"Don't know," said Rafe, snugging his Colt into its holster, looping the hammer. "I'll make it up as I go."

Their heads whipped around when a whoop followed a random shot that spanged off a rock not thirty feet from where they sat. It had been fired from one of the far-off band closing in. Cookie and Rafe spun, hugged gravel and slowly peered through the sandstone again.

They heard boots on gravel behind them and turned in time to see Jack Smith swinging up into his saddle, one hand clutched to his side, a grimace of tight-set teeth pulling his mahogany features into a mask of barely controlled pain.

"Jack! No!" barked Rafe, not daring to rise. But it was too late. The man's heels dug into the horse's barrel hard, drumming quick counter-rhythm to the horse's pounding hoofbeats as they angled downslope, then northwest.

"He's riding out to do what you was going to . . ."

"The fool's going to get himself shot to ribbons."

Cookie said nothing, but swallowed hard. "Yeah, but he wants to prove himself, I reckon. He's a good egg, that Jack."

"Stubborn, is what he is."

"You're one to talk," said Cookie.

For some moments they could only listen for the occasional echoed reports of Jack's horse's drumming hooves far below and to the northwest. The riders, the pursued and their pursuers, drew closer.

"Should we up and shoot 'em?" said Cookie.

"Can't do that, Cook. We don't really know their intention. And until we do, killing a man isn't right."

"Oh, pish posh. You think they're here for tea and biscuits?" Cookie's face reddened as he sighted in his rifle. "Ain't like I want to go and kill people for the fun of it. And you can bet your boots they're after us. Or at least me."

Then there was no time for talk, for the two men in the lead were a hundred yards from the boulder that marked the half-concealed curved entrance to the ranch valley. At that moment a bolting form shot up and over across from their right, pounding northeast. It was Black Jack Smith, and he rode low, hugging the Palouse's neck.

He bolted by the two men being chased, and shouted, "Follow me!" and though they looked startled and had been forced to slow up when he cut across their path, they reined after him with little hesitation.

Jack smiled and offered a two-fingered hat-brim salute as he rode by Rafe and Cookie, a mere forty yards away, pounding the earth and sending grass clods flying.

"Crazy bastard," said Rafe, but a slight grin played on his face. "But he has style, I'll give him that."

CHAPTER 33:
WHAT'S A MAN'S WORTH, ANYWAY?

Black Jack Smith wondered, not for the first or last time, what in the hell he thought he was doing. Here he was, a man who, since buying his freedom with hard-won gambling money, swore he would never, ever again be any man's down-at-the-mouth cur of a work dog. He was a man who had taken more beatings and still clawed his way back to life after each one.

And yet he was out in the middle of nowhere at all, his side not healed from the last brutal thumping he took. But here he was, bent low over a horse — he had to admit it was a fine beast — risking his nervous neck to save a handful of folks he hardly knew.

Now, that's no way to think, you ungrateful whelp, he told himself, letting a wry grin widen on his face. These folks are your friends — neck-saving friends, at that. And this is what you do for friends, right?

In this case his job was to provide a distraction, usher these fools from the path of hot flying lead, and at the same time draw them and their pursuers from the entrance to the ranch's twisty hidden lane. It still didn't make much sense to him. Best not think about it, he told himself. Treat it like a fine hand at the tables. Everybody's anted up and it's your turn, Jack. Dump your hand or raise the stakes.

He thundered up out of the rising wash to the northwest of the ranch road, the Palouse not yet laboring. Despite the whistling bullets, Jack mused that he truly did love to ride. Had he not been born into slavery, he might have been happy riding the range, working with cattle.

But then there was the other, his mistress, that fickle, heady queen known to him as Gambling, with a capital G. He loved the soft ruffling slap of shuffled pasteboards, the snap as they are set down in confidence on green baize. Then there's the blue haze of cigar and cigarette smoke, floating above the heads of intent players, men and women, too, as they carry on the sometimes-noble profession of gambling.

The clinking of chips, tiles, and glasses fill the air along with the forever-present murmur of gamblers, spiced with the breezy motions of perfumed ladies, more of them willing to bed with a man of his color than he had expected.

But it was the gamblers, his fellows, he had to keep an eye peeled for. Despite his impeccable, dandified clothes, they were unwilling to take him seriously until he tugged free his impressive wad of cash that he plunked down with as much reserve as he dared.

And he showed them, too, all those dandies he envied for so long. Now he was one of them, at least in his eyes. They didn't like it, having to share table space with a black man, but more often than not, money won out, the sniffing, drooling, desperate scratching need for it.

Jack liked what money could do for him, liked the clothes, the good liquor, fine cigars, and, whenever he could get it, usually through hefty bribes, a fine room in a hotel. But amassing cash for its own sake had never appealed to him. Life, as he knew, was fleeting.

He'd seen his parents both lose their lives. His father, whipped to stinging, bloody shreds, had died of his wounds. His mother, at the end all skin and bones, had succumbed to scarlet fever because she'd worked too hard and far beyond the point of exhaustion for people who didn't care about her, beat her for their amusement.

He had a sister, too, Evangeline, sweet young Evangeline, ripped from him and sold when his mama died. He'd been but a young boy then, and Evie even younger. Where was she now? Alive or dead? The lack of an answer was a hole in his chest that never filled, never healed over, collapsed anew with each sunrise and ached an ache of the ages in the small hours when no distractions were available.

So money was to be used for fun, for finery, and whenever possible, for humiliation of fat-faced white men who thought more of themselves than anything else in their lives.

The whine of a ricocheted shot yanked Jack from his seconds-long reverie. Nearly to the men. "Follow me! This way! Follow me!" He windmilled a long arm, beckoning the men, his white shirt snapping with the breeze the thundering horse whipped up.

Passing by them now — a white man in the lead, a Mexican close behind. The third had taken a tumble and his horse had cleared off, but the unlucky man had not risen from the dirt. Likely dead or winded. But Jack had no time to ponder the man's fate, for their pursuers were closing in, a mass of ugly men firing harder and faster as they pounded closer.

They wore heavy black leather vests, chaps, boots, dark hats, all clanking with conchos glinting and winking with hard points of sunlight. They reminded Jack of the eyes of serpents in the darkest hours, where tormenting dreams thrive.

"Ride hard! Let's go!" Jack shouted anything that came to mind, the grim truth of the situation zinging by his head, the smells of horse and sweat tingling his nostrils. There was the slick feel of his horse's hide beneath his palms as he hugged the beast low around the neck in a weak effort, he knew, to keep himself from earning a bloody hole in his ribcage or guts.

The other two men closed in on him, and he was thankful to see they flanked him. A quick glance to his left, and there was the hardscrabble, leathered gang thundering closer in a boil of dust. This glance also showed him the blond cowboy, sweat-stained tall-crown fawn hat now riding on the man's shoulders, tethered by a stampede strap across the man's throat.

The fool, thought Jack. Should have chosen the other side with the Mexican, put whatever he could between himself and the thundering trouble. Then everything changed — Jack's world slowed. He felt his horse tremble as if sledged from behind by some unseen force, some almighty hand slap.

The beast bucked, crow-hopped, bellowed horrible, drawn-out moans like nothing Jack had ever heard before. The blond cowboy and the Mexican shot past him, turning their heads slowly and looking back at him with widening eyes.

Jack lost his seat on the horse's back, arced up, reins whipped from his hands. There was air all around him now. There was the sky, no horizon, no grand ol' green hills, no peaks in the distance, no sandstone jutting proud and raw, blue forever, with drags of white cloud to break it up. And there was nothing he could think of to do about this odd situation.

Then Jack dropped fast, and time sped up. It was joined by a rattling chorus of harsh, punching, driving sounds once more. He slammed downward, felt his teeth rap together. Something inside his body felt as though it had busted into a million little pieces, more than all the double eagles he could imagine winning at the lap of his baize mistress.

A spray of grass and dirt feathered skyward, and Jack saw the last of his horse's somersaulted body hit, saw the wide neck slam, disappear in sage. From the angle he knew there was no recovery from such a tumble. The beast had been shot, most likely, then its speed collided with the pain and confusion it felt, and the Palouse's footing was lost somewhere in the tumult.

Dust spumed, clouding everything in sight.

CHAPTER 34:
WHAT ROUGH BEAST . . .

They heard the growls and shouts, drumming hooves and rapid, straining breaths of the horses, and the increased volley of gunfire from the pursuers who, Rafe now saw, numbered eight. He was certain of it now — they were the men who'd attacked them that night on the trail. They had the look of wolfish men, clad in black and howling and firing as if the end of time had come.

Cookie was right, they were wearing a god-awful combination of leather and chain and straps over their begrimed tunics. A few wore black chaps over loose-fitting peasant trousers tucked in all manner of footgear, from stovepipe to moccasin.

They thundered closer . . . closer . . . their outliers hammered to within a dozen yards of Rafe and Cookie's hidey-hole. They rode hard, pursuing their quarry without let up, finally angling northeastward after Jack and his two charges.

And then, in a fingersnap, it changed.

Cookie saw the shot that took down Jack's horse. Seconds later he watched as the swarm of black-clothed banditos swarmed the man. One of them slowed. The others whipped their horses onward toward the two escaped men.

The rider who'd eased up bent low and snatched at the fallen gambler. He missed, circled around, and clawed again. In seconds he'd found purchase in Jack's clothes and dragged the flopped black man along. Jack's legs bounced in the dust before the rider gave a heave, yanked Jack up, and flopped him across his saddle horn.

"No!" shouted Cookie as he watched, prairie-dogging too high and likely giving away his spot, as shots from the black riders still ripped the air. Cookie didn't care. Rafe's big hand rammed his shoulder, drove him back down.

"You can't help him that way, dammit."

"But they're taking Jack!" Cookie struggled under the big man's fist, balled in his shirt at the chest. "Let go of me, dang you!"

"Knock it off, Cook. We need a plan or we'll all end up dead."

The old man relaxed, nodded, and Rafe released him. "You think they killed him?"

"No, not yet. That fall might have. I never reckoned on this. We need more firepower, more repeaters, cartridges."

"Thought that was where you were headed. If you want, I'll go," said Cookie, easing back from the rim.

"No, I should. You . . ."

"I know, I'm too dang slow. I never could get the knack of high-speed riding. Git, go on. I'll be here and I won't do nothing foolish whilst you're gone."

"Promise?"

"I promise I won't risk Jack's neck, that's all. Now git gone — I can still see them. I'll wager they're making for that arroyo yonder. You know the one."

"Yep, and now that they know we're here, or someone is, they'll be back, sniffing."

"You reckon it's those ghouls who were on our trail from way back?"

"The first three looked like your old railroad cohorts. Those others, the banditos in black, they're the ones who attacked us that night."

"That warden fella sent 'em, didn't he?" Cookie grinned. "Well, we whupped 'em once, we can do it again, right?"

"Maybe. Could be we were lucky then. Or that fella in the lead was toying with us. Stay low."

"Either way, let's go." He chucked Cookie on the shoulder and, keeping low, bolted downslope. "Don't want to waste the lead he bought us."

Rafe slid down the slope, then mounted up, keeping low in the saddle, gave the old man a quick nod, then hammered it for home. Cookie glanced back once, saw his partner's dust trail, and spit once as he eyed the retreating backs of the black riders. Then he, too, eased away from the rim.

"What the hell do they want with us, anyway?" said Cookie to himself, though he knew what the men being chased wanted. That third man was surely dead, when that horse rolled him hard moments before. Had it been Manny or Miguel? Either way, the bitter taste of guilt rose up Cookie's gorge.

Plain and simple, they wanted revenge for Cookie and Rafe costing them their livelihoods. That revelation brought a grim nod to Cookie. He had to respect that sort of dogged pursuit. Even if it was stupid.

He'd dog the bandits, all right. And past the rendezvous point, too, if he needed to. Ain't no way was he going to sit safe and pretty and wait for Rafe to collect him like a tot. Rafe would just have to track him.

What Rafe didn't tell Cookie was that in

those seconds when the black-cloaked riders hammered by — seconds that seemed to stretch out like hours — one of the riders, a tall, thin form, more boy than man, riding on the outside edge of the pack, swiveled his head southward and stared for the briefest of moments into Rafe's eyes. Straight in.

It took a whole lot these days to chill the big man's marrow, but that gaunt youth's stare — those glinting dark eyes — had done it. He'd been caught out, and Rafe knew in that dead moment they should have laid them all out in an unexpected volley of lead from the concealment of the ridgetop, even as the leather-wearing gang thundered by. Knew it, but something stayed his hand. Something he knew he might well regret before long.

"Timmons," growled Rafe as he drummed his heels and slapped the reins. If he lived through this mess, Rafe knew he was going back to Yuma — this time on his own terms.

CHAPTER 35:
A TIME TO PLAY,
A TIME TO PAY

Jack came around — fuzzy noise bubbled together with blurry vision. A sound circled, something like birds, lots of birds, no, not birds, deeper sounding, like voices, voices of men, many men. And there they were black shapes, like huge vultures, flapping and shouting. What were they doing? Then one of them stepped aside. Jack's sight sharpened, and what he saw took on a sharper shape, and he wished it had not.

A thin groan escaped his lips. One of the men turned toward him and laughed. "Don't worry, you are next! Ha ha!"

The shape he'd seen was, like him, a man on the ground. But that's where much of it ended. He wasn't certain, but he thought it might have been the white cowboy who had followed him, then flanked him. But there was not much more to see that he could associate with that riding man.

The shape he saw now was a quivering,

bloodied wreck of a man, stripped down to his skin and covered in what looked like hundreds of thin cuts. The man was still alive, and kept trying to push himself backward along the bloody ground away from the men in black, but they shoved him back to the center of them with their boots.

Each time they did, he screamed. The noises he made were not those of any grown man Jack had ever heard. They were the sounds of a child, terrorized past any point of returning to something normal again. The bloody wreck was gone in the head, and likely in the body, too, he didn't know it yet.

As soon as the burly, scar-faced man turned back to the gruesome sport playing out at his feet, Jack tried his legs — they tensed. He flexed them, and lances of pain like blades of smithy-heated steel, seared upward, bloomed hot and angry deep in his gut, flashed up his spine. God, no, no, must be something's broken inside. Must be I'm a cripple. Thrown from a horse and into the midst of torturing killers.

This life, he thought. This life is a vicious, bastardly mess. And then he forced himself to think back on the best times of his days. Of the fine and intense games of chance seated around that fickle baize bitch, his temptress, his mistress, his goddess, and he smiled.

Good games they were, when bubble-filled wine flowed and women rubbed his shoulders and whispered in his ears and the men with whom he played those games no longer saw him as a brown-faced man with curly hair, but a man. A man who was in the midst of kicking their asses up and down and all around that green tabletop. Then taking their money for the pleasure of it all.

And Jack felt his hands clench, and he smiled and rammed them into the earth, found purchase and pushed. His throbbing, agonized body slid backward. He might be a cripple, he might be wearing dirty clothes with no crisp creases, no fine folded silk handkerchief, lavender in color, in his breast pocket . . . Yes, he might be a wreck of a man, he might never know what happened to his little sister . . . He might be a whole lot, but he was not going to give up this ghost without at least trying to fight, or flee, as the case may be.

He slid backward another six, eight inches. And again. And again — then his head bumped into something. He looked up.

Staring down at him from a ways up was a long, thin face with two eyes such as he'd not seen before. Eyes of a goat or a cat. No, no, they were plain black eyes. Like the eyes of something dead inside. Something dead that still saw everything, but showed nothing.

Once more Jack moaned and didn't know he'd done it. He tried again to scooch back with his hands. But the long face with the dead eyes shook slowly side to side. No, it was saying. No more.

And that's when the burly man with the scarred face walked over. He grinned down at him. "I have a few questions for you. And since you are an uninvited guest to my camp, I believe you should answer those questions, eh? That would be polite of you. Nod if you understand me."

Jack stared up at the man, said nothing. The man's cigarillo drooped. He puffed on it, issuing a series of blue-black clouds, then smiled again. "Okay, my friend."

With no warning, the man delivered a hard kick high up on Jack's ribcage. Jack felt something inside him snap and his breath wheezed out between his clenched teeth. At the same time he tried to draw in breath — it didn't work too well, and he ended up gagging. With each wrenching cough the pain dug its spurs deeper into his wrecked body.

"Hey! You wake up now and listen to me

or it's going to be so much badder for you, eh?"

Jack heard the voice and forced himself to focus on that leering face. Had to show the man he wasn't an easy kill. Never had been. He'd been through too much in his life to give up like anything but a man.

"That's better," said the homely man looking down at him. "Now, I think I seen sign of you before. Up north of that Platte River, eh?"

Jack tried to speak, tried to form spit, but all he could do was shake his head back and forth.

"No, no, no. Don't lie to me, black man." El Jefe kicked Jack's right boot hard. "I can track, too, you know. Oh yes, and these fancy boots of yours, they leave tracks like the one I saw some weeks ago, well north of here, like I said." El Jefe hunkered down and stared straight into Jack's eyes.

"Yes, yes, I see now that I am correct. You are that man. Then your tracks left the others, went away, you rode your way, they went theirs. So where are the others?"

Jack said nothing, tried to regain his breath before the next kick — or worse.

The burly Mexican stood and spread his arms wide. "They came to here! Somewhere out here. But I cannot find them. Not yet.

But now you are here. And I say to myself, 'El Jefe' — that's me — I say, 'Jefe, this man' " — he held up a warning finger, wagged it in the air — " 'this man with the flat-bottom boots, the boots of a dandy man, a gambler, a city man, he knows something, or else why would he be back here?' Yes? I think finding you today was a sign from God. It was God telling me we are on the right trail."

He bent low again. "Now," his voice uncurled like a snake, slid out of his mouth, curled around Jack's head, and slipped into his ears. "I think you should tell me where it is these men are now. I have a feeling they cannot be far, eh? Oh, and they will have a girl with them, too. But what am I saying — you know this already."

Jack stared up at the man, saying nothing. It's a game, Jack, my boy, he told himself. Nothing but a game of chance. And you know how that works — sometimes you win, sometimes . . .

"I tell you what," said El Jefe. "If I like what you say, you get a nice drink of cool water, eh?"

Jack looked at the man, made as if to speak, opened his mouth wider, whispered, "Closer."

El Jefe leaned in. "Yes?"

Jack smiled wide. "I fold."

The effect was not immediate, but it did amuse Jack to see El Jefe's face contort and bungle through the steps it took until the meaning of Jack's answer struck him.

"You bastard." El Jefe grunted upright, then bent again so quickly Jack barely had time to clench before the gruff gang leader's leather-gloved knuckles swiped hard, whipping Jack's head to one side.

No matter how many times I take a beating in this life, Jack thought, it will hurt and it will never get any easier. One of them, one day, will be the last one. As he looked up at the scowling Mexican's face, crimson in rage, it became eclipsed by a fast-descending blackness of boot sole straight at his face.

Today is it, Jack old boy. All in, all done.

CHAPTER 36:
BAD ODDS, BIG SMILE

Cookie made his way along the rim, carving his own trail along the tumbledowns, angling too damned slow for his taste toward that arroyo. He hoped they would be there, holed up and considering their next move. For a good quarter hour he picked his way closer, not yet daring to venture upslope and check his progress. He knew enough of the landscape to make a decent guess as to his progress. He looped reins over a jutting arm of stunty, wind-dried pine.

It took him another few minutes to make his way back up the rim, where he crouched, listening for stray sounds of gunfire, shouts, anything out of the ordinary. Nothing.

He couldn't stand hunkering down below the sandstone rim anymore. He risked a peek over the rim toward where he hoped the arroyo lay.

There was no warning as a bullet furrowed its way into the sandstone, spraying snags of rock into Cookie's face. "Gaah!" he howled, dropped down, and clawed at his cheeks. He wanted to swear a blue streak, howl flinty sparks that struck fear into the black hearts of the ravaging banditos, but it didn't work out that way.

Instead he stopped himself, feeling as if Rafe was still there, the reassuring weight of his big hand pressing him back down into safety and security. "Dang it, Rafe," he mumbled, drawing a blood-spattered hand away from his face. He blinked a few times to clear the sand from his eyes and checked his revolver. Good enough, but . . . then a smile spread wide on his face. "Got me a little friend, ain't I?"

He slicked out the slender paper-wrapped stick of dynamite, flicked up the protected nub of fuse from beneath its paper covering and then stopped, frowning. No way he could light this and give it a well-directed lob. What if he hit Jack? Was Jack even still alive?

"Oh hell." Cookie stuffed the stick back into its protective holster, closed the leather flap back over the top, and secured the thong. Now that he knew where the bandits were — or at least one of them — it was time to move. He'd get at them another way. No telling how long Rafe would be.

Cookie looked downslope. Half the rump of his old mustang showed from behind a boulder. The dumb animal was probably cropping rock. Cookie slid sideways, not sure what his next move was going to be, annoyed that his one relied-upon bit of fun was taken from him. He dearly wanted to toss a stick of something that might explode. As soon as he got confirmation that Jack was out of range, he was sure as hell going to light something and throw it.

"Hey, gringo!"

The call was a taunt to draw him out, he knew. But he sorely wanted to respond. Still, he held his tongue and kept moving sideways, sand sifting down between his un-tucked shirt and his belt. Teach him to be a skinny-loo all his life.

"Gringo! I'm talking to you! Nobody ignores El Jefe, eh?"

That did it. "Like hell! I'll ignore you if'n I want to."

He never got the rest of his thought voiced because a fusillade of lead rained at him from across the span of sage and grass. He slid low, raked his hands over his head, tug-ging his old, worn hat low, and cowered, hissing through his teeth as gravel and sand sprayed around him.

"Should know better. Hate it when Rafe's

right. Always telling me I'm hasty, take life slower, blah blah. Wasn't for Jack, I'd give them rascals a few notions to consider." Cookie continued crawling along the slope, keeping his head low enough, he hoped, so it wouldn't get shot off. Might be they would think they'd got him. If he could move over far enough he could wait them out. Surely they'd send over a man, maybe two, scout him out, see if they got him. He'd snipe them then. "Wish I was a better shot," he said in a mumble.

Beggars ain't choosers, though. He cranked back on the revolver's hammer and waited. Silence like he hadn't heard in a month of Sundays lowered over the plateau. They were waiting him out and he knew he had to do the same to them. At least until Rafe poked his mangy head up from some varmint hole.

Where was he, anyway? And what was his plan? Leave me out here to wither in the sun like an old chili pepper while he hoo-raahed it up with the ladies?

Cookie bit the thought off even as it tumbled out of his mind. That wasn't fair of him and he knew it. But neither was the prospect of getting his noggin shot off.

CHAPTER 37:
CIRCLE THE WAGONS!

Despite the raw, unexpected events peeling apart up on the rim, Rafe's heart snagged in his throat as he hammered into the yard. Sure, the sun was still a high, searing orb, half-blinding him, but he could have sworn he was seeing Maria standing before him at the hitch rail with her horse, tugging confidently on the cinch.

She stood tall and thin, so certain of everything with those quick movements. Her back was to him, men's trousers cut slim, still baggy in the seat, a pretty blouse with small blue flowers, and the back of her fawn beaver-felt hat.

But it wasn't Maria, never would be. The figure turned to face him, one hand visoring her eyes — it was Sue, of course, so alike and yet so different from his Maria.

Sue was nearly done saddling a solid roan mare with a willful edge that annoyed Rafe. But the girl was as worrisome and as pig-headed, so he had concluded when he'd given her the horse that they were a decent match.

He'd told Cookie to bring back a quiet, safe horse from town that the girl might ride. Cookie had told him he saw the beast at the livery and it reminded him of Sue.

"Did you find out what it was? Hunters?"

Rafe shook his head, slid out of the saddle as he loosened the girth, and hustling the horse to the trough for a drink. "No, worse," he said, scanning the yard. "Where are the others? And why are you saddling up?"

"I was going to look for you. Arlene's in the kitchen, and I saw Doc a while ago up at the cabin site, by the log pile, sleeping off a toot. He must have found one of Cookie's jugs."

Rafe shook his head as he hastily whipped the reins around the pump handle. "You're not going anywhere. We have trouble and I need you here. Jack took off hell-for-leather to —"

Sue cut him off. "What sort of trouble?"

"Follow me, I'll talk as we go." He strode for the storeroom off the back side of the bunkhouse. It was all Sue could do to keep up with the big man.

"I can't be sure but I think it's the men I told you about who jumped me and Cook before we got to Deadwood. They're likely the same ones who dogged us out of Deadwood and much of the way here."

"I didn't know anybody had followed us for certain."

"We didn't tell you," he said, though they both knew the real reason had more to do with the rank hold of the drugs in her system while on the journey.

"What can I do to help?"

He cranked open the padlock to the small storeroom and swung the door wide. It squawked on steel pin hinges. Inside rested a trove of implements and hand tools, from shovels and hoes to bucksaws and two scythes. And much more stood stacked under tarpaulins, crisscrossed with thin bands of light leaking in through gaps in the board siding.

Against the wall of the little makeshift house, tucked well back from any possible danger of the weather, stood a wood-and-steel-strap cabinet. Rafe unlocked it, slid the wrapping chain free, revealing six Henry repeating rifles, two shotguns, three revolvers, and two hefty wooden cases brimming with cartridges, enough brass to hold off a siege for days. Which is exactly what Rafe had had in mind when they laid in the store of goods.

Up on a table, double wrapped in canvas, four kegs of gunpowder stood at the ready for anything — or anyone, namely Cookie. Beside them, two cases of dynamite sticks, also double wrapped, stood poised for service.

"What's doing, folks?"

Sue and Rafe both spun at the voice from the doorway. It was Doc Jones.

Rafe strode up to him, taking the little potbellied man by surprise. He leaned close to the man's face, sniffed.

Jones sighed. "I'm not inebriated, if that's what you're wondering."

"But I saw you sleeping up by the log pile," said Sue.

"Yes, I'm sure you did. But that's only because I was up most of the night working on a . . . project."

Rafe nodded, turned back to rummaging in rapid-fire fashion in the gun cabinet. "What sort of project?" He handed various weapons out, without looking, into Sue's waiting hands.

"Oh," said Doc leaning against the doorframe. "Remember when I told you about my curiosity of the various minerals hereabouts —"

"Never mind," said Rafe. "Hold out your arms." He laid rifles and boxes of ammunition in them. When he'd finished he faced the two of them.

"After I leave, I want you three to ferry the rest of these crates and barrels and guns into the house. Anything that can be used to kill, maim, or blow up anything that isn't one of us. Tools included. Bring it all into the house and bolt the door from the inside. Don't open it for anyone unless it's me or Cookie."

"What about Jack?" said Doc.

Rafe ignored him and kept talking. "I should have done it before now, but I hadn't thought that far ahead." He snatched up a small hand axe, strode out and bade them follow him around the side of the building.

"Stay put. Cook and I have been through this sort of commotion before, too many times to count. We'll do our best to . . . deal with them. If we don't come back, do your own best. There's no other place for you to go right now that's safer than holing up right here." He patted the wall with a big hand. "You'll have a whole lot of firepower. Make the most of it."

"What do you mean if you don't come back?"

By that time they were in the kitchen and Arlene was dumping an armload of firewood in the woodbox beside the stove.

"No time," said Rafe, stuffing dynamite, cartridges, an extra repeater, and two revolvers into a canvas satchel with a shoulder strap. "Sue will catch you up." He walked to the door. "Sue, help me with the horse, will you?"

When they were outside, by the watering trough, Rafe handed her a small bundle wrapped in oilcloth. "Here."

"What is it?" she said, unfolding the dark cotton.

"It's called a pepperbox."

"I remember where that came from," she said, wrinkling her nose at the memory of the fat man in the dugout.

"Not important right now. It's a six-shot, see that barrel? Be careful with it. I had intended to show you how to use it safely before now, but there's no time. Keep it on you, plenty of shells here." He handed her a hundred-count carton. "It's only effective for close-in fighting. Last resort before a knife. But it's more deadly than it looks, so be careful with it."

"I can take care of myself, Rafe Barr, thank you very much."

Rafe said nothing, but stared at her, both of them knowing what she'd said was not true. At least not yet. Perhaps in time. But for now they both knew she was dependent on him and beholden to him for saving her from Swearengen, and from herself.

She looked up at him. "Oh." She jumped up on her toes, threw her arms wide around his neck, and hugged him tight, briefly. "Please be safe. I . . . can't . . ." She stepped back.

The big man nodded. "I know."

"This fight, it's about me, isn't it?"

He paused. "No, not just you." He looked eastward, toward the spot where Sue knew his wife and son were buried. "They were . . . killed. Murdered," he said, looking at her, "because of me, something I did years ago, maybe in the war. I was blamed. I don't know who was behind it, but somehow this is connected. Somehow, and I'll find out — I have to."

He hoisted himself up into the saddle. "Don't worry." He smiled. "And unsaddle that horse." He heeled his buckskin, then reined up, looked back at her. "Take care of those two in there — I'm counting on you, Sue."

Seconds later, horse and man — followed by a low cloud of dust — receded into the distance. Sue watched a moment more, then clutching the oilcloth-swaddled bundle to her chest with one hand and gathering her horse's reins in the other, she led the horse to the bunkhouse, confused but determined not to let Rafe down.

She planned to get the "old folks" settled and safe, then slip out and scout the perimeter — she would help Rafe and Cookie. It was the least she could do.

CHAPTER 38:
BULLETS ARE FOREVER

"Okay, okay. Enough with the beatings, idiots. We have more important matters to tend to. I am sure there is a ranch down there somewhere. During the hot sun of today I looked around and could not believe the pretty grazing land below us. Why, I might take up ranching, once I have liberated this place from the fools who don't know what they have."

"But first?"

El Jefe looked around the campfire. "Which one of you interrupted me? Which one said that?"

The Kid stood up. "I said it, El Jefe."

"You?" For a moment the boss let confusion trail across his face. "What is this? You joke with me at a time like this, eh?"

Unblinking, the Kid regarded El Jefe. Finally he spoke. "No jokes, El Jefe."

"What is this?" repeated the boss.

"It is time to go . . . eh?" said the Kid.

El Jefe's eyes narrowed. Before anyone else could move, let alone speak, El Jefe yanked free a Dragoon revolver and thumbed back the hammer. "You dare to mock me, boy? You are nothing." El Jefe's top lip arched high on one side of his mouth. His sneer was short-lived as he looked into those dark, blank eyes that didn't blink even as the pistol waved at him.

"Without me you would be a dead animal." El Jefe walked forward, doing his best to avoid looking straight into those vile eyes. When had the Kid become this way? Surely not always, for El Jefe would have noticed, wouldn't he?

The Kid stared right at him. "Who says I am not?"

"Diablo!" shouted one of the men, which one, El Jefe could not tell, nor did he care. For at that moment the Kid's black eyes widened and something that may have been a smile widened the youth's slit of a mouth. Then it slipped away again.

"Oh, God," said El Jefe. He nearly reached up to cross himself, but a greater fear won out and he tensed his left arm and squeezed the trigger. The revolver barked even as the Kid's arms whipped up to either side, as if he were mimicking flying. His eyes grew wider, and his mouth stretched top to bottom in a long, dark hollow of disbelief.

The shot, from such close range, lifted the Kid off his feet and spun him around, pivoting on one boot toe. He collapsed backward as if slammed by an invisible hand swatting him to the earth before dropping backward beside the smoking fire. He didn't move. His last breath stuttered out at the same time his eyes fluttered closed. His chest stopped moving.

No sound was heard for a minute or more. Then someone coughed, tried to cover it up, coughed again. That snapped the spell.

"Kid. Bah," said El Jefe, still standing with the revolver at his side, a last string of smoke curling upward from the barrel. "Leave them here," he growled, scanning the scene, taking in the still bodies of the yellow-haired gringo cowboy, the beaten, broken black man, and the Kid. "We ride down into that valley to get that girl. Then we leave. I have had enough of this place."

CHAPTER 39:
OF RESCUE AND REVENGE

Bleary eyed and suppressing the urge to let out a ripper of a yawn, Cookie McGee glanced up with furrowed bushy brows at the darkening sky. He'd intended to spring Jack from the grimy paws of the bandits, but they'd pinned him down, waited him out. He had to admit they were good at it. Whenever he'd made what he hoped was an unexpected move to confuse them, they'd been right there with a well-placed shot.

He had more damn rock splinters in his face than he could likely ever count in his life. And he had lost them. Didn't know how far they'd gotten away from him.

He had about decided to lob a stick or two of good ol' boom-boom when he heard a scuffing sound behind him. He spun, digging his bony backside even further into the gravel. And there was Rafe, lugging a shoulder satchel and making his way fast up the slope.

" 'Bout time," whispered Cookie.

Rafe regarded his partner's face. "Looks like you found them."

Cookie shook his head. "Had 'em, then lost 'em. Somewhere down that arroyo, I hope. They caught sight of me a ways back, pinned me down, sprayed me with rock. I kept trailing."

Rafe plunked the satchel down. "I brought a few supplies."

"Any biscuits?"

Rafe shook his head as he scanned the darkening landscape before him.

"Let's move," said Rafe, handing Cookie shells, a carbine, and three sticks of dynamite.

Cookie tucked the sticks into his shirt. "Ain't they pretty, though?"

They kept moving, walking the horses on the last stretch along a series of clefts that marked the eastern edge of the upper range, looking for sign, and for Jack.

Impatient, Rafe wanted to range it alone, said he could make better time that way, but Cookie insisted they take it together. He was concerned about Rafe, had to keep the lug on the trail and keep his mind off bulling in there and taking them on all by his own self.

Cookie knew what would happen — Rafe

would find the nest of backtrailing killers and open up on them, come what may. The man had never seemed so reckless in the past.

After an hour, and near dark, they'd found precious little to let them know they were on the right trail — or any trail at all — when Cookie held up a bony hand to hold Rafe back. "Smoke." Then he stuck up his nose, mimicking sniffing the air.

Rafe did the same, drawing in a silent breath. The breeze felt good on their sun-burned faces. Then they had a sure sign, right in the direction Cookie had seen them all ride. He'd been doubting himself for a while, though, as he had not expected those banditos to have ridden so far before setting up camp.

"What you think they want with Jack, anyway?" he whispered.

Rafe didn't answer.

Cookie looked at him, saw the big man jerk his chin ahead of them. Cookie followed the direction with his eyes and shaded by a low rock knob with sage clumping about it, sat a bulky shape, dark and unmoving. Cookie felt the light breeze on his face once again. Then his nose wrinkled and he nearly gagged.

The dark shape near them grunted and

they heard a god-awful series of low, splat-
tering sounds, only outdone by the stink
rolling their way on the cursed breeze. Then
the man groaned. He was emptying his
backside, and right upwind of them, too.
Before Cookie had a chance to whisper his
disgust, Rafe was on the move.

"Oh no," hissed Cookie, following. He
hoped he didn't step in anything foul.
Whatever the man had eaten in the last day
or so had obviously not set right with him.

By the time he caught up with Rafe, the
big man was two strides from the squatting
man, who was nearly finished and looked as
though he was commencing to stand up.
Rafe moved in fast.

Pepe heard something — a boot on gravel?
— and spun as he rose, tugging up his
trousers. "Who is there?" He held up the
pants with one hand and shucked his wide-
bladed sheath knife, waving it back and
forth before him.

His voice was weak. Fear tickled Pepe's
innards. Perhaps El Jefe was right when he
said that some men were cowards, not cut
out to be Hell Hounds. Every time they
faced a fight, Pepe was gripped by a cruel
hand from the inside, something that
squeezed him terribly, forced him to hunch
up in the bushes over and over again. It

413

would one day be the death of him.

He looked up in time to see a monstrous shape grow out of the blue darkness and descend on him. He thrashed and lunged with the knife, desperate to stab this intruder.

Pepe tried to scream, but a big hand closed about his face. His last thought was that the ghost of the Kid had come back to kill him, to kill them all. Then hot pain bloomed fast up from his neck, covered his head like boiling water dumped over his head. Then Pepe knew no more.

"A neck sounds the same every time . . . like a carrot," whispered Cookie, looking at the pudgy man facedown at their feet.

"Didn't want to do it." Rafe toed the man. "He pulled a knife. Turn him over, see if you recognize him, will you? I'm going to scout the camp, try to find Jack."

"He fell back in his own leavings!" Cookie hissed. But Rafe was already gone, vanished into the dark.

"Sure, leave it to ol' Cookie to deal with." He set to work, holding his breath and rolling the neck-snapped man to one side.

Rafe crept slow as a hunting snake toward the edge of the arroyo. He heard no voices, but did see the dim glow of a small fire, and smelled the smoke. They were not taking care to hide themselves. That means they are either stupid or drunk or don't care if they are found. Or want to be found — is this a trick? The sudden notion froze him. He was out of practice. Was a time years back that he'd have sniffed that possibility right away.

Pay attention, Rafe, he told himself. Jack's life is at stake — unless it's already been forfeit. He shook off that thought and made his way forward. He'd find out soon enough. He gained two more yards, then dropped to his knees and lifted off his hat. He peered up over the lip of the arroyo . . . and saw no one.

He held his breath and once more scanned the scene. Beyond the small fire, now more coals than flame, lay a prone man, far to the left in the shadows. Rafe backed down and knew what he was seeing, and he didn't like it.

They were either being watched and this rube he'd ambushed was bait, or the rest of the bandits were . . . where? Where would they be? The ranch? How could they know about it? Perhaps they'd been spied on for days already.

The idea of it balled his guts like a fist of stone. He'd check on the man by the fire, see if it was Jack, and if he was alive. But it had to be fast.

He gave a look over his shoulder and there was Cookie, ten feet away and low walking closer. "What you see?" said the old man, crouching beside him.

"Man by the fire, might be Jack."

"The rest of them?"

Rafe shook his head.

"Think they know about the ranch?" Even in the low light Cookie's face showed the alarm they both felt.

"Stay here, cover me. Might be a trap. I have to see if it's Jack. If he's alive, we'll get him back to the horses, ride home as fast as we can."

Cookie nodded and raised his carbine. Rafe was already halfway down the slope toward the stretched-out form.

Cookie did his best to see in all directions at once. No one else came, no bandits popped up from behind rocks. Rafe motioned to him.

Cookie scrambled down the embankment and came up breathless beside Rafe. "It's Jack, ain't it?" Cookie bent low, checked on the man. "Don't hardly look like him, though. They whomped on him something fierce."

Rafe nodded. "Still breathing, but he's in

bad shape. Busted up, from the looks. I'll carry him and you double up with him on back to the ranch. Stick to the trail or you'll jostle him off. I'll ride overland. Help me get him up on my shoulder, then take a look over there at that other fella. I didn't give him much attention, but I think he's gone."

Cookie looked at the vandalized corpse. "Oh God, no. It's Carl, I'd know that towhead anywheres. Aw hell, they tortured him. Them three never would have come out here if it weren't for me."

"You can't blame yourself for their actions, Cook. They were grown men, knew the risks of riding the revenge trail, but they did it anyway."

Cookie was silent as they hotfooted back to the waiting horses.

CHAPTER 40:
STAND BACK, BOYS, SHE BITES

Sue rode hard, hell-for-leather, toward the east. Armed with a rifle and the pepperbox pistol Rafe had given her, she felt certain she would be of more use than sitting at the ranch with the two old folks. Besides, she had to do something, anything, and whatever it was that had Rafe all worked up was the excuse to prove to Rafe she wasn't a simpering girl.

The horse carried her smoothly toward the east edge off the valley. The mare, normally fidgety and rambunctious, seemed to be right in her element. Sue smiled when she recalled how Rafe said she and the horse were well matched.

She kept to the rough trail only used by Cookie on his trip to town, but on a flat stretch she let the horse run all out, regret at lying to Arlene and Doc slipping away with each hoofbeat. It had been easy — she told them Rafe asked her to ride eastward to keep an eye on the road in. Simple as that, they did as Rafe said and holed up in the little bunkhouse, looking worried but resolute, and armed for whatever may come.

One glance over her shoulder toward the setting sun told Sue the ranch buildings and corral were now gone from sight. This was the farthest she had ventured since arriving weeks before. She felt better, stronger with each day that passed, but wanted more. She wanted to do her share — more than helping Arlene with the damned women's work in the little house.

She could ride, felt sure she could learn to shoot, help with the stray cattle Rafe and Cookie had been scaring up all over the surrounding countryside. Surely Rafe had seen promise in her efforts so far. After all, hadn't he trusted her enough to give her a gun?

And then, as she crested a rise, she faced a bigger challenge than she could ever have imagined. Not twenty feet ahead, a half dozen black-clad riders thundered straight at her. And judging by their wide eyes and open mouths, she had surprised them as well. The men in the lead shouted and pointed — at her.

She cursed, and though she yanked hard on the reins, in seconds she was surrounded by these frightening riders. They wore black leather vests, chaps, boots, and grimy, sweat-rimed hats. They were large men, fat, muscled, hairy, swarthy, and howling and shouting in the boil of dust they brought with them.

"Chiquita!"

"Hey, mama!"

They whistled and hooted and laughed as they circled her. Sue felt their legs, their horses ramming into her, felt their boots bounce off her legs, pushing, crowding. Her own horse whinnied, reared, but one of the men grabbed the reins and yanked, ripping them from her hands.

Sue heard a scream, her own mixed with that of a horse, more than one, all the horses stamping and milling in confusion, guided by these wild men.

Voices shouted in Spanish all around her, howls and laughter jumbled with words she did not know, but guessed at. Filthy gloved hands grabbed at her. Their stink that of sweat and booze and rancidness — food and bad teeth, rank breath, unwashed hair, it all clouded her, smacked at her senses along with the grit of dust churning up by the stomping, wheeling horses. One second she saw purpling sky, the next leering faces, rough hands reaching for her, horses . . .

"No! Get your hands off —"

It didn't matter, they grabbed at her, all over, snatched at anything they wanted, feeling her as if she were something for purchase in a street vendor's stall. The rifle left her grasp the same time as the reins . . . at least it left her hands free to swat at them.

Then an idea, a nugget of hope came to her — she had secreted the small pepperbox pistol, which she'd loaded before climbing into the saddle, into a pocket of her chore coat, a gift from Arlene. It had belonged to her husband, a slight man.

Sue felt the reassuring slap of the hefty little pocket gun against her thigh. It would be but a matter of seconds before she was yanked from the saddle and . . . she knew what would happen then.

Should have listened to Rafe, never should have gone off on my own.

She used her left hand to swat at the groping hands of the leering, laughing men, even as she groped with her own hand, the right, beneath the coat. Her fingers closed around the grip and she scrabbled with her fingers — hands wrenched her arm backward, smacked at her breasts, nails raking her bare skin.

She didn't let go of the pepperbox, but gripped it with all her strength, strength that was fast being sapped from her. She didn't think she could stay in the saddle much longer.

What did Rafe say to do with it? She felt the trigger, squeezed, and the heavy little gun fired. It didn't make as much sound as she thought it might, but it left a smoking hole in her coat and shirt. But it was the screech from the man to her left that smacked silence onto the roiling mass of animal-men.

"Ahh! Shot! Who shot me?" The man patted his side where he'd been grazed.

Sue used the stunned moment to drum her heels hard against her horse's belly and yank the tiny pistol free of the confines of the now-holey pocket.

It snapped free of the coat, and she let the weight of the little brute carry her hand arcing up until the thick cluster of barrels smacked the nearest savage across the face. The man's nose snapped and the impact jerked her finger once more against the hair trigger.

Ka-blam! Off it went, drilling another black rider, this time in the chest.

Sue didn't wait to see what might happen next. The man she'd shot was the one who'd been holding her horse's reins. Sue bent low, gripping the mane with her free hand, gripping the pepperbox with the other, and shouting a ragged "Hee-yaa!" — and it worked.

Her horse bolted from the nest of confusion. She knew they'd likely shoot her in the back as she rode away, but she didn't care. She'd try anything to get away from these beasts.

No shot came, though bellowed shouts and the pounding of hooves filled her ears. She rode eastward, not wanting to risk cutting cross-country and snapping her horse's legs in a hidden hole.

For a flicker of a moment she thought she'd broken the nerve of the attackers. But no, she heard their horses pounding hard behind her. "Bastards!" she sobbed and ground her heels harder into the horse. "Run, damn you! Run!"

But her horse stumbled, righted itself — Sue saw the trailing reins whipping, slapping the mare. Still she kept low, her face tight to the mane. She smelled the horse's sweat, beneath her hands she felt the wet hide of the gasping, lunging animal.

She drummed a fist against the lathered horse's neck. It didn't help. The horse slowed and a dark shadow fell over Sue. She raised the pepperbox, pulled the trigger, and a shot echoed. A man's laugh brayed closer than she expected. She looked up, saw a black shape outlined in the day's dying light.

Something fast and hard hit her out-stretched gun hand. She shouted in surprise, in pain as the pepperbox was smacked from her grasp. Still she drummed her heels but the horse had stopped.

"Enough!" The voice was loud, from in front of her. She squinted up, saw a man holding the reins, one she didn't believe she had seen in the whirling melee of moments before. He came up facing the opposite direction, onto her left side, and stopped next to her.

"The *puta* has teeth, eh?" The man laughed, baring a wide mouth filled with gleaming teeth. "So does El Jefe! Ha ha!"

He snapped them together as if he were eating the air between them, darting his wide, oily face at her with each bite, a raspy low cackle riding beneath the frightening action.

"I am not certain," he said. "But I would bet all the money and jewels I wish I had stolen over the years that you are the sweet little *chica* that Swearengen wants so badly. The same man that pig of a jailer, Timmons, also wants so badly, eh?"

He leaned closer.

Sue smelled the man's breath, she turned her head, and the man laughed once more, his teeth inches from her face.

"So I say to myself, 'El Jefe' — that's me, El Jefe, leader of these old women who call themselves the Hell Hounds — I say to myself, 'El Jefe, why is it all these people want this little *puta* so much?' Hmm?"

His voice was low and curling, rasping and grating close to her face. She wanted to scream, spit at him, bite at him as he had mimicked seconds before. But it was all she could to keep from crying. That she would not do, could not allow herself to do.

Quick as a viper strike he snatched her by the arm and heeled his horse. The beast grunted, lunged, and Sue felt herself being dragged from the saddle. Her left foot caught for a moment in the stirrup, but she kept moving forward and with a burst of hot pain her foot slipped free. Her arm hurt worse — she felt something pop inside and knew the shoulder had come out of joint.

Her cries of pain, of rage did nothing but spur the man on to greater bursts of laughter. She tried to get her feet underneath herself, but couldn't keep up. Soon she was dragged alongside, trying to keep from getting a hoof to the head by the rampaging horse while the Mexican's grip grew tighter and he worked her arm up and down, as if toying with her. Sue gasped as hot tears rolled from her eyes.

Then as suddenly as he spurred his horse into action, the Mexican dragged back on the reins and his horse churned to a stop.

The dust clouded, rose, settled and Sue struggled to her feet. "What do you want with me?"

He ignored her and let go of her wrist. Sue held her arm close to her chest, only then realizing her shirt had been torn open by the pawing bandits. She staggered for the safety of a nearby outcropping of sandstone, glancing back at the man. He climbed down from his saddle, seemed in no hurry, not bothered that she might run away.

But Sue knew there was no way she could outrun him, no way she could outrun a bullet.

"So, little girl, you got any more tricks in your coat, eh?" He walked toward her slowly, as if he were strolling in a city park. "Anything that might hurt El Jefe? Hmm? Maybe I should take a look myself, maybe strip you down, for my own safety, eh?" His laugh was forced, as if he wanted her to know he had a sense of humor.

Sue looked past him, back along the short distance they'd traveled. There was no sign of the others.

El Jefe saw her glance. "Oh, my men, yes,

they will not trouble you any longer. They have gone on to wherever it is you rode from. All but the man you shot in the chest, he will die a long time, blood blood blood. These wounds are messy. But that is all your doing, none of mine."

"Good!" she shouted, overcome with anger. She backed up, one, two steps, then tripped over a rock. She landed hard, her strained arm still held before her chest like a bird with a wounded wing. Her other hand clawed at the dirt to steady herself. She felt a rock, the right size for her fingers to curl around. She grabbed it, not caring if he saw.

"No, no, no." El Jefe continued slowly picking his way toward her, in no hurry. "That is bad, you see? You cannot hurt me with that rock, but you will try. Like all the others. I cannot admire this in a person. It is stupido." He tapped the side of his head with a dirty finger.

Sue shrugged, and let go of the fist-size rock. She leaned back on her good elbow. Ignoring the urge to wince at the flower of pain from her injured arm, she forced a smile and squinted up at the Mexican a dozen feet away.

She spread her button-free shirt to expose her breasts and the smooth belly below, now

427

crisscrossed with fresh scratches from the pawing men. Then she let her legs flop open.

"Oh ho!" said El Jefe. "So this is how it's going to be, eh? You lure El Jefe in and then smack me with a rock when I am like a goat in heat!"

Sue nodded, forcing a smirk. "Something like that, yeah." But she knew it was working, because El Jefe had slowed his pace and let his eyes linger too long on her bared chest. The tip of his tongue darted out, licked his lips.

"Might be worth the risk." She winked. God, thought Sue, her breath coming in stutters. I can't believe I'm doing this. The man's worse than a foul beast, disgusting from the boots up.

In two quick strides El Jefe stood before her. With a grunt he dropped to his knees between her parted legs, his eyes still on her dust-flecked breasts, a wide smile on his mouth, and his eyes even wider.

Without looking he drew a heavy pistol, cocked it, and snugged the tip of the barrel against her left temple.

"I think if you hit me in the head with a rock I will shoot you — it would hardly be my fault, but that is the way of these things, eh?"

The snout of the barrel pressed into her

head and all Sue could think of was Al Swearengen and how bad her life had been — and how much better it had become since. A sudden anger she had never known filled her.

CHAPTER 41:
A VISIT FROM LAZARUS

Sue kept her eyes closed, smelled El Jefe's foul breath gouting at her, felt his piggish, grimy hand pawing her belly, her breasts, mashing, squeezing roughly. It hurt, but not as much as the gun barrel jammed hard against her head.

She knew what was coming, knew the man would rip at her pants, knew there was nothing she could do about it, though part of her wanted to reach for the rock, hit him with it, even though it might mean her death.

But what if she could somehow jerk away from him at the same time? After all, as she told him minutes before, it might be worth the risk.

She reached, her fingertips crabbing in the dirt for the rock while El Jefe panted with lust, his free hand clawing at her pants, gouging her belly with his nails.

The rock, the rock, she told herself. She

CHAPTER 42:
MEANWHILE,
BACK AT THE RANCH

It took Cookie a long time to get Jack back along the west trail to the ranch. It was all he could do to hold the man upright before him in the saddle. He considered lashing the dandy gambler to him, but figured if he ever lost his balance they'd both topple out of the saddle. Cookie knew he would smack his head and end up simple all the rest of his days. That would not do.

But he had to make haste — Sue, Arlene, and Doc were at the house, maybe needing help by now. Riding in the dark was a dicey move at best, even with a lantern — which he did not have — and without a sick man flopping back and forth like a sack of meal. There was enough light from the dying day that he could still make out the narrow trail that cut down the valley before that last hard left to the ranch.

Jack had not so much as groaned, but his head was a swollen mess with lumps and cuts. Lord knew what else ailed the young man. "Soon enough, Jack," said Cookie.

He judged he was a quarter mile from the ranch when he heard a single shot, then a few seconds later another.

"Don't sound good," he said, and drummed his boot heels into the mustang's sides as much as he dared, all but a full-out gallop.

Whether they'd been had or followed a cold trail, it didn't really matter to Rafe now. All that mattered was getting back to the ranch as fast as he was able. He rode his horse hard, with no intention of sparing the beast.

And when the buckskin faltered once, nearly stumbling and throwing him, he hung on, a thousand and one thoughts punching holes in his vague plans. There had been no chance to take the fight to these intruders, instead it was falling apart.

Jack was beaten all to hell, might not live, and what shape would he be in if he did? Rafe had left three helpless people alone at the ranch, and now it appeared as if they were being descended on, forced to defend themselves with weapons they didn't know how to use. And here he was, riding a damn good horse to death in a thin effort to hold the threads together, to stop the intruders somehow.

Rafe barked a harsh, wordless curse at his own stupidity, and heeled the horse harder. They devoured the landscape, man and horse, pounding the earth and raising spumes of powdery dust that slipped in dervishes on a slight breeze.

Full dark would soon be on them. He had to get close, to that second swell of land behind the buildings. He'd leave the horse there and trail down on foot. That should put him at the bunkhouse in a couple of minutes.

He heard shots from somewhere ahead, didn't dare stop. And then the horse stumbled once more as the land rose up before them. Rafe knew the rise, knew most of the landscape like he knew his own mind. This place had few secrets from him. The damnable bandits did, but not this ranch. He couldn't tell Cookie that he didn't consider it his anymore, despite the old man's kind gesture of maintaining the payments. For now it was a place to stop and figure out what to do next.

"Whoa, fella, whoa." Rafe patted the lathered horse's neck and slipped out of the saddle. He lifted the satchel loop from the saddle horn, slid out his rifle, and left the heavy-breathing horse to its own devices.

Another twenty yards, Rafe topped one last rise, and below he saw the dim outline of the bunkhouse. No light from inside shone through cracks, a good sign. That means Sue, Arlene, and Doc were locked inside, ready to defend. He hoped.

Rafe bent low, hustled down the slope as fast and as quietly as he could. He had no idea if the invaders had found the place, or if they ever would. But he didn't want to take any chances.

He made it to the lean-to on the back of the little building, and laid down the satchel. He'd lugged all that extra weight all that way and most of it had gone unused, unneeded. Better to be safe, he thought. Then that pet phrase of his wife's popped unbidden into his head — in for a penny. Here we go, he thought, as he low-walked around the side of the building, well below the window where someone spooked inside might fire out at him.

In the dark shadows as he was, he did not see the man on the ground until he walked into him. Rafe backed up, tense, his rifle aimed. The person hadn't moved. He shifted forward, poked with caution at the form. It jostled, laid still.

Covering the body with the rifle, Rafe reached forward, felt leather beneath his hand. He poked again at the form. Nothing but the softness of sagged fat beneath clothing. Dead? His hand trailed along, up a shoulder. The form was . . . mustaches and grizzled unshaven face . . . a stranger, a man. His hand spider-walked further and felt a telltale stickiness, likely blood, sopping long, stringy hair.

Rafe gritted his teeth, felt the unpleasantness of a collapsed skull beneath his fingertips. Not shot, but hit, and hard. By what or whom? It was beneath a window — perhaps someone from inside had dropped this scoundrel as he skulked?

Still, if one got this close, little would stop others from doing the same. Rafe hurried to the front corner of the little home, and paused there a moment. He hugged the shadows and scanned the yard, but saw nothing unusual. "Sue? Doc? Arlene?" he whispered their names, nothing.

Rafe repeated them, then leaned over and, straining, managed to knock softly on the bottom of the wooden door. It squeaked, moved inward an inch. He froze, waited.

He inched forward, his boots making a slight grating sound in the dirt. He pushed the bottom of the door again. It opened wider, a low squeak sounded. He whispered their names again. No response.

The crack of a pistol shot sliced the night air close before Rafe's face, and the door shuddered beneath his fingertips, the bullet embedded in a chewed hole of its own making. He felt hot, slicing pain across his chest. He touched fingers there and felt wetness. He'd been shot, likely grazed. Wasn't the first time. He'd worry about it later.

The shot came from across the yard, over by the stack of firewood. Should have kicked it over earlier, he thought. He raised up on one elbow, and returned fire, driving two rifle rounds at the stacked wood.

"Gaah!"

The shriek was followed by a soft, thudding sound, then the plunk of wood toppling. Got one. Then footsteps told him there had been two, and the second man had run from the wood, maybe toward the corral? He couldn't be sure.

Rafe heard no further cries or shouts, but pushed off with his feet and rolled onto his shoulder, legs arcing up through the doorway and slamming down into the dark of the little kitchen. He rolled fast to the right side of the doorway and hugged the wall. "It's Rafe — anybody in here?" he whispered.

No response.

Cold nails of regret clawed at his gut.

Where were they? Taken? "Sue?"

He scrabbled around on the floor, swiping a free hand along the planks in wide gestures, searching for another body, but he found none.

All Rafe heard was his own rising heartbeat, felt it thudding in his throat, his neck, echoing in his head. Where were they? What had he done? Cost more innocents their lives? He squeezed his eyes closed, fighting the welling confusion, the anger, the doubt — feelings that used to be foreign to him. What had happened to him in Yuma?

"Rafe!"

Cookie — it was Cookie. From the west side of the bunkhouse. He walked on his knees, one hand ahead, guiding him in the dark of the little structure, every nail and mud brick holding it together, all hammered and stacked by him years before. Yet he felt a stranger here. He rushed to the far end of the building, into the little bedroom, Arlene and Sue's room now, to the shuttered window.

Shuttered but he couldn't pry them open. What had they done to wedge them closed? "Cook?" he shouted.

"Rafe!" his friend's shout barked again, was clipped by a rifle shot from a different spot in the yard.

"Dammit!" snarled Rafe. His only friend needed him and he was stuck in this little house, trapped save for this window and the one at the other end. He reached over his head, pushed against the shutters again. They didn't budge.

Anger filled him and he drove the carbine's butt hard into the center of the double shutters. They burst apart, whipping outward. Night air flooded at him and a trio of shots hit the little house. He heard them thudding into the front, powdering stucco and splintering wood.

"Rafe!" Another shot.

Cookie was out there, likely pinned down behind the water trough, the only structure of substance in that direction. Rafe risked a peek out the window. It incited no shots. Good, he was in shadow, not seen by whoever had them hemmed in.

Diagonally across from the bunkhouse, Rafe saw a wide, dark shape close down and low by the base of the misshapen mesquite that had, despite awful damage from the fire five years before, manage to claw its way skyward, though in a stunted, gnarled fashion. But that dark shape was not natural, not something he remembered being there. Might be the second man from the woodpile.

"Cook!"

"Rafe! The trough — I'm pinned."

The big man heard the anger in Cookie's voice. With any luck that also meant he wasn't injured, not enough, anyway, to keep him from throwing lead — or dynamite. And that thought gave Rafe an idea.

He shouted over to Cookie: "One stick — the tree."

Two, three beats, then Rafe heard a low, drawn-out chuckle followed by a quick, bright match flare, then it winked out.

The crack of a rifle shot sounded, and brief blast of explosive light burst from beneath the shadowed tree. He knew enough about Cookie to know the old man would already have deduced, as if second nature, which way to duck and roll so his position in the dark would not be given away by the brief match light.

He heard a quick "Ha!" and then saw a hissing spark of light whip end over end toward the target — no one could throw a stick dead-on like Cookie — right at the base of the tree. Before it hit, Rafe saw the shape shift, split in two, heard clipped shouts of shock, then *BLAM!*

The stick hit and there weren't even screams, only hunks of debris whipping skyward, raining down on the ranch yard, pounding the earth with the force of fists on soft flesh.

Two more men down. Plus the one beneath the kitchen window. How many to go? Rafe tried to run through the figures in his head, recalled seeing at least six of the black-garbed men ride by earlier. That devilish-eyed skinny youth included.

Later, he'd think about it later.

Cookie used the lull to hightail it to the bunkhouse. He made his way around the back, and Rafe met him at the front door.

"I don't know if that's all of them, but I can't wait any longer. You stay with Jack. I have to find Sue and the others."

"No need," he said, nodding beyond Rafe's shoulder. The big man spun, and in the moonlight saw Doc and Arlene walking side by side, scanning the night to either side. They stepped as if on glass, toward the bunkhouse.

Arlene held a Winchester repeater poking straight out, her apron ruffling slightly in a soft breeze. Doc gripped a double-barrel Greener, the end of which he worked side to side like a snake's head. Cautious relief crept into Rafe's mind.

The pair made it to the little house, Arlene walked over to the form beneath the window and she nudged it once with her boot. "Is he dead?"

"Yes, ma'am. But where's . . . ?"

"I left the shutters open for air, not thinking anybody was really going to come around. Then I saw this" — she sneered down at the man — "brute, skulking along. I don't much like guns." She handed the rifle to Rafe. "But I've never gone wrong with my iron skillet."

Doc cradled the Greener in one arm and rubbed his head. "You have never seen the like, gentlemen — she walloped that man square on the bean!"

Cookie said, "Hoo doggy —" but Rafe interrupted.

"Sue, dammit! Where's Sue?"

Arlene's eyes widened. "You mean she's not with you?"

"No, I told her to stay here, with you two. I told her . . ." Rafe's gaze raked the dark yard. "Sue!" he shouted.

"Rafe," said Arlene, reaching toward him. "You're hurt, bleeding."

"Let's get in the house, might be more of these rascals lurking." Cookie jerked his chin toward the door.

Rafe ignored him. "Arlene, do you know where she went?"

"Yes, she said you told her you needed help, that you wanted her to ride the east trail, wasn't it?" Arlene turned to Doc, who nodded.

"Cookie, where's your horse?"

"Tied yonder by the corral, but —"

Rafe took off on a run for the corral. "I have to find her. There's still at least one more outlaw loose out there, I know it."

In seconds, he thundered by on Cookie's horse, and shouted, "Tend to Jack!"

"What's happened to Jack? Where is he?" said Arlene.

Cookie hurried them over to where he'd laid the man down. To his surprise, Jack was awake. "No more horse riding for a while, okay, Cookie?" He tried to smile, ended up coughing and moaning.

"Don't worry," said Arlene, nudging the old trail hound out of the way. "One of you two make yourself useful and fetch a blanket, something to carry him to the house on. And hurry up about it!"

CHAPTER 43:
BIRTH OF A LEGEND

The Kid listened to the girl's receding footsteps. After a while he walked around El Jefe and picked up the revolver from the man's relaxed hand. He tossed his own to the ground. Two more steps, then he looked down at El Jefe again. Finally he unbuttoned his fly and in a few moments urinated on El Jefe's face.

The wetness revived the swarthy man. His eyes opened, fluttered, worked to stay open. His mouth sputtered weakly.

The Kid thumbed back the hammer on the oversize Dragoon. Heavy iron and wood from tip to butt, but the Kid's thin arm held it steady as a jut of stone. It pointed at El Jefe's focusing eyes.

The man on the ground looked up, his eyes centering, comprehending. "Kid," he wheezed. "What . . . are you doing? It can't be! I —"

"Yes, you shot me. Eh?" The words slipped

from between narrow lips that barely moved. The Kid lifted an edge of his ratty leather jacket to reveal an oozing blood smear far on his left side. "But I am thin, sí?"

There was almost something of humor in his words, but no smile on his face. That's when El Jefe realized with the surprise that accompanies sudden clarity, that in all their years together — how many had it been? Ten? Twelve? — he had never once seen the Kid smile. No matter, he thought. I am broken, yes, but I am still El Jefe of the Hell Hounds. I have been in worse scrapes.

"So you want to be El Jefe now, is that it?" A chuckle, dry like old tree bark, rattled out of him.

The Kid's head moved side to side slowly. "No. There is no more El Jefe." The tendons in his wrist tensed . . . tensed . . . the trigger following, tighter.

The man on the ground watched as if time had slowed. His bloodshot eyes widened, his mouth stretched, a scream dragged up the parched throat, ready to fling itself skyward.

But it never got the chance.

The bullet smeared the middle of the man's face, a pudding of bone, blood, and brain vomited out, leaching around the deflated head of El Jefe. A halo of gore spread wide, staining the place forever. The bloodied eggs of his eyes stared skyward.

"There is only . . . Hell Hound."

Smoke wisped from the barrel even as the wraith slipped the gun into his holster. He walked straight for the horse that had skittered a dozen yards away at the gun's roar. He gathered the reins and kept walking, the horse trudging along behind, *pajados* on his oversize Mexican rowels chinging an off-kilter tune to his steps.

A single, thick, rolling gunshot cleaved the air of the rising moonlit night.

"No!" Rafe shouted, grinding his teeth together. The deadly sound came from somewhere ahead. He jammed his heels hard into the ribs of the little mustang, urging her on faster. The stalwart horse, already tired from a long day on rough ground, gave even more to the big, relentless rider.

He saw her before he thought he would, but it was Sue, had to be. Of that there was no doubt in Rafe's mind. He was still a dozen yards from her when he jerked the reins and the horse jammed to a halt.

"Sue? Sue!" Rafe stood a moment, looking toward the staggering person.

She stopped her loping walk, stood still,

weaving in the narrow, overgrown lane, hugging one arm to her chest with the other.

He ran to her, and looked her up and down. "Are you okay?"

She nodded, took the last step between them, and leaned against him. They stood like that in the moonlight for long minutes. They exchanged no words, but walked back to the mustang, standing where Rafe had left it, head down, no longer breathing hard.

Rafe helped Sue into the saddle and he led the horse, walking ahead, back to the ranch.

Miles away, the Kid walked northwestward. Moonglow turned his shape into a harsh, stark shadow. He walked on until the night swallowed him. And still he kept walking, his black eyes all-seeing in the dark.

CHAPTER 44:
PARADISE REGAINED

The next few days brimmed with activity, each person's mind filled with thanks that their injuries could have been worse, damage to the ranch more severe. Even Jack Smith, though battered, broken, and bruised, was pronounced by Doc likely to heal, given time and more bed rest than he wanted.

He tried to protest, but his jaw was swollen. Cookie threatened to take a knife to what was left of the man's meager pile of clothes if Jack didn't keep quiet and simmer down.

Somehow, an unspoken change came about where Sue was concerned. Though her arm was tucked up immobile in a sling, silently and methodically she set about helping Cookie and Rafe in tidying the place, repairing damage caused in the ruckus. They retrieved the bodies they could locate, eventually satisfying themselves that they had found them all. Of the renegades, Rafe was certain two were missing, and hours of tracking confirmed that they had made good their escapes.

Cookie insisted on digging the two graves that Carlton and Manuel needed, side-by-side resting places atop a knoll. They were buried with as much honor as Cookie could muster. He spoke over them from the heart, saying they would not have taken to the revenge trail had he not driven them to it.

It was a cross he felt he must bear, no matter the efforts of Rafe and Sue to persuade him otherwise. He gathered what possessions of theirs he could, vowing to sell them and send the money to their families, who he felt sure would be reachable through the railroad offices. He was heartened only by the fact that Miguel had, he hoped, made good his escape, since they'd not found his body.

The outlaws they now knew as El Jefe and the Hell Hounds — from Sue's encounter with the man and the lettering on their vests. These they buried in a mass grave, laid out free of flourish but with bare respect. As with the other graves, they mounded stones atop to prevent coyotes and wolves from digging up the corpses. It was long, tedious work, but it needed doing.

"We'll keep what horses we can round up," said Rafe. "Sell the gear we don't need, and split the money. The bastards owe us that much."

By the end of that second day, a day filled with much digging and labor all around, they gathered at twilight around the table in the little kitchen. Jack slept soundlessly in the bedroom, now affectionately dubbed Jack's Quarters. Doc, ably assisted by Arlene, had tended Rafe, Sue, and Jack, setting the gambler's broken leg and arm, as well as broken ribs. He was in rough shape, but would heal.

Cookie stood at the window and scanned the purpling skyline. He yawned. "Another day shot in the backside. I tell you, I have seen all the hard times and the rascals who bring them I care to."

"Amen," said Arlene, setting a plate of biscuits on the table.

Doc and Sue nodded, murmured weary agreement. Only Rafe said nothing.

The others, still gun-shy and tense, looked to him. Something about the big man's silence unsettled them. Something about him foretold of coming change.

Cookie's statement had been wishful thinking, and they all knew it. Others would come, for Sue, for Jack, for Rafe. For any reason at all.

Cookie turned, his bushy brows drawn together. "You all right there, son?" His voice was unusually quiet.

Rafe nodded.

"Tired, huh?"

"I expect so." Rafe's eyes fixed on a knot in the smooth log wall. The dark, polished thing seemed to stare hard at him, like the unblinking gaze of death itself, the same look on that gaunt boy he'd seen up on the plateau.

He closed his eyes. "It's nothing. Nothing at all." Rafe raised his cup and sipped long, savoring the fleeting taste of cool water.

He seemed to come back to himself then, and looked around the table at his friends. "There is a time and a place for brooding over uncertain days ahead, of all the enemies who won't stay quiet forever. But this is not that time or place."

He smacked his big hands on the tabletop, and cups and cutlery bounced and clinked. "Let's try not to forget the good that has come of all this, too."

Weary, tired looks began to be replaced with cautious smiles.

In the pause that followed, Doc rubbed his eyes beneath his spectacles, then stood. "Ladies and gentlemen," he said. "In the spirit of Rafe's fine statement, I have an announcement that I have wanted to make for some days now. You will recall, Rafe and Cookie and Sue, that I have disappeared now and again of late. I am sure you all thought me inebriated and sleeping it off."

Sue began to protest but Doc held up a hand. "Rightfully so, I am a man who is fond of his liquid encouragement, shall we say. But this time, it is . . . oh, confound it, you know that spiny giant knob of rock behind the place? Well I was up there not long ago, snooping around for various minerals for an experiment I have in mind when I discovered this." He held out his palm and three thumb-size rocks of varying shades and dull gleams sat atop his pink palm.

"Is that what I think it is, Doc?" said Cookie.

The pudgy medicine man nodded, a smile on his face. "High-grade gold ore, or I'm not Doc Jones. And what's more, I believe there's a promising vein. And it couldn't be situated in a more convenient place."

"How so?" said Rafe, holding up a hunk of the ore and eyeing it.

453

"As I said, I was up there nosing for minerals when I found a vertical cleft in the rock face. I stuck a hand in, never a recommended maneuver, let me tell you. And what did I find?"

They all looked at him, eyes wide, shaking their heads.

"I found nothing. That is to say, air, dead space. I went back with a lamp and do you know what? It is a cave, the opening quite narrow, and a portly fellow like me has his work cut out for himself in squeezing in there. But once inside, it's a wonderful space, fully three times the height of this room and at least fifty feet, more or less, in diameter."

"That's where we went when it looked like we were about to be overrun by those bandits," said Arlene. "A risky move, but this place didn't seem so safe once we were faced with real bandits."

Cookie narrowed his eyes. "You went with him up into this cave of his?"

She nodded, a slight smile and color rising on her face.

Doc held up his hands. "I can assure you, Cookie, nothing untoward, that is to say, um . . ."

Cookie crossed his arms. "Hmm. And this cave. That's where the gold is at?"

"Indeed, my good man," said Doc. "And it's all yours, gents."

Cookie regarded them both, then smacked his gnarled old hands together. "Hoowhee!"

"Cookie McGee!" said Arlene. "You'll wake Jack!"

A voice from the dark bedroom said, "I'm awake — and I heard everything you all have said. Now maybe you can buy yourselves some decent clothes."

"Sure," said Cookie, throwing his arms wide. "Why not? Clothes for all. Heck, might be enough to set us up nice as you please in the cattle business, don't you think, Rafe?"

All the big man could do was nod and look at the hunks of ore. He passed one to Sue and grinned. "How do you like those apples?"

Arlene stood, held up a lone finger and turned to the cupboard over the long wooden work counter. She shoved aside cans and jars of various ingredients and lifted down an unopened bottle of whiskey. From the colorful label, with curlicues and a picture of a castle, it looked to be mighty fancy. Cookie and Doc both licked their lips.

"This was Stanley's," said Arlene. "He always said he was going to crack it open when we found our heaven on earth. I don't know about the rest of you, but I think he would agree this is it."

"Here here," said Rafe, smiling.

Sue helped Arlene pass around drinking glasses.

Rafe raised his glass. "I toast to you all, friends new and old, and thank you for breathing life back into this place."

They all raised their glasses, then sipped.

Cookie raised his own glass next, puffed up his chest, and made quite a show of clearing his throat. "Me and the boy here have traveled a whole lot of trail miles together, and I can honestly say that in all my years a-rovin', this here is a house full of top hands."

Rafe nodded, sipped, then over the rim of his glass, caught Sue's gaze. "Yes, sir," he said. "We have ourselves quite the outfit."

CHAPTER 45:
KEEP IT SIMPLE

Warden Timmons reread the telegram a fifth time. The words hadn't changed — all his plans had come to naught. He crumpled the yellow scrap and tossed it to the floor.

Such a simple undertaking, and yet it bore no fruit. Barr and the girl, that's all he had asked for. He ground his teeth together. Think, think . . . there has to be a way to get that damned girl and dispense with Barr and still come out the victor, the hero. So much depended on it.

Simple, it should have been simple.

A slow smile crept onto the warden's face and one eyebrow arched high. That's it, perhaps he was trying too hard. "Feeney!" he shouted. "Feeney!"

The thick-muscled plug of a man entered the warden's office, floorboards creaking under his girth.

"It's time you took a trip. This office has made you soft, and it has clouded my judgment. I see now that less guile and harsher measures are required to dispense with Rafe Barr for good. You do want a chance to deal with Rafe Barr, don't you?"

The burly guard's nostrils flexed and he nodded once. He grunted the low, menacing sound a bull makes just before it stomps a man to death.

"Good, I thought as much. But first? First you shall go to Denver."

The guard's eyebrows rose in question.

"You know who's there, don't you?" said Timmons. He smiled as Feeney shook his head.

The warden struck a match, set alight a cigar, turning the end slowly in the orange flame, puffing quick clouds of blue smoke. "Our old friend, Turk. You remember Turk?"

Feeney's eyes narrowed, and for the first time in his long employ as the warden's right hand, the plug of a man smiled. The open little cave of his mouth revealed a ragged wet stump where his tongue had once been.

The warden's own smug grin slipped at the sight. He turned to the window. "But remember, Feeney, you must play nice with Turk Mincher. Our futures depend on it."

The end.

The Outfit will return . . .

ABOUT THE AUTHOR

Matthew P. Mayo is an award-winning author of more than twenty-five books and dozens of short stories. His novel, *Tucker's Reckoning,* won the Western Writers of America's Spur Award for Best Western Novel, and his short stories have been Spur Award and Peacemaker Award finalists. His many novels include *Winters' War; Wrong Town; Hot Lead, Cold Heart; The Hunted; Shotgun Charlie,* and others.

Matthew's numerous nonfiction books include the bestselling *Cowboys, Mountain Men & Grizzly Bears; Haunted Old West; Jerks in New England History;* and *Hornswogglers, Fourflushers & Snake-Oil Salesmen.* He has been an on-screen expert for a popular BBC-TV series about lost treasure in the American West, and has had three books optioned for film.

Matthew and his wife, photographer Jen-

nifer Smith-Mayo, run Gritty Press (www
.GrittyPress.com) and rove the byways of
North America in search of hot coffee, tasty
whiskey, and high adventure. For more
information, drop by Matthew's Web site at
www.MatthewMayo.com.

The employees of Thorndike Press hope you have enjoyed this Large Print book. All our Thorndike, Wheeler, and Kennebec Large Print titles are designed for easy reading, and all our books are made to last. Other Thorndike Press Large Print books are available at your library, through selected bookstores, or directly from us.

For information about titles, please call:
(800) 223-1244

or visit our Web site at:
http://gale.cengage.com/thorndike

To share your comments, please write:
Publisher
Thorndike Press
10 Water St., Suite 310
Waterville, ME 04901